FARVIEW

KIM FIELDING

Tin Box
PRESS

Cover Art: Reese Dante reesedante.com

Chapter One

Thirty minutes into the journey, Oliver Webb knew he should have splurged on a first-class ticket, but by then it was too late. He spent another six hours on the hard wooden bench, squashed between a portly older man and a young woman who glared daggers every time Oliver's long leg jostled hers. Even if he had found a position comfortable enough to attempt sleep, he would have been kept awake by the din of crying children and the conversations of excited holiday-goers. The third-class car smelled of sweat and onions and soiled nappies, a nasty combination even for a man used to the reeking air of Greynox.

Oliver nearly cheered when the train came to a shuddering stop in Bythington.

Shouldering his bag, he pushed through the crowd and made his way to the counter marked Coach Tickets. Or more accurately, *oach ickets,* since the two initial letters—likely painted originally in color—had faded to obscurity.

"Croftwell," he said to the gray-haired woman behind the till.

"Five coppers for the return ticket."

"Just one-way."

For the first time, she actually looked at him. "Three," she said after a pause and then accepted his coins. "The coach leaves from bay six in twenty minutes. If you want to eat, do it now. It's two hours to Croftwell and the coach won't stop."

Oliver eyed the queue at the pasty stall and decided against it. He wasn't truly hungry, although he'd had nothing that day except tea and a stale biscuit. Instead he made his way to bay six, where two dusty dragons stood tethered to a shabby coach. There was no sign of the driver.

Within a few minutes a middle-aged couple arrived, accompanied by a porter with a cart. He unloaded their considerable luggage and hurried away as they stood straight-backed, speaking neither to Oliver nor to each other. Oliver had the impression they were in the middle of an argument—or perhaps their relationship had soured into hatred and they were always like this. A young man in much-mended clothes appeared soon afterward. His eyelids drooped and he swayed as he stood, as if he might collapse into sleep at any moment.

Oliver did not possess a pocket watch, and the station clock was out of sight, but it was far more than twenty minutes later when the driver showed up. He had puffy red cheeks and the slow, careful gait of a drunken man, but the dragons seemed happy to see him. He paused to murmur at them and feed a treat from his palm.

"Tickets, please!" the driver said loudly, as if addressing a large crowd. He peered closely at the slips of paper they handed him and, apparently satisfied, loaded the couple's suitcases onto the back of the coach. "There's room for your bags inside," he said to Oliver and the young man.

The passengers climbed into the vehicle.

It was a bumpy ride—the coach seats long since sprung—but it could have been worse. The young man fell asleep almost immediately and the couple glared angrily at nothing, leaving Oliver in blessed peace. The dragons, who'd looked overfed, kept up a surprisingly fast pace. They were probably eager to get home to their barn and dinner.

Uncaring of the blue skies and sea views, Oliver retreated into a formless gray space deep within himself. As far as he was concerned, he could stay there forever, feeling nothing but a numbing chill.

The coach reached Croftwell just as the sun was ready to dip into

the ocean. Many people would have paused upon disembarking to admire the tidy little harbor backed by a sky of delicate pinks and oranges. Oliver faced inland instead, quickly scanning the few blocks that constituted the town's business district. There was, as far as he could tell, nothing threatening: a high street more mud than cobbles, a handful of shops with weathered signs, a few pedestrians in no particular hurry. Houses, some ramshackle and some neat and tidy, but all modest. Behind the town, a rocky cliff topped with tufts of grass.

It was an alien place to Oliver, city born and bred, but that was the point of his coming here.

A part of Oliver wanted to make a more careful inspection of Croftwell, poking into the dark spaces behind the shops and peering into the harborside shacks. But he reminded himself that none of that was any of his business. What he needed now were directions—and a meal to fill his empty belly.

Croftwell had three pubs, as far as he could tell, but none of them had a sign. The locals undoubtedly knew which was which, and really, it didn't matter to him. He chose the nearest one, which boasted a maroon-fronted ground floor and yellow plaster walls on the two floors above. A grinning, sharp-toothed merman had been painted on one street-level window, so perhaps that was the establishment's name—or simply decoration.

The door creaked when he opened it but shut without a sound.

He stood just inside, allowing his eyes to adapt to the relative gloom. The interior smelled of ale and of fish—not surprising since the entire town smelled of fish. Nothing fancy about the décor or customers, who ranged from their late teens far into wrinkled decrepitude. They wore the plain clothes of working people, but there was none of the poverty evident in Greynox's seedier establishments, and although everyone stared at him, their faces weren't hard.

"Help you?" asked a blond man carrying a tray of filled glasses, who Oliver assumed was the landlord.

"Can I get dinner here?"

The man gave a half smile. "Sure, if you've coppers to pay for one."

Oliver nodded and took a table in the far corner; the light was poor, but he could sit with his back to the wall. There was an exit nearby as well, likely leading to the pub's yard. After delivering the drinks, the landlord walked over. He had a severe limp but managed well enough.

"Got a fish stew tonight," he announced. "Or meat pie."

"What sort of meat?" Oliver had long ago learned to ask and to indicate with his expression that he expected a truthful answer. Unimaginable unsavory ingredients were frequently hidden between layers of pastry.

The landlord looked slightly offended. "Mutton and knucker, of course. The knucker was caught just off our harbor on Tuesday."

Oliver had never been fond of most sorts of dragon meat, but knucker—water dragon—wasn't too bad. And he supposed he'd be having more than his fill of fish soon.

"Pie and a pint."

"Have some lovely currant cakes for after, if you like. My partner makes 'em."

"All right."

By the time the landlord left Oliver's table, the other customers had returned to their discussions. The pub wasn't crowded, but it wasn't slow either, and it was clear that the patrons knew one another well. They called from table to table, and sometimes a person relocated from one group to another. Near the front of the place, four young men played an elaborate dice game that involved a great deal of boisterous wagering. A happy enough crowd. None of them looking over his shoulder or casting a furtive glance.

After a short time, the landlord brought over Oliver's ale along with a little bowl of dried fireberries. "Dinner'll be along shortly," he announced.

"Can you tell me something?"

The landlord shrugged. "Depends what you want to know, I expect."

"Do you know where Farview Cottage is?"

That brought narrowed eyes and thinned lips. "You're not one of those people, are you?"

"What people?"

"The ones that want to poke about in things that don't concern them."

"I am not one of those."

Apparently not fully convinced, the landlord jerked his chin toward the back of the room. "That way. Up on the cliff."

Oliver should probably have surmised that from the name. He wasn't certain whether he was pleased or disappointed that the cottage was some distance from the village. He'd have to make the climb in the dark now, but there was nothing to be done about that.

As the landlord limped away, a man detached himself from a group watching the dice-players, patted the landlord's shoulder in passing, and came to stand next to Oliver's table. He looked to be in his midtwenties, with corkscrew-curly dark hair that needed cutting—or at least taming—and unfathomably dark eyes. He was very pretty, but not like the dandies in Greynox with their oiled mustaches and peacock clothing. This man had a scruffy beard, as if he'd forgotten to shave for a few days, and his well-worn shirt and breeches were varying shades of tan. He looked, in fact, quite a lot like a wild man who'd popped into civilization for a brief visit.

"You're a puzzle," the wild man announced.

Oliver, who didn't want conversation, tried to ignore him.

But that didn't seem to matter. The man pulled out the opposite chair, turned it around, and sat astride, his gaze firmly fixed on Oliver's face.

"You have the look of a Crofter, you do," he said. "You've got the same build and coloring and square face. Blue eyes instead of brown, but there's some here with those. Put you in some fishing gear and you'd fit right in. But you don't sound like one of us. You sound like a Noxer." He seemed curious rather than hostile, his voice having an almost musical lilt.

"I am a Noxer."

"I was there for a bit. Everything was dirty and gray, the air so thick I could hardly breathe. Everyone rushing round with scowls. Nasty place."

If he expected an argument from Oliver, he'd be disappointed. The last thing Oliver would do was defend his former home. He took a long swallow of ale and said nothing.

"What's your name, then?" asked his unwanted companion. And before Oliver could answer, he continued. "I'm called Felix, of the Corbyns. You might've seen our name on the biggest harbor shed when you came in. But there's a lot of us, so if you want me specifically, you'd best use my given name. Otherwise half the town might answer your call."

If they'd been in Greynox, Oliver would have assumed the man was flirting and would soon offer private services in exchange for some coppers. But this was Croftwell, and Felix was likely just bored. Or perhaps this was the normal method of conversation here.

With Felix waiting expectantly, Oliver grunted. "Webb."

"Do you have a given name too? Or are they out of fashion in the city?"

"Oliver."

Grinning, Felix scooped a number of fireberries out of the bowl and tossed them into his mouth.

"Pleased to make your acquaintance, Mr. Oliver Webb of Greynox. Why are you looking for Farview Cottage?"

"My business, not yours."

Felix seemed to think this was very funny. "You're in Croftwell now. Everyone knows everything about everyone else. Our soil's not rich enough to grow secrets."

Oliver was suddenly relieved that the cottage was isolated. He'd be able to minimize his interactions with the locals and avoid most of the gossip.

After tapping his cheek thoughtfully, Felix winked. "Tell you what. Buy me a pint and I'll tell you about Farview while you're eating."

"Don't be filling strangers' ears with nonsense," scolded the landlord, who'd arrived with a tray of food. He efficiently set everything onto the table. The pie smelled good, and there was plenty of it, even for a big man like Oliver. There were vegetables too, and three small hard rolls.

"It's not nonsense," insisted Felix. "It's the absolute truth."

"You always say that. I don't think you know the difference between stories and real life."

If Felix was offended by that, he didn't show it. "Who says there's a difference, and why should there be? Every person holds his own truth." Ignoring the landlord's snort, he turned to Oliver. "There's a good tale there, mate. Worth far more than a pint, it is."

Most likely, everything he had to say would be a load of dragonshit. But he *was* pretty, and Oliver hadn't had a proper conversation with anyone in ages. And it might be ages again. The ale here was cheap; he might as well be entertained while he ate.

"All right," Oliver said, then nodded at the landlord. "But just one pint."

Chapter Two

While Felix waited for the ale to arrive, he turned the chair back around and settled in with a satisfied sigh. He was on the thin side, Oliver noted, which was unusual in this land of robust people. Oliver, in contrast, was sturdy: tall and broad-shouldered, heavily muscled. In his youth, he'd earned a few extra coppers by winning wrestling matches, until he'd run out of willing opponents. He would have likely had better competition here in Croftwell. But not from Felix, who looked to be made of skin, bones, and restless twitches.

With a sigh, Oliver dug into his pie and nodded at Felix to begin.

"It's tasty, isn't it?" Felix pointed at the plate. "Tural's a good cook."

"Is that the landlord?" It was a strange name, but perhaps it was common around here. Or perhaps Tural came from somewhere else. He had lighter coloring than a Crofter and his accent wasn't the same.

Felix nodded. "And the Merman has better food than our other pubs, although the others aren't bad. You chose well."

"I'm not paying for your dinner," Oliver warned.

"No, mate. Our agreement was a story for an ale, fair enough."

Tural brought Felix's drink a moment later. "Just raise a hand if you want more," he said, pointedly addressing Oliver. "Or if you want me to drag this nuisance away." His expression suggested fond exasperation before he turned and left the table.

Felix took a long swallow. "He's a good man, Tural is. Came to us years ago from I don't know where, missing one leg. But lots of folks round here have lost a bit or two of themselves—fishing's a dangerous business. Tural, though, he arrived with his partner, who's a wind person."

Oliver blinked. "Wind person?"

He'd heard of them, of course—people in the far north who allegedly flew through the skies like birds. But he'd never seen one or known anyone who had, and he'd doubted they really existed. Maybe this was one of Felix's wild tales.

But Felix nodded earnestly. "He's beautiful. But he has a ruined wing, so he's as bound to earth and sea as the rest of us. Gets along well enough, though, and he's right interesting to talk to. Plus he bakes—"

"You said you'd tell me about the cottage."

"That I did."

Felix ate the last of the fireberries and washed them down with more ale, while Oliver mulled over the description of another man as *beautiful*. Customs here were certainly different from back home. No, not home. Oliver would never return to Greynox.

"It starts long ago," Felix said, mercifully interrupting Oliver's thoughts. "People have lived here in Croftwell longer than anyone can remember."

PEOPLE HAVE LIVED HERE in Croftwell longer than anyone can remember. For generations far too many to count. A few years ago some men arrived from one of your universities and started creeping around in cellars and up on the moor, digging holes like dogs searching for bones. They got very excited about some of the rocks they found, specially the ones with the odd little scratchings they said were a kind of writing. They told us that people made those scratchings over five thousand years ago.

All of which goes to show that Crofters are as tied to this place as are the sea waves. Kings and queens come and go, but we stay put. And even if we wander, we're like the tide—we always come back. That bit's important now, so mind you remember it.

Nothing much grows here. You came in from Bythington, didn't you? You saw the fields over that way. Corn and sunflowers and barley, mostly. But round here and most of the way up to Urchin Cove, our soil's too poor for farming. A few of us keep sheep up on the moor, but mostly we fish. Always have. Those university men say we were fishing five thousand years ago. And even those of us who aren't fishermen, we're the next thing over. We repair nets or boats, or we get the catch ready for market when it comes in. Or we sell supplies to the fishermen, or ale and dinner; or we keep their homes in good shape.

I know that in Greynox the residents get food on the table with a hundred different occupations, but here it's fish. That's an important bit too.

The story of Farview cottage begins a long time ago. Oh, not so long ago as those stone-scratchings. But... perhaps round the time our grandparents' great-grandparents were born. No trains back then. You traveled by boat, by dragon, or by your own two feet. And none of those nasty machines you Noxers love so well, the ones that belch filth into the air night and day. But I reckon Croftwell wasn't much different back then than it is today.

There was a girl called Lyra Moon. There's still plenty of Moons round the town nowadays. My oldest brother married one of 'em. And this Lyra, she was pretty and smart and could've had her pick of suitors, but she turned 'em all down. Said she'd dreamed of a blue-eyed lad and she was going to wait for him. And wait she did, even though everyone told her she was being foolish. In Croftwell back then, blue eyes were rare as sapphires. Nowadays they're a bit more common. But she insisted, until finally her parents and everyone else gave up on her ever marrying.

And then one fine afternoon, someone spotted a strange ship far out beyond the harbor. Crofters have always kept an eye open for pirates, although they haven't much bothered us. We've nothing worth stealing, I expect. But these were no pirates. It was a ship such as nobody had ever seen, with a hull that gleamed in the sun like diamonds, and sails as fine as cobwebs but in all the colors of the rainbow. Although the whole town had turned out, it didn't come into our harbor but instead tacked back and forth out past the rocks.

And then, at long last, someone with sharp eyes saw a little wooden boat coming in—just big enough for three or four passengers and with a single gossamer sail. All the Crofters waited. It was likely the most exciting thing that had happened here in years.

The boat tacked in, proud as you please, right up to the docks. Only a single man aboard. He threw the mooring rope to someone on shore and then hopped off.

And wasn't he a sight! Tall and slender, with long hair paler than winter butter. A sailor's skin should be roughened by salt and sun, but his was as white and smooth as a dish of cream. He wore nothing more than a few bits of jewel-toned silk set with pearls. And his eyes, they were like the sky on a warm spring day. Like yours, Oliver Webb.

He said his name was Aymar Iceshadow, and that he'd come to stay with the Crofters for a time. To learn about them, he said. His accent was strange to everyone's ears, all rolled *r*s and breathy vowels. And he showed the people an emerald as big as a hen's egg, which was enough to get him a nice little home near the harbor and to fill it with all the modest comforts Croftwell had to offer.

Just like everyone else, he went out fishing every morning—but only by himself—and he always returned with a fine catch indeed.

Ah, but you can guess where this tale is heading next. Aymar's house was next to Lyra Moon's. He had blue eyes, just as she'd dreamed of. And soon enough they fell in love. He warned her that someday he'd have to leave, but since when do new lovers worry themselves about the future? They married. Sometimes she went out fishing with him and sometimes not, but either way they were so happy together that it almost hurt to look at 'em.

They had four children—two boys and two girls—all of them as bright and lovely as their parents. Aymar and Lyra grew older. Her black hair became streaked with grey and his yellow turned to white. Their children grew up.

And then one fine afternoon someone spotted a ship with a

sparkling hull, out beyond the harbor. Aymar turned to Lyra and said he had to go. He begged her to go with him. But sorrowful as she was, she refused. She was a Crofter, and here she'd stay. She told him that if she was away too long, she'd wither and die like a plant yanked from the soil. She begged him to remain. But he couldn't. He had an obligation to his people, which he said he must fulfill.

What could they do? Everyone was crying, but Aymar hugged his children and kissed his wife. He promised her that he'd always love her, and that he'd do everything in his power to return.

Then he sailed away in his little boat with the gossamer sail.

Understand, Lyra certainly mourned him, but she was otherwise well-set. Over the years, she and Aymar had tucked away coppers—or perhaps it was emeralds. I don't know. She had her children as well, but by then they had their own lives. So she announced that she was going to wait for Aymar to return. But instead of waiting in their house near the harbor, which I reckon had too many memories, she planned to build a cottage up on the cliff. So she'd be the first to see Aymar's ship when it returned.

Her children and friends said she was foolish, but she'd never taken advice from anyone and wasn't about to start. She bought a patch of land on the clifftop that nobody'd ever had any use for. Hired people to drag stones there to build a modest little house, hardly more than a hut. And you know, stones are heavy and hard to move, so the people she hired chose the handiest ones. They didn't much notice or care that those stones had funny scratches on them, or that long ago they'd perhaps formed the walls of an ancestor's home.

As soon as it was ready, Lyra moved in. She came down to the village now and then for supplies, but the path is steep and she eventually grew unsteady on her feet. So mostly her children and then her grandchildren brought things up to her. She didn't need much. When the weather was fine, she'd spend the day on a bench outside her cottage, looking out to sea. When the weather was foul, she'd watch through a window instead.

She grew old and then older. Her hair was all gray now, her back stooped, her hands gnarled. Some days one or two of her many grandchildren came up with food for her and she couldn't remember their names. But she remembered Aymar and her love for him, and she refused to come down off the cliff. Her eyes became rheumy, yet she insisted she'd still see Aymar's ship when it arrived.

Lyra's children, well, they grew old too, and eventually they died. Even her grandchildren had creaking joints and wrinkled skin. She lived on, however, always insisting that Aymar would return for her.

And then one autumn morning, Crofters awoke and knew a storm was coming. A bad one. The clouds hadn't showed up yet, but we can tell. None of the birds were singing or flying, and the sprites were hunkered down in their nests. Up on the moor, the sheep huddled close. Down in the village, dogs and cats refused to go outside. Dragons remained in their stables, stamping their feet restlessly. Imps didn't come scavenging round for crumbs and scraps. The sea was as smooth as glass. The air smelled thin, and sounds didn't carry as they ought to. Babies cried.

The Crofters knew what to do. They checked their boats to make sure they were firmly moored and the sails furled and tied. Then they closed up the harbor shacks good and tight and shuttered all the windows in the shops and homes. They made sure they had plenty of firestones stacked indoors and that anything that might blow away was secure.

And then they waited.

I've sat inside, waiting for storms like this, and it's awful. It's hard to breathe, and your muscles want to twitch and jump. No use trying to get any work done, or read a book, or even have a chat with anyone. Certainly no use trying to sleep through it, although I've tried that. Crawled into bed and pulled the blankets up high, but then I grew too warm and my eyes wouldn't stay closed.

That day, once the winds finally shrieked their way in, it was almost a relief. Sometimes waiting is worse than the blow itself. Oh, but it was a good one. The sky went green first, like moss, before the clouds swept up—so thick that it was like the middle of the night—and then the rain blew in sideways and mixed with the ocean spray until anyone foolish enough to be outside wouldn't know if they were on land or in the sea. The waves came up so high that they pounded the shutters here, in this building, and all up and down High Street.

Two boats broke from their moorings. One floated loose and the other crashed into its neighbor, sinking them both. The Crofters found the loose one after the storm, washed all the way down High Street and into the little park near our school. They had a devil of a time dragging it back to the water.

And one of the shacks along the harbor collapsed, leaving nothing but a few pieces of wood. That's where my family's shack stands now. We've a business there sewing and repairing sails.

People huddled inside near their lanterns and fires, blankets round their shoulders, children and pets pressed close. Did anyone think of Lyra up on the clifftop? Perhaps. But nobody could do anything for her even if they'd wanted to. If they'd tried to walk up the pathway, they'd have been blown away.

Oh, there'd been worse storms before and we've had worse since, but still—it was a bad one.

After three or four hours that felt much longer, the winds stopped as suddenly as a candle snuffed. This was only a lull, though, not the end. Crofters knew they had thirty minutes' grace at most before the other end came through, and it was likely to be even worse.

People hurried out of their houses, under a sky like pewter, and checked to make sure their neighbors and dragons were all right. They tightened shutters that had blown loose. Perhaps paused for a moment to marvel at the mysterious things that had washed ashore. Took a few minutes to simply stand and wonder at the world's great forces and be happy they'd survived so far.

Nobody was looking out beyond the harbor, nor did they notice the solitary figure making her steady way down from the cliff. How did she manage it on the rain-slick path? I don't know. I expect she had a walking stick. Perhaps she even had a small spell to help her.

But when she had nearly reached the harbor, somebody did notice her, a lad who at first thought she was a wraith. Then he recognized her—as he should; she was his great-grandmother—and he called her name. Others took up the cry, so even the people who'd remained indoors came out to see what was happening. They watched as she walked to the piers, to the very one where Aymar had moored so long before.

One of her granddaughters hurried to her, took her arm, and tried to drag her away. "You must get inside, Granny! The storm!"

Lyra pulled herself free with shocking strength and pointed out toward the mouth of the harbor. No more cloudiness to her eyes now. "It's time. My love has come for me, just as he promised."

Everyone looked, of course. And there, beyond the rocks, was a ship. The hull, once shiny, looked dull and cracked. The sails hung in tatters, and the masts were broken. But the ship was tacking back and forth nonetheless. And anyone who looked carefully could see a small boat on the still waters, its sail straining toward them despite the windless air.

A bolt of lightning rent the sky, making everyone jump.

"Granny!" cried the granddaughter, whose hair began to stir in a breeze. "Hurry!"

Lyra turned to face her. The old woman was smiling now. And perhaps it was the weird lighting, but it appeared as if her hair was again jet black and her skin smooth.

"It's time, my dear. I've been waiting so long."

"The storm!"

"The storm doesn't matter to me. Not this time. Go inside. Be safe. Be happy. I'll come back someday, you know. Crofters always do. But now I need to go."

And just then, the little boat reached the dock. Nobody could see who was in it. Well, maybe Lyra could. She gave her granddaughter's cheek a quick caress and then turned, ran toward the boat, and leapt into it with all the power and grace of a young athlete.

More lighting flashed. The wind began to blow in earnest. Although it was blowing inland, the boat turned and sailed toward the harbor mouth. Toward the waiting ship.

Perhaps some of Lyra's family members made as if to follow in their own boats, but other people certainly dragged them away. Coaxed them to safety indoors as the storm resumed its fury. A good number of people drank heavily while they waited, but the storm raged all night, and eventually they had to sleep.

Dawn came, soft and meek as a baby sprite. The villagers spent the morning cleaning up and assessing the damage. There was no sign of the strange ship, of course, nor of Lyra Moon. When a few people climbed the cliff, they found her cottage empty.

And this was all before my granny's granny was born. There are still members of the Iceshadow family in Croftwell, and some of 'em have eyes like yours. Sometimes one or two of Lyra's descendants have taken up residence in the cottage, though most prefer to stay down here. On occasion someone unrelated will try it, but they never stay for long. Haunted, they say when they return to the village. Not by Lyra or Aymar but by something else, something that makes them uneasy. Maybe it's to do with Lyra, or maybe it's those stone scratchings at fault. Maybe it's nothing but the sea wind sighing over the moor.

Nobody ever laid eyes on Lyra again. But she was a Crofter, and you'll remember what I told you: however far we wander, we always come back.

Oliver's food was long gone, including the bread rolls and the currant cakes. He'd lost count of how many times his glass was refilled. Tural had also poured several pints for Felix, and Oliver hadn't stopped him despite the limits of the original agreement. It seemed a small enough price for good entertainment.

And it had been entertaining. Felix was pretty, true enough, but even better, he was a gifted storyteller. While he was speaking, Oliver had nearly forgotten the rest of the world. It had been even better than the fuzzy gray space in his head.

But now the tale was over, the meal eaten, the ale downed. And Oliver was exhausted. So when Felix grinned at him and offered a story about pirates invading the nearby village of Urchin Cove, Oliver shook his head. "I'll pay my bill and be on my way."

Tural, who'd hobbled over to collect dishes, nodded. "If you need a room for tonight, we have two for let upstairs. Not fancy, but clean and comfortable."

In truth, it was a bit tempting. But Oliver's journey was almost complete, and there was no point in waiting until morning for the last part.

"Thanks, but I have a place to stay."

"Where's that?" Felix leaned forward.

"The house I inherited. Farview Cottage."

Chapter Three

Felix tried to ask a lot of questions, but Oliver paid him no attention as he handed coppers to Tural and gathered his bag. It was harder to ignore Felix out on the street; he planted himself in front of Oliver, nearly jumping up and down in his eagerness to learn details.

"But who did you inherit it from? Oh, I knew you were a Crofter—I told you that from the start—but you're from Greynox and that's odd indeed. And why did you decide to come here and move into Farview? What will you do here? How long will you stay?"

Oliver, who could have simply pushed him out of the way, waited for the words to run out. Finally Felix just stood there, coatless and shivering in the cold night air. In the harbor, ropes and boards creaked.

"Move," Oliver said.

"But I want—"

"I don't care what you want. Move."

Ten years of work experience in Greynox had taught him how to imply future use of force while keeping his tone low and even. *Your voice should be your first and best weapon*, his boss used to say.

And the boss was right. After a brief pause, Felix huffed his disappointment and stepped to the side. But he wasn't quite finished. "I could tell you more about your ancestors. About how Aymar Iceshadow used to—"

Oliver brushed past him without responding. As he continued down the pavement, he heard the hinges of the Merman's door squawk as Felix went back inside.

The night smelled of salt and fish and wet wood, and clouds scudded past a pale sliver of moon. The shops were closed and shuttered and there was nobody else in sight, although lights still shone in the pubs. If Oliver looked out past the boats in the harbor, he could see faint green glows dancing just above the water. He didn't know what they were and wasn't especially curious to find out.

Hitching his bag securely over a shoulder, he turned toward the cliff.

The pathway was difficult enough to find that he almost wished he had asked Felix for directions. He found it at last: nothing more than a narrow dirt trail dug into the rock, steep and without a railing. He wouldn't have wanted to hazard it during a storm, and even now he was careful with his footing. Despite everything, he wasn't ready to meet his end splattered on the stones of Croftwell.

There was a time when Oliver could have sprinted all the way up the path and arrived at the top breathing smoothly, ready to rush down and back up again. Not tonight. Tonight he slogged, his lungs working hard and his big body as heavy as granite. When he reached the end of the path, he stopped, telling himself he was enjoying the view. But it was too dark to see much apart from those green glows and a sparse scattering of now distant houselights.

After a few minutes, Oliver turned away from the sea and faced the moor. It smelled different up here. Although a hint of brine remained, there was also the heavy scent of mud, the sharp aroma of herbs, and the sweet fragrance of grass. All infinitely better than Greynox's reek. Despite the poor visibility, something to his left loomed, large and unmoving. Farview Cottage, he presumed.

He felt no sense of homecoming as he tromped closer. And why should he? He'd never been here before. Until today, he'd heard Farview mentioned only briefly, without descriptors. For all he'd known, it was a grand manor like the ones proudly lining the streets near Jayne Park in Greynox, a stone's throw and only a few social classes down from the royal palace.

Farview Cottage was definitely not a grand manor. He could make out that much even in the dark. It was squat and solid, with a hefty door that resisted as he pushed it open. Inside there was no light at all, so Oliver sighed, pulled a matchbox from his coat pocket, and struck a light. The feeble flame did a poor job of illuminating the interior. All Oliver could make out were a few pieces of cloth-shrouded furniture, a lot of cobwebs, and what he suspected was a great deal of dust.

"Fuck." The fire scorched his fingers and he dropped the dying match to the floor; he didn't bother to light another. He'd have to sleep rough tonight. Luckily he was drained enough that it wouldn't much matter.

He pulled a couple of cloths smelling of mildew onto the floor, blindly arranged them into a makeshift nest, and lay down without removing so much as his coat or boots. His bag made a hard but serviceable pillow, and he fell asleep to the sounds of creeping mice and distant waves.

"YOU SHOULD HAVE TAKEN a room at the Merman."

Oliver jumped up, slipped on the cloths, and nearly tumbled onto his arse. The only thing that saved him was a heavy wooden table, even though it tilted alarmingly under his weight.

"What the fuck are you doing here?"

Felix smirked at him from the open doorway, with a bright sky behind. He wore the same scruffy clothes as the previous night, or ones very like them, and didn't appear to have used a comb or razor in the interim.

"Checking to see if the ghosts got you."

"There are no bloody ghosts."

Oliver tried ineffectually to brush the dust off his coat. His back ached, either from the stone floor or his abrupt awakening, and his mouth tasted like gutter water.

"Not yet, perhaps. You took them by surprise. Give them another day or two." Felix tilted his head. "You do intend to stay for a day or two?"

"Permanently," Oliver growled.

Clearly uncowed, Felix clapped his hands. "Excellent. You'll need to hire me, then. We can discuss it over breakfast." He lifted a basket from the floor in front of him.

Oliver knew he should push Felix outside and then slam and bolt the door. But, well, he was hungry. And unless he ate whatever Felix had in that basket, Oliver was going to need to make himself presentable and descend the cliffside path into the village before he could have breakfast. And even then, no doubt Felix would tag along the entire way.

When Oliver looked around, he spied a sink and pump against one wall. He had to work the pump several times, but after its loud metallic protests, he was finally rewarded with a stream of cold, clear water. He scooped a few handfuls into his mouth and then splashed his face. After that, he thought about tea, but since he didn't know whether he possessed firestones and a kettle or pot—or cups or tea leaves, for that matter—he dismissed the idea. "We'll eat outside," he announced.

"A picnic for breakfast! What a clever idea. You Greynoxers are so daring."

Oliver scowled as he pressed past Felix and out of the cottage. But it was impossible to remain too choleric when the morning greeted him with brilliant skies, wheeling gulls, and a view to the end of the world. Down below, fishing boats sailed through the harbor's rocky mouth or bobbed in the open sea, mere toys among sparkling wavelets.

"You can see how the cottage got its name," Felix commented beside him. "I would've expected Lyra Moon to have more imagination, though."

"It's a lovely place."

"I know Croftwell's a boring little fishing village, but on a fine morning such as today, I'd wager there's no place better."

Oliver took several deep breaths and turned to face him. "You brought breakfast?"

"Indeed." Felix grinned broadly, every bit as untamed and beautiful as their surroundings.

They sat on a stone bench against the cottage wall. Felix's expression said Oliver should understand that this was *the* bench, the one where Lyra watched and waited for her beloved to return. It was old enough for that, Oliver supposed, and worn from use, but otherwise entirely plain and ordinary.

Felix laid out dishes, cups, and cutlery and then unwrapped the food. He'd brought flaky pasties stuffed with spiced meat and potatoes, a hunk of salty cheese, two hard sausages, glass pots of clotted cream, and a couple of handfuls of tiny strawberries. There was even a crock of brewed tea, wrapped in enough layers of quilted fabric that the liquid was still quite warm.

"That's a lot of food for two people," Oliver pointed out.

"We have a morning of hard work ahead of us. Besides, the imps will be wanting their share."

Sure enough, a small tribe of the creatures lurked nearby, chittering quietly as they eyed Oliver and Felix. Their bright orange fur looked thick and well-groomed, nothing like the mangy, disreputable-looking creatures that skulked in Greynox's alleys.

"You can't feed them," Oliver said. "It only encourages them to beg."

"Perhaps. But I believe in staying on their good side. When the pirates attacked Urchin Cove, for instance—"

"What hard work?" interrupted Oliver, who had no intention of being lulled into another of Felix's stories.

"Making the cottage habitable, of course. We'll have loads of cleaning to do and likely some repairs. And we'll need at least one trip down to the village for supplies. You can pay Tural for breakfast then."

Oliver fixed him with a glare. "Why would you help me?"

"Because you're going to pay me for it. You can't possibly do it all yourself. I come cheap enough—ten coppers a day plus breakfast and lunch."

"I don't need an assistant."

"Sure you do. Do you want to spend another night sleeping on a dirty floor? Besides, I can be your guide—show you where to find everything you need in town. That's efficiency, that is."

With only about three blocks of shops, Oliver would certainly find his way around just fine. He didn't need much anyway: just a few basics and some groceries. But with the good food in his belly and the sun warm on his head, he lacked the energy to argue.

"Just for today. After that you'll leave me in peace."

Felix smiled.

THEY DIDN'T GET to work right away. It was simply too pleasant to sit and watch the sea. And for once, Felix was quiet, seeming as appreciative of the view as Oliver was. The imps crept closer and closer. Felix tossed them some pieces of pasty and the last of the cheese, blithely ignoring Oliver's grumbles.

Finally, Oliver stood. "Not paying you to sit about all day."

"No, although it would be a lovely vocation to have. I'd be quite good at it."

Oliver began with a thorough inspection of the cottage exterior. He was certainly no expert on such things, but it looked generally sound. It looked, in fact, as if the structure was as ancient as the moor itself, a natural thing risen straight from the earth and no more likely to crumble than the cliffs below. He opened the shutters. A few of them were loose and only a few flakes of green paint remained, but that would be simple to repair. The glass panes were all intact. The door and frame, which also needed repainting, were resolutely solid, and although he couldn't see the roof well from the ground, he didn't spy any obvious problems.

Aside from the cottage, the only visible structure atop the moor was the outdoor loo a number of strides away. It was made of stone as well and, as far as he could tell, would suit its purpose adequately. He'd brush away the cobwebs later.

"Do you know how much of this land is mine?" he asked Felix, who'd been following him closely. "I don't know how to judge its extent."

Felix shrugged. "Does it matter? Nobody else comes up here except for an occasional shepherd, maybe a tourist or two. Claim it all, if you fancy." He tilted his head at the expanse of grass and low brush. "What would you do with it anyway? Build one of those manufactories to spew poisons into the air? Or perhaps you want a warren of stinking closes packed with the hungry and the sick. Or a palace."

"Do I look like a prince?"

"No." Felix grinned. "You look like a Croftwell fisherman in dusty Greynox clothes."

Oliver stomped into the cottage. He pried open the windows to get rid of the stale, musty smells, and he finally had a good look around. There wasn't much to see. The cottage consisted of a single large ground-floor room and a ladder leading to a loft above. The loft held nothing but spiders, mice, and dust, but it would be big enough to serve as a sleeping space if he chose.

Felix helped pull the rest of the dusty cloths off the furniture and dump them in a heap outside. Oliver would wash them later and then tuck them away for the next time the cottage was vacated. The furnishings were sturdy but minimal: a large bed frame without a mattress, a table and five chairs, two armchairs with the upholstery and stuffing in tatters, a chest of drawers, and some shelves near the sink. A cupboard held a broom, bucket, and scrub brushes.

"Not even a chamber pot," Felix observed. Dirt smudged his face. Probably his clothing as well, but due to their color, it was impossible to tell.

Oliver, who had removed his overcoat, suit coat, and vest and rolled up his shirtsleeves, slumped against a wall. This was a larger task than he'd imagined. "I can't live here," he moaned.

But Felix was dancing around like a puppy. "Of course you can. We'll scrub everything down and make a list, and then we can go down to the shops and find the things you need. I'll help carry. We might need a few trips, but that's all right. Your ten coppers have me for the whole day."

"The two of us will haul a mattress up that cliff?"

"Oh, don't worry about that. I'll get some of my brothers and cousins to help. You'll have to wait until tomorrow for that, though. They're all out there." He waved a hand in the direction of the sea. Then his expression grew serious. "How much copper've you got to spend, mate?"

"I don't have an emerald."

"Pity." Felix waited for a more specific answer.

Oliver had never been good with sums, but he did some calculations in his head. X number of coppers divided by Y months, where Y was an unknown quantity. "Not much," was his eventual conclusion. Which he'd known from the beginning, really.

"All right then. We'll be thrifty. I don't expect you'll need too many things to get started. What kind of work will you be doing once you're settled?"

"None."

That was enough questions for now. Oliver grabbed the broom and began to dislodge webs from the rafters and corners. After a moment, Felix followed suit with a scrub brush.

It came as no surprise that Felix was not a diligent laborer. He'd been working less than an hour when he tossed the brush aside and perched atop the table, legs crossed and palms planted flat behind him.

"You must be an Iceshadow," he announced.

"Webb."

"Right. But what was your mother's name?"

"Rowe."

"Ah! The Rowes are all mixed up with the Iceshadows. Truth be told, we all are. There aren't that many of us and we've lived here since time began, so I expect we're all cousins of some sort. But there are a lot of Rowes in with the Iceshadows."

Oliver was down on hands and knees, attempting to clean beneath the chest of drawers. It was a massive thing, much larger than a modest home should need. Most of the drawers had swollen with damp and couldn't be opened. He'd tackle that some other time. It wasn't as if he had much to put in them.

"What were your mothers' parents' names?" Felix asked.

"How should I bloody know?"

"They're your grandparents."

"Never met them."

Felix didn't even pause. "But surely your mother must have spoken of them."

With a grunt, Oliver rose to his feet and glared at him. "My mother died when I was two, so if she ever mentioned them, I was too young to remember. And yes, she was from Croftwell. My father wasn't. He didn't tell me anything about her family either, except to mention that she'd left me a place in Croftwell called Farview Cottage."

Felix's untidy brows were drawn into a vee and his eyes looked especially dark. "That's awful, to not know anything about your past, where you came from. We can ask around. I'm sure some of the older folk will know your story. Some of them must have known your mother, in fact."

Oliver thought about entanglements, the fetters of obligation and expectation that could tie a man down, and he shuddered. "I know where I came from—Greynox. And I know my story perfectly well. I don't want anyone else involved."

Although Felix looked perplexed and maybe a bit concerned, he didn't say more. He remained on the table a few minutes longer, peering at Oliver, before hopping off and taking up his brush again.

Chapter Four

By the end of the day, Farview Cottage was clean, with even the windows sparkling in the waning sunlight. Oliver and Felix had made three round trips to the village, and now Oliver had kitchenware basics, food and tea to last several days, and firestones for heat and light. A woman who Felix claimed as a distant relative had promised to come up the next day to reupholster at least one chair. Delivery of the mattress was going to take a few days more, which was slightly inconvenient, but Oliver had bought a few thick blankets that would serve as his nest in the meantime.

"It still doesn't look like a home," Felix said, hands on hips. "No rag rugs on the floor, no pictures on the walls. You don't even have curtains."

"I don't need those things," Oliver said as he moved to stand near the large window that overlooked the sea. A stone seat worn smooth and shiny had been built into the wall below. He could imagine an old woman sitting there, gazing out and waiting to spy a ship with a diamond hull. An image which was ridiculous, he chided himself. That had been nothing but one of Felix's stories.

"Why did you come here today?" Oliver asked without turning to look at him.

"Because you paid me ten coppers and two meals."

"That's not so much. Couldn't you do better on a fishing boat?"

"Oliver, look at me." When Oliver didn't comply, Felix stomped over and pulled at Oliver's shoulder until he turned. "Do I look like a fisherman?" He spread his arms wide.

Reluctantly, Oliver looked. All day he'd avoided staring at Felix because his pretty face was too distracting, too much a reminder of what he would never have. But now he let his gaze roam over Felix as if he were considering a dragon for hire. And no, Felix with his unweathered skin and slender frame didn't look like a fisherman.

"You're too skinny."

Felix barked a laugh. "You sound like my mother."

"I've seen what your neighbors look like: as if they could pull in a kraken single-handed. Not you."

After a moment Felix stepped in, much closer than two men ought to stand, near enough that Oliver could smell the sweat and dust on him, see the salt water trickling through the earth on his fine-pored skin.

"I was a sickly child," he said, barely above a whisper. "My mother planned my funeral more than once. She even bought a coffin. But I lived, as you can see. I'm not strong enough to fish."

"You could work harborside. Didn't you say your family repairs sails?"

"I've tried that. It didn't work out." Slowly Felix raised a hand as if he meant to stroke Oliver's face.

But then, quick as a flash, he rushed to the door. "You can pay me next time you see me. Good-night, Olly." And then he disappeared into the deepening dusk, leaving the door ajar.

Olly?

SORE AND TIRED, Oliver had gone to sleep early. Now he awoke well past midmorning. For the second night in a row, he'd escaped his usual nightmares. Perhaps his exhausted brain had been unable to dig up any horrors.

Since it was another beautiful day, he decided to breakfast again on the outdoor bench. He wasn't at all surprised when the imps made an appearance partway through his meal.

"I told Felix not to feed you. You lot look healthy enough without my scraps." Undeterred, the imps chittered at him. "You remind me of the rich young men and women who stroll about the shops near Jayne Park. Always nattering away at one another and demanding things from the salesclerks." He tossed them the crusts of his toast and stood, shooing them away with his hands.

Oliver spent about a half hour strolling the vicinity of his cottage. There was very little to see, although he did notice large stones in what seemed to be regular patterns, as if a village had gone to ruins long ago. The stones were covered in mosses and lichens, but when he peered closely, he could see chisel marks and other remnants of long-forgotten masons. A few stones had more purposeful inscriptions, although Oliver couldn't make any sense of them. They reminded him of the scratchings Felix had mentioned, so perhaps he hadn't made that bit up.

On his way back, three jewel-toned sprites flitted past, making him stop in his tracks. They seemed such joyful things, nothing like the bedraggled, listless specimens in the Greynox zoological gardens. He grew angry at the thought of anyone caging such delight. But that was the way the vast city worked; it beat down and slowly destroyed everything and everyone except the elite. It took everything good and twisted it into something foul.

He was frowning when he reached his cottage.

"Is something wrong?" asked the thirtyish woman waiting near Lyra's bench.

"Ah. Mrs....."

"Bellflower," she reminded him. Seeming to note his befuddlement, she added in the sort of tone one might use for simpletons or small children, "Here for your chair?" She toed the overstuffed satchel at her feet.

"Of course. I'm sorry. I hope I didn't keep you waiting."

"Oh, it's no problem. I haven't been up here in ages. I forgot how splendid the view is. Look, you can see my rooftop!" She pointed down at the village, although it was impossible to tell which specific house she was indicating.

"Er, the chair's... just inside."

"Of course it is, dear."

She looked around curiously after he let her in, clucked at the condition of his furniture, and did a quick inspection of the chairs. "Oh my, this won't do at all. Mice and moths. The frames are sound, though. I can fix the rest." She opened her satchel and began to dig inside, humming something tuneless under her breath.

"Can I get you some tea, Mrs. Bellflower?"

"In a bit, perhaps. But you needn't worry yourself about me. You can go back to your work."

His work. The problem was, he didn't have any. He'd already tidied his makeshift bed and breakfast things, and he'd realized he was going to need a washtub before he could tackle the soiled furniture cloths or his besmirched clothing. He hadn't yet bought paint or tools either. That left him with nothing but time on his hands—a thought that almost made a bitter laugh escape. Well, at least Mrs. Bellflower wasn't a chatterbox like Felix. Silence was much better. Oliver decided that more time outdoors could be beneficial.

Sure enough, the sunshine and the air felt good, as if his skin might soak them in and consequently rejuvenate. The beautiful view was constantly changing as winds, clouds, and light shifted, as boats moved to and fro. Before coming to Croftwell, he'd seen the open sea only once, during a childhood visit to Eelmouth. But the beaches had been crowded with other holiday-goers, and every time Oliver waded into water deeper than his ankles, his father and stepmother had hauled him out again. He'd ended up sitting on the sand for hours, bored and frustrated, while the adults conversed.

The ocean was a glorious thing, Oliver decided today. He felt almost as if he could dive straight from the cliff, over the Croftwell rooftops, and into the harbor, and then swim away like a dolphin.

"I'm a fool," he informed the hopeful imp skulking nearby. It seemed to agree.

For a time he strolled the moor. It wasn't as gorgeous as the sea but was interesting in its own way, with meandering footpaths and more piles of stones with scratchings. Birds—he didn't know what kinds—swooped and twittered, and sometimes sprites flitted about as well. But he saw no other people. As far as he could tell, he and Mrs. Bellflower were the only people on the moor, which felt odd to a Noxer. He'd never before been out of earshot of other humans. But then, he reminded himself, solitude had been one of his objectives.

Eventually his boots felt heavy and his legs grew tired, so he made his way back to the cottage. Mrs. Bellflower was sitting on the floor surrounded by what looked like acres of fabric.

"I'm sorry," Oliver said. "I've been very rude, abandoning you like that. Can I get you some—"

"I'm fine." She held a needle between her lips but spoke around it. "I brought my own lunch. I did help myself to some tea, however." She pointed at the cup on the floor beside her.

"Of course."

"D'you want to take a look at the fabric?"

He didn't especially. When he and Felix had met with her yesterday, she said she had materials left over from a previous project, making his cost considerably less. He didn't much care what the chair looked like as long as it was comfortable. But refusing to look now would be rude, so he stepped closer and peered at the folds of green and pink.

"Is that—"

"Octopuses with roses. Yeah." She held up a length and squinted at it. "Fernica Moon ordered yards and yards of it. Had me do her entire parlor, curtains and all. It's not so bad if you don't look at it too close. Colors are nice."

Moon. Oliver wondered if this was a distant relative. "I won't be looking at it at all—I'll be sitting on it. So it's fine."

With an expression that said she approved, Mrs. Bellflower put down the fabric and picked up her scissors. "I'll finish this chair today, but I'll have to come back tomorrow for the other."

"You only need to do one." He'd store the other frame in the loft.

She lifted her eyebrows. "What will you do when you have guests?"

"I'm not planning to have any."

"You will, though," she said with a cluck of her tongue. "Whole town's bursting with questions, so I expect they'll start finding excuses to pay you a visit soon enough. Unless you're planning to chuck 'em over the cliff, I suggest getting your other chair done. I won't charge you nothin' for it. It'd make me itch, thinking of you up here with only one chair done."

Oliver sighed. "Fine. But please no octopus curtains for me."

Mrs. Bellflower chuckled, either at the thought of the curtains or because she was pleased with her victory—he couldn't tell which.

Realizing that he was hungry, Oliver put on the kettle and set about assembling some lunch. As he did so, he remembered that Mrs. Bellflower was Felix's relative, which explained the similarly insistent natures.

"Felix Corbyn is your cousin?" he asked, pausing with knife in hand.

She shot him a sidelong glance without pausing in her fabric-cutting. "Some sort of cousin, aye."

"What does he.... Does he have a job of some kind?"

"He gets by, I expect. Moves about from one family member's house to another, does occasional work. Talks people into buying him ales in the pubs."

"Ah." He didn't know why he'd asked. It made no difference to him.

"Mr. Webb, Felix is a good lad. Has a good heart, and he can light up a room, can't he? But...." She sighed. "You'll want to stay clear of him, as much as you can."

"Why?" Oliver demanded, wondering if Mrs. Bellflower somehow sensed his secrets.

"He... he brings trouble. Not on purpose, mind you, but it follows him like a wake after a boat. And anyone caught in it is likely to get pulled under."

Mrs. Bellflower arrived early the next day, and this time Oliver was ready. "I'm going into the village to pick up a few things. Help yourself to tea and whatever food you fancy."

"When you get to the grocers, make sure you get yourself some waspfish. There's a real nice catch of it this morning. Fry it up with some moor-herb on top and potatoes on the side, and you'll have yourself a lovely dinner tonight."

He thanked her, put on his coat, and set out.

Villagers began greeting him as soon as he reached level ground. He'd met a few of them during his expeditions with Felix but couldn't remember any names, so he simply nodded and wished them a good morning. He noticed how differently they moved, their gaits slower and looser than Noxers. They didn't hold bags and parcels tight against their bodies or peer nervously about, but they paused often to chat with one another, sometimes creating blockages that other pedestrians stepped around, uncomplaining.

He went first to a shop that sold tools, building supplies, and a bewildering array of things probably intended to be used on boats. There he chose some paint, nails, brushes, and a hammer, and he escaped with only a few prying questions from the mustached proprietor. Next came the grocers, where, following Mrs. Bellflower's advice, he bought waspfish and potatoes.

"Do you have moor-herb as well?" he asked the clerk, looking around uncertainly. He had no clue what they looked like.

She laughed. "Moor-herb! Who'd buy that when you can pick all you want for free?"

"Oh."

Perhaps taking pity on him, she held her thumb and finger about two inches apart. "It's yay high, so it hides a bit under the grasses. Tiny leaves, and at this time of year likely little purple flowers as well. You'll know it by the smell when you find it. It's nice."

"Thank you."

"I expect there's not much moor-herb in Greynox."

"Not much."

"Look. You want to know the best way to cook that waspfish? Go down to the harbor and ask the first fisherman you see for some sea-fern. He'll have some in his boat—it gets caught on the nets and hauled in. Sprinkle moor-herb on the fish, wrap the whole thing in sea-fern like a parcel, and set it in a pan high up from the flames. Don't leave it too long. Ten minutes at the most. It'll be lovely."

Overwhelmed with the unsolicited advice, he tried a smile. "So I eat the sea-fern too?"

"Oh, no," she cackled. "It's tough as old leather. Toss it away. Or give it to the imps if you fancy it—they do something with it, although I don't know what."

Feeling a bit as if the villagers were leading him on a wild goose chase, he walked to the harbor. A grizzled man was just tying up his boat.

"Ah, yer the new one, ain't ya?" he said by way of greeting. "Felix was right. Ya look like a Crofter."

Oliver wondered what else Felix had told the villagers about him.

"Um, I was just at the grocers—"

"That's Envina Corbyn's place."

A Corbyn. Oliver wasn't surprised. "Right. She said I should ask for some sea-fern for my fish?"

"Got yerself some waspfish, have ya? Well, she's right. Hang on." He hopped into his boat with surprising agility for a man of his age, tugged at something near the back, and returned with a handful of green stuff.

It was slimy, but Oliver tried not to look disgusted. "Thank you."

The fisherman clambered back onto the dock. "Now what ya want to do, lad, is sprinkle some fireberries on the fish afore you wrap it. Fresh or dried, won't make no difference, either's good. And soak the whole thing in saltwater for an hour afore you put it on the fire."

Apparently everyone in town had advice on how to cook. Oliver repeated his thanks and hurried away before the fisherman started suggesting more ingredients.

His final stop was a household goods shop. Fabric, pots and pans, small pieces of furniture, a few pieces of basic clothing, towels, cutlery, picture frames, firestones, boot scrapers, and hundreds of other items were piled on shelves and counters or hung from hooks in the ceiling. The shop had a strong odor of cleaning powders, and at least two enormous tabby cats wandered the place imperiously, rubbing against customers' legs.

"Mr. Webb!" cried the girl behind the counter. She wasn't yet grown, and she'd been almost beside herself to meet him two days earlier, as if he were someone famous. "You came back!"

"Hello, Pearl. I need a washtub, please."

She clapped her hands, showing far more excitement than the request merited. "'Course you do! My sister Anrilla takes in washing sometimes, but you wouldn't want to carry it up and down that cliff, would you? Besides"—she dropped her voice to a stage whisper—"she's with child right now and not doing much washing. Big as a house, she is!" She said the last part loudly, with giggles.

"I'm fine doing my own. If you could just—"

"Of course." She skipped out from behind the counter, braids swinging. Over an orange dress she wore an improbably vivid apron with splotches of color, as if someone had thrown paint at it. She would have been visible even in Greynox's worst gloom, and it was even easier to spot her in the brightly lit shop. Oliver had to take care not to trip over anything as she led him to the back of the large space, where there resided an assortment of tin and copper vessels ranging in size from teacups to small boats.

Oliver reached for one just big enough to encircle with his arms. "This one will—"

"Too small by far, Olly."

He spun around to find Felix leaning against a shelf and grinning. How did the man keep his hair and whisker scruff in the same precise state of disarray?

"This one is fine," Oliver said.

"Not if you want to wash your bedding or those furniture cloths." Felix pointed at one of the larger ones. "Get that one and it can double as a bathtub."

"I don't need a bathtub."

"You don't mind going around smelling like fish and mud, then?"

"I can wash up at the sink." Oliver glanced at Pearl, who was trying to hold back laughter, her palm against her mouth. "And I don't care if I stink."

"Well, others might. And you'll want to come into town now and then. Greet civilization, remind yourself how to speak to people, drink some ale. That sort of thing."

"I'm fine."

"I'll even help you carry it up to the cottage."

Although Oliver didn't want the big copper tub and couldn't remember agreeing to it, he somehow found himself a few minutes later leading Felix up the path, the tub—filled with his other purchases—heavy between them.

"You needn't look so glum," said Felix, who couldn't see Oliver's face. "I got you an excellent bargain."

"I don't want this enormous tub."

"But you do! You can set it outside the cottage, fill it with water, and throw in a few firestones. Then you'll soak in luxury with the finest view in the county."

Oliver huffed with mingled effort and annoyance. "It would take a week to fill."

"Ah, don't exaggerate. Only three or four days."

Although Oliver intended to make the rest of the journey in silence, he huffed again. "I'm not paying you for this."

"You wound me! I'm assisting out of the goodness of my heart. Besides, I don't need your money. I earned five coppers this morning."

Don't ask. Don't do it. It doesn't matter. Oliver heeded his own advice until they had almost reached the top of the path.

"How did you earn five coppers?"

Felix didn't answer. When they got to the flat part, he let go of the washtub, which wrenched itself from Oliver's sweaty grip and landed on the ground with a thud. Then he grinned and fished the coins from his pocket, angling them to glint in the sun.

"It's not many, but they'll feed me for a few days, I reckon. And it's five more than I had when I woke up today."

"How did you earn them?"

Felix cocked his hips and fluttered his eyelashes exactly like one of the girls on Lily Street in Greynox. When Oliver responded with what must have been a shocked expression, Felix burst out laughing.

"I wrote a letter for my great-aunt. Her eyesight's mostly gone, and she likes to correspond with her brother in Urchin Cove. My grandfather, he is. We'll send the letter to him next time the coach goes there."

"Five coppers for a letter?" Oliver asked skeptically. "Must be quite a missive."

"Oh, it is. She told him everything that happened here for the past month, she did. And he'll send one back with the latest news from Urchin Cove."

Oliver squinted at him. "How much news could there possibly be from either place?"

"Oh, you'd be surprised, Mr. Noxer. A few years back they had a pirate invasion up there, and—"

"You mentioned that already."

"Hmm. But I didn't tell you the whole tale, did I? It's a good 'un. And lately, we've tidings here. A brand new Noxer among us, tucked away like a hermit in Farview Cottage."

Unsure how he felt about being part of the local news, Oliver scowled and picked up his end of the washtub. "I have work to do. Come on."

Mrs. Bellflower didn't look surprised to see Felix, although she did cast Oliver a meaningful warning glance, which Felix either missed or ignored.

"I was just getting set to leave," she said, closing up her satchel. "I ran out of the blue thread I need. I'll be back with it in the morning. Should take me only an hour or so to finish."

Oliver looked at the chairs, now resplendent in their ridiculous new upholstery. "They look fine to me."

"Look fine, but need reinforcing. You want my work to last, don't you? If you take care of these chairs, you won't need to recover them within your lifetime."

Oliver barked a bitter laugh. "Right. I'll see you tomorrow then."

She nodded at him, glared at Felix, and left.

While Oliver put his purchases away—shoving the washtub into a corner for now—Felix examined the chairs. "Nice pattern."

"It was cheap. Left over from something."

"Fernica Moon's parlor. I know. But did you know there's a reason she chose it?"

"I expect everyone chooses fabrics for a reason. I chose this because it was cheap."

Oliver found himself staring at the fresh waspfish and debated whether he should go out in search of moor-herb. If it even existed and wasn't part of an elaborate joke on the newcomer.

"There's a story about this octopus. He was swimming along near the harbor when he spied a young woman sitting on the harbor wall and reading a book. She wasn't very pretty by human standards, but he liked the look of her—she was tall, with long arms and legs—and he was impressed with the book. Mollusks are envious of literacy. So the octopus decided to woo her, he did. He went searching along the sea floor for—"

"You're making this up as you go along."

Felix pressed a hand to his chest in mock offense. "I am *not*. All Crofters know this story. It's *beloved*. We teach it to our babies when—"

"You've finished helping me with the washtub. You can go now."

"With all the lovely waspfish just sitting there? No, you're going to have me to dinner."

A part of Oliver wished he could have this impertinent man *for* dinner. He was so beautiful, with such animated features, and so unlike anyone Oliver had known before. And there were those thick curls, which no doubt would be good to tug on, and that busy mouth he'd enjoy silencing.

"I have work." He turned on his heel, grabbed paint and a brush, and stomped outside.

Of course Felix followed him, leaning against the stone wall while Oliver painted a shutter. He stood closer than he should have—near enough that Oliver was tempted to color him green as well—and watched as if Oliver's movements were entirely fascinating.

"What *is* your line of work, Olly?"

"It's Oliver. Or Webb."

"You're not a fisherman, that's clear enough. And if you hired Mrs. Bellflower to sew your chairs, I expect you're not a sailmaker either. You don't own any tools—or have any other signs of a profession. And you've moored yourself here above the village, which is damned inconvenient if you intend employment harborside."

"I don't."

Oliver didn't owe Felix any answers, but giving them seemed faster and easier than being endlessly harried. Felix was very like an imp, only instead of crumbs he wanted... attention, Oliver supposed. Or entertainment.

"So I ask again, Mr. Webb. What is your line of work?"

"I don't have one. I'm going to live in my cottage and mind my own business." He said the last part rather pointedly.

"Ah. You're no aristocrat or industrial baron, but you're also far too young to retire. You can't be more than thirty-five."

Oliver shot him a glare before moving a few feet to the next shutter. "Twenty-eight."

"Did your mother leave you enough fortune to keep you for the rest of your life?"

"She left me this cottage and, I guess, some of the surrounding land. Nothing else."

"Then how—"

"I had a position in Greynox. I set aside most of my pay and now I've enough to manage. But not to pay you."

Felix smiled and sank down against the wall as if he were too lazy to stand. The ground was soft, and Oliver was tired. He wouldn't have minded a rest himself. But not with Felix watching him.

"What was your position in Greynox, I wonder. I don't think you were a doctor or a solicitor, and you don't seem the type to be a clerk. But you've an education—I can tell by the rare words you choose to grace me with—so not menial labor. You seem too hardy for factory work. Those poor sods all look so sickly. And you're a large man who fancies stamping about and barking orders. Were you a policeman, Olly?"

There were at least a half dozen parts of that little speech that Oliver wished to object to, and a few more that made his chest feel too tight. He opted for a simple and mostly accurate denial. "I was not a policeman."

"Well, that's good. All the ones I met were nasty sorts who couldn't decide whether to beat you to a pulp, extort all your money, or both."

Oliver almost asked how many policemen he'd met and in what capacities but stopped himself in time to avoid another nonsense tale. He took a step back to evaluate his work. The green looked nice against the stone, and although the color was darker than the moor plants, it connected the cottage to its surroundings.

Felix squinted up at him. "Gods, you weren't a wizard, were you?"

That nearly made Oliver choke. "No. There's nothing magical about me. Besides, what've you got against wizards?"

"Nothing. My granddad's one. It's only.... You've got me on your hook, Olly, and I'm gasping for oxygen. Be merciful. Tell me what you did for a living."

Well, that was both a ridiculous metaphor and a gross exaggeration. But Felix did look oddly vulnerable, slumped against the cottage with his legs sprawled and his hair falling into his face.

"You were wrong about the factory bit. I worked at Hillard's woolen mill."

"You operated the looms?" Felix looked highly skeptical.

Suddenly so exhausted that his eyes swam, Oliver shook his head. "I was a security officer."

"Which involved what?"

"Making sure nobody broke in to steal anything or damage the equipment. Accompanying shipments of funds to and from the bank. Protecting Mr. Hillard when he visited less savory parts of the city." Oliver made a face. "Breaking up fights between the workers, now and then."

"So... you were a policeman. Of sorts. I was right."

With no energy to argue, Oliver simply shook his head and gathered his things. He could finish the painting tomorrow; he had that much time, at least. At the doorway he stopped suddenly, causing a near collision with Felix. "Is there really something called moor-herb, and will it taste good—"

"On your waspfish. Of course. Hang on."

Felix loped a few yards away and bent at the waist, displaying an arse that Oliver should not be staring at. It was surprisingly well-rounded considering Felix's general thinness. He plucked something, turned with a knowing grin—as if he was absolutely aware of Oliver's unwilling admiration—and sauntered back.

"Moor-herb." He held out a few sprigs that precisely matched Envina Corbyn's description.

When Oliver sniffed at them, he realized he'd been smelling them all along, crushed underfoot as he strolled the moor. The scent was sharp, as if it might make him sneeze, yet also pleasant.

Inside, Oliver washed up and then eyed the fish. It was already gutted and cleaned, but its blank eye seemed to stare up at him reproachfully. Oliver spun to look at Felix, who was gazing at Oliver's makeshift bed. "You cook it," Oliver said.

"Wha'?"

"I paid for it. If you're going to eat half, you should cook it."

"Look at the size of you and the size of me, mate. I won't eat half."

"But still."

Felix shifted awkwardly from one foot to another. "The thing is—"

"I've never made fish in my life, but Envina Corbyn said it was easy. I can give you directions." He wiped his hands on a towel and walked over to the almost-completed chairs. It felt wonderful to collapse into one of them. Mrs. Bellflower had done a good job with the stuffing. He wondered if he could somehow manage to sleep in the chairs until his mattress arrived.

"I know *how*," said Felix, wringing his long-fingered hands. "But you won't want me near your hearth."

Oliver yawned so widely that his jaw cracked. "Dunno why not. It's just stone. Plenty of firestones in the basket. Don't fall in."

His eyelids, too heavy to keep open, slid shut. He was like a young child or an old man, worthless without a daily nap. He never used to need them. He used to wake up before dawn, take some exercise, eat a hearty breakfast, and hurry to Hillard's, where he'd be on his feet all day. He traversed the iron stairs to Mr. Hillard's office at least twenty times per shift. And once his work was over, he'd meet up with friends for food and ale before finding an evening's entertainment. A boxing match, perhaps, or more drinks, or sometimes a willing stranger in the darkened back of certain pubs or against the bricks in a narrow alley. The sweat-and-ale scent of those strangers, the sensation of heavy clothes parting to reveal select bits of hot skin, the sounds of moans and panting muffled against sleeves and backs. Gods, the life coursing through his veins then, his heart beating like the engines in a factory, his cock hard and heavy, his—

"Help!"

Oliver leapt from the chair, nearly falling over his own feet, and came very close to tripping into the conflagration that engulfed his hearth. The flames were high enough to lick the ceiling beams, and the heat made his skin feel tight. Felix scurried to the sink and began frantically working the pump.

"Not that!" Oliver bellowed. In three huge strides, he'd reached the untidy pile of furniture cloths still waiting to be washed. He grabbed two or three, lunged back to the hearth, and tossed the fabric onto the fire, smothering it at once.

After a few steadying breaths, he turned to Felix, who was motionless by the sink. "How many bloody firestones did you use?"

"Just two," came the murmured answer.

Oliver couldn't believe that. But when he lifted the cloth and patted out a few stray sparks, he saw that, indeed, only two firestones sat on the hearth, still glowing a little.

"Did you pour grease on them?"

"No. I only.... I'm sorry."

Felix looked miserable, and when Oliver peered at him more closely, he realized Felix was scorched as well. Oliver checked to make sure the cloth wasn't going to combust and then stepped over to tow Felix to one of the chairs. "Sit. Let me have a look at you."

He had to clean Felix's face with a damp cloth first, and during that intimacy Felix wouldn't meet his gaze. Some strands of hair were a bit singed, and his cheeks and forehead were red, as if he were sunburned.

"I'm fine," Felix whispered.

"I might have some heal-all ointment. I'll just go—"

Felix grabbed Oliver's wrist. "No. I'll be fine." And then, piteously, "Please."

Oliver scrunched up his mouth. "Then let me see your hands."

For some reason, handling Felix's palms and fingers seemed even more personal than touching his face. Short, ragged nails made Oliver suspect that he chewed them. Felix's skin was uncalloused and smooth save for a small blister on the pads of two fingers and a thumb. "Could use some ointment here too," Oliver said.

"No. Just.... I'll go."

Felix started to stand, but Oliver gently pushed him back down. "Stay. You wouldn't want to miss dinner after all that, would you?"

Chapter Five

Oliver would have been entirely within his rights to interrogate Felix. The man certainly hadn't hesitated to inundate him with questions. And it was Oliver's cottage that Felix had somehow nearly burned down, after all. But something about Felix looked vulnerable as he huddled among the octopuses and roses, his hands swaddled in cool, damp towels.

So Oliver simply set a proper fire and, seeing that Felix had already wrapped the waspfish in sea-ferns, started water boiling for the potatoes. He decided he might as well set a proper table while he was at it, at least as much as his limited possessions permitted. He put out his only two plates, all his cutlery, and a wooden salt-cellar that, he'd been assured, contained crystals processed from the sea right here in Croftwell. He didn't have butter for the potatoes, so he set out a bottle of olive oil.

As he waited, the silence felt so heavy that he almost begged Felix for a story.

But it was Felix who finally spoke first, clearing his throat and keeping his head bowed. "I'm sorry."

"No harm done aside from those cloths, which I don't especially need for anything."

"You acted fast."

"Fires break out in a mill now and then. All the dust. You learn to move quick before the whole place goes up in flames." He shuddered, remembering the smoking remains of another mill he'd seen a few years ago. Dozens of workers had died in that fire. He gave Felix what he hoped was a firm nod. "Smothering it is more efficient than using water, especially if there's any grease involved."

Felix nodded without looking up. "I knew that. I panicked."

"You got hurt."

That made Felix lift his gaze. "Only a little. I'll be—"

"Fine. Yes. You said that."

He saw that the water was ready and dumped in the cut-up potatoes. Ten minutes for the fish, Envina had said. He wouldn't put it on the fire until the potatoes were nearly done.

"Moor-herb's nice on potatoes as well," Felix said. "I'll get some more if you need it."

"I have enough. Are you sure you don't want ointment? It's good stuff. Comes from one of the best chemists in Greynox." Although it turned out that its name was inaccurate—it didn't truly heal all. Hadn't done him a bit of good, as a matter of fact. But it would work well for Felix's minor burns.

"Is it bespelled?" Felix looked resigned to some terrible fate.

"I expect so. The chemist is meant to be an excellent wizard."

"Then none for me."

"Whyever not?"

Instead of answering, Felix shook his head. Silence settled in again. Oliver was relieved when he poked at the potatoes and found them softened. He put the pan with the fish over the flames, realized he had no good way of telling when ten minutes was up, and shrugged. He'd have to guess. Perhaps he could measure it in his heartbeats, which seemed noisy in the quiet cottage.

How was it that Felix took up so much more room with his mouth resolutely shut?

Oliver's estimate must have been sound, because when he set the food on the table it looked good and smelled delicious. Felix, sitting across from him, sniffed appreciatively. "Lovely. I am very fond of waspfish. Are you?"

"I've never had it."

"That's right. You can't find it in Greynox unless you're ridiculously rich. Did you know some of the aristocracy pay mountains of coppers to have waspfish brought to them via coach and train? It's swimming in our harbor in the morning and gracing the lords' golden plates by dinner." For the first time since the fire, the corners of his mouth lifted. "We're eating like princes tonight. Minus the jewel-encrusted goblets."

"I'll make sure to pick some up next time I'm in the village."

Felix snorted. "Listen to that. Olly Webb made an actual joke. Who'd have thought?" He raised his glass of cider in a mock toast.

Oliver's friends used to say he was funny. He'd have them roaring with laughter when they gathered in the evenings, and they'd clap him on the back and even buy him rounds. That seemed centuries ago.

"Why did you come here?" Felix asked, interrupting the memories.

"I inherited the cottage."

"Years ago, sounds like. Why now?"

Oliver shrugged and popped a forkful of fish into his mouth. It was... delicious. Rich and smooth and salty, it smelled of the sea but tasted like heaven.

Felix ate some of his as well, a few sounds of enjoyment escaping as he chewed and swallowed. "Very nice. Well done, Olly." Then he set down his fork and took a deep breath. "It's a curse."

"What is?"

"My granddad—the wizard, aye?—says it's not, that it's just the way I am. Like some people can't carry a tune and others can barely walk without tripping over themselves. But I think it's a curse. It feels like one."

Setting down his own cutlery, Oliver leaned forward. Felix was trying to tell him something important, although Oliver didn't understand what. "What feels like a curse?"

"It could be worse. I know that well enough. I had an ancestor, oh, back a few generations before Lyra Moon's time. Blaynel Corbyn. He was the best fisherman Croftwell had ever known. He could bring in a catch when no one else caught a thing, and he did it right fast, so he'd fill up his boat, come back to shore, and spend the rest of the day lolling about. But he never helped his wife with the chores, and she grew angry. She was a Loowin, and you don't want to have *them* against you. Blaynel woke up one day and, out of the blue, just thinking about water made him so seasick that he couldn't hardly stand. Well, he went to his wife and—"

"Felix. What's your curse?"

That earned him a bleak look and a sigh. "I'm... allergic to magic. Or more accurately, I suppose, it's allergic to me."

"Pardon me?"

"Let's... let's just eat, shall we? And I'll tell you a story after."

Felix looked so miserable that Oliver gave a small nod and continued his meal. It was delicious—perhaps more so because he'd prepared it himself—and he had two generous servings. Felix had only one, but he drank enough cider to make up for it. He drank enough, in fact, that a man of his slender build should have displayed blurred eyes and slurred words, yet everything about him remained crisp and sharp, as if alcohol were his whetstone.

After dinner, Felix helped with the washing up. There were only a few scraps left of the fish, and since they wouldn't keep anyway, Oliver tossed them to the imps. Judging from their excited chatter, the creatures were very pleased with the gift.

"I've spoiled them already," he muttered as he stood in the open doorway.

"They're good to have around." Felix pushed gently past him, some of the furniture cloths heaped in his arms. "Will you sit outside with me for a bit? It's a lovely night."

That was true enough. Oliver took a spot beside Felix on the bench and opened his senses. The sky was entirely clear, the half-moon reflecting off the sea far below. A light breeze carried the sweet scent of some kind of flower, and the waves slapped along the distant shore.

Chuckling, Felix arranged the scorched, dusty cloths around their shoulders and over their laps. "Your clothes will need cleaning."

"Good thing I bought a washtub."

"Why did you leave the factory and Greynox and come here?"

Oliver shook his head. "You were going to tell me a story, remember?"

"Ah. Yes." Felix's teeth flashed white in the moonlight. He slouched a bit more deeply and gazed out at the dark horizon. "There was a lass from Urchin Cove, you see."

THERE WAS a lass from Urchin Cove, you see. She was the sort of young person we produce in great numbers around here: sturdy, strong-willed, clear-eyed. The sort who can withstand a gale without a fuss and doesn't want anyone telling 'em what to do or how to do it. Her name was Merwica Andox. Still is, halfwise.

Everyone expected Merwica to marry a local fisherman, 'cause that's what lasses from Urchin Cove do. But she said no. Didn't fancy any of the local lads, and besides, she preferred a husband who stayed put on land. Maybe that's because her father wasn't a fisherman either —he was the village wizard. Still is.

So Merwica came to Croftwell, where she had an aunt who'd never married or had children. Merwica moved in with her, worked about the house, made some coppers helping out at the grocer now and then.

She was working at the grocer, in fact, when a lad came in to buy some oil and tinned tomatoes. He wasn't especially handsome, but he made a few jokes and she thought he was funny. Oh, you know how this part goes, I'll wager. They went for strolls along the harbor, he showed her his family sail-mending business, she met his family. And in due time they married. His name is Samuel Corbyn.

This isn't an interesting story so far, is it? Nothing exciting at all—just two ordinary people in a little village starting a family. Which they did straight away. They had three strapping boys, followed by two strapping girls. And they were as happy as any family, which is to say they sometimes quarreled and sometimes money was tight but mostly they were content.

Ah, but the next time Merwica got pregnant, she lost the baby. And the time after that. Next baby came to term but died that same day. The other children were a comfort to Merwica and Samuel, but still they mourned long and hard.

So when she became pregnant again, well, you might imagine that everyone was on tenterhooks about it. But she and the baby came through the pregnancy just fine, and he was born squalling and healthy as could be. The Corbyns were so pleased and relieved that they named their new son Felix. It means happy or lucky, aye?

Samuel went whistling back to his sail-mending. Merwica kept the large household afloat and orderly. That boring sort of contentment returned.

But when Felix was two years old, he caught the croup. Stray bit of cold sea air got into him, perhaps. Loads of children have that happen, and I daresay you did too, what with nothing to breathe but that foul Noxer air. It's nothing much to worry about.

Merwica *did* worry, though. Much more than she should have, and no doubt on account of her lost babies. She slathered Felix with heal-all ointment, made him drink a dose of curative elixir, and even tried a bit of a medicinal spell she'd learned from her father. All of which should have helped or, at the very least, done no harm.

Instead, Felix became suddenly and critically ill. His body turned red and swelled all over, he coughed so hard he could barely take in air, and he ran a fever hot enough to trigger convulsions. Croftwell didn't have a wizard or a healer then—still doesn't—so Merwica sent a message to her father, who came at once, tearing down the coast road on the back of a borrowed dragon like a knight of old.

The wizard arrived before the child died, which was a small miracle in itself. After examining his grandson, though, he ran out of the cottage as if chased by demons. Merwica caught up with him in the garden.

"What do you mean by this, father?" she yelled, her voice raw from sobbing. "Make him better!"

The old man shook his head sadly. "I'll only make him worse, my dear. Even being close to him is dangerous."

"Why?" she wailed.

"It's a quirk in his system. Some people are born with it, and nobody knows why. It's very rare. But when that boy gets too close to magic, he... twists it. Makes it go wrong. It's not his fault, not at all. But it's very dangerous."

She looked at her father gravely. "I used magic to try to treat his croup. That's why he's so... so ill now."

"You didn't know. You couldn't. What you did would have been fine for any other child."

She was crying, Merwica was, but that didn't stop her from tackling the problem head-on. "How do we cure this?"

"We can't. There's nothing to be done for this affliction. Go inside and do the best you can to keep him comfortable. A cold oat poultice might help his skin and the fever, and if he can swallow, try hot fire-berry tea with honey for his cough. Love him, Merwica, as you do so well." The wizard was crying too, you see, because this was his grandson.

Merwica did what she had to. She walked back into her home and did everything she could to save her son's life—without magic. It worked. He didn't die. He was very sick for months, though, and he never fully recovered. For the rest of his childhood, he remained small and weak—nothing like his big, strong family. Other people would catch a bit of a sniffle and feel better in a day or two; Felix would be laid up at death's door for weeks. And of course anytime he was too close to magic, disasters happened.

He surprised everyone by surviving to adulthood, but that raised a fresh problem. What was he going to do with his life? He wasn't strong enough for most positions, especially fishing. And the others.... Well you know, there's nearly always a bit of magic about. The firestones for heat and light. The lockspells that keep things secure. The charms woven into nets to help with good catches or sewn into sails to help find favorable winds. Everything Felix attempted turned out badly.

Nobody particularly wanted him in their homes either. Not that they didn't care about him. None of these people were cruel or cold-hearted. But if he stayed longer than a few days, inevitably his curse would kick in and... and he'd have to move on.

The wizard informed the Corbyns that printers don't use magic in their trade. It spoils the inks. So Felix's oldest brother worked very hard and finally found him an apprenticeship with a printer in

Greynox. Felix moved away from the sea to the city, determined to succeed. For a while he did. He even managed to avoid most magical mishaps.

But, oh... problems arose. Not from the curse, but problems nonetheless. Felix couldn't abide being so far away. He returned home, as all Crofters do.

He got by as best he could, earning a few coppers here and there, moving from one house to another every few days. Sometimes an accident happened and his curse caused damage, but at least nobody died from it.

One night Felix tried to cook some nice waspfish for a newcomer, but he got too near the firestones for too long. Nearly burned down the newcomer's cottage, which would have been a great shame. Luckily, the newcomer was quick of mind and fleet of foot, and he doused the fire at once. They had a very fine dinner after all. And afterwards they sat outside and Felix told a story while they gazed out at the velvet sea.

FOR WHAT MIGHT HAVE BEEN hours, they sat on the bench in silence. It wasn't exactly an easy peace—Felix's tale carried too much pain for that—but neither was it awkward. The salt air seemed to help, and the ripples of moonshine on water, and the faint scent of crushed moorherb evident even over the scorched cotton of the furniture cloths.

Anything Oliver might say in comfort would have been false. He'd never been good with words like that, and even if he were, what could you say to a man who was forced to live like flotsam in his own hometown, among his own family?

"Are there places in the world with no magic at all, do you think?" he asked at last. "Like a desert lacks water?"

"I don't know. I couldn't leave here anyway, at least not for long." Felix stood and stretched, allowing the cloths to fall. "You look done in. I'll leave you be."

"I'm—" Oliver stopped himself, not sure what he wanted to say next. He *was* done in. His bones ached and his body felt leaden.

Felix patted his shoulder. "Come on down to the Merman tomorrow night."

"I don't think so."

"Aw, c'mon. Have a few pints. Perhaps you'll meet Tural's partner, the wind person. He has even more stories than I do, when he's in the mood. And he has the most gorgeous face you've ever seen—including in paintings or statues. Doesn't mind being looked at, either." Felix gave a small chuckle.

"I don't want—"

"—people to bury you with questions and weigh you down with their scrutiny. I can see that. But no worries. I'll tell them to fuck right off if they press too much."

Oliver thought about an evening in a pub with friendly conversation and good ale, with cozy warm lighting and laughter and the feeling of being... connected. Then he shook his head. That was all over for him.

He stood too, as careless with the cloths as Felix had been. The imps could nick them for all he cared. Or tomorrow he'd wash them in the stupidly big tub Felix had convinced him to buy. He'd clean up the soot from Felix's disaster and finish painting the shutters, and really, that was a good day's work right there. If he found the energy for it, he'd have a walk on the moor. And he'd ignore the hollowness in his heart the same way he ignored the pains in his joints and the weakness of his muscles.

"Thank you for the story," he said as Felix started to walk toward the path.

Felix stopped. He turned back, crossed the distance between them, and kept *on* coming until Oliver was pressed back against the stone wall of his cottage, Felix standing so close that you could have barely slid a newspaper between them.

Oliver noted that Felix was shorter by a few inches. His eyes were inky pools, his breath somehow sweet while redolent of waspfish. Oliver could feel the heat of Felix's burns still emanating from his face. Or no, perhaps that was Oliver's own warmth, the blood rushing just beneath his skin.

"Do you think my stories are nonsense?" Felix's voice was so quiet that Oliver wouldn't have heard it, had he been a step further away.

"No. At least, not all of them."

"But stories are the most truthful things of all, even the ones that aren't entirely accurate. Do you see?"

Frozen yet burning, Oliver didn't see. He could barely think. And he didn't know what Felix wanted from him, their faces so near that a small movement would end in a kiss. Men didn't act like this toward one another, not unless they'd met in a very particular sort of establishment and were positive they shared a certain understanding. They didn't smile in the moonlight at another man, lips soft and slightly parted, tongue flicking out to leave a sheen of moisture in its wake.

"Maybe," Felix whispered, "you'll tell me your story soon."

Then he spun and ran away, disappearing almost at once down the path at the edge of the cliff.

Chapter Six

By all rights Oliver should have fallen asleep quickly, makeshift bed notwithstanding. His belly was full and his body fatigued. Unfortunately, his brain still sizzled like water on a hot frying pan. What did Felix want from him? Some free food and a fresh audience for his stories? Or something more? And why should it matter anyway, since Oliver didn't want a friend or a lover. He wanted to be left alone in his cottage atop the cliff, with its views of the sea and the odd little scratch marks on its walls. He wanted to be free of memories and devoid of aspirations.

"I don't even want the fucking imps!" he rasped into the darkness.

Yes, well, wants were one thing and needs something else entirely. Ever since Felix had pinned him against the wall, Oliver's cock had been heavy and aching. All the skin on his body felt as if it had been put on wrong, a poorly fitting garment that needed smoothing out. He needed... gods, he needed to be touched.

He had to do it for himself: rough angry strokes with one hand while his other clenched into a tight fist and his eyes squeezed closed. He climaxed so quickly that it stole his breath. When he could draw air again, he let loose a long, loud howl. And then he fell asleep with his seed cooling and sticky on his groin.

The dream fell on him almost at once, as if it had been waiting to pounce since his arrival in Croftwell. He'd hoped that he would escape it by moving here—perhaps it might disembark at the wrong train station—but no, here it was.

Maybe he'd invoked it by talking about Hillard's, because that was where the dream began, inside a vast brick building where dust swirled thickly in shafts of sun that beamed from the skylights. All around him, machines whirred and thrummed like a great creature's lungs and heart. Which is what they were—not only was he inside Hillard's but also in the gut of a voracious beast. People moved about him, industrious in their work. They had no faces. Just hands and feet that served the beast.

He couldn't breathe inside the mill. Never could at this point in the dream. He lurched for the nearest door, almost surprised when it fell open under his weight. He was outside on a Greynox street now, sucking in lungfuls of the dirty air. Except for him, the street was deserted. He had to get somewhere, though. Had to give someone an important message. If he failed, people would die. Yet he was lost and couldn't remember where to go, so he staggered from doorway to alleyway, searching.

He tried to run, but his legs were leaden. Then suddenly a crowd pressed around him. Hundreds of voices rose together in an angry, wordless chant. He couldn't push through them, and when he shouted to clear the way, he couldn't hear his own voice.

No! No, he had to—

A flash of light seared his eyes, followed by hundreds of shrieks. People clutched at him, begged him to save them, even as their bodies shriveled, twisted, and desiccated, falling into piles of dust. The buildings crumbled too, followed by the street, and the pavement he stood on. He then felt the horrible tingling within his own body and—

"Get out of that dream, boy."

He blinked his eyes open, untangled himself from a knot of blankets, and sat up. A man sat in one of the octopus chairs, his gnarled hands clasped in his lap, his wrinkled face looking mildly annoyed. Oliver could see the pink roses right through him.

"I'm still dreaming," Oliver said. He gave himself a vicious pinch on the thigh, but that didn't wake him, and now the transparent man seemed amused.

"Your dream is over, thanks to me. You should stop torturing yourself with it. Does you no good at all."

"You.... What language are you speaking?" It wasn't Oliver's own, yet he recognized it. And, apparently, could speak it as well. He was very clever in his dreams.

"Of course you understand me, boy. This is the tongue your ancestors spoke. Most of them, anyway. The rest, well, I can't wrap my mouth around their words. They love vowels far too much." The man wheezed a laugh.

"Who are you?"

"A ghost, of course, you daft thing. Don't recall my name. Forgot it centuries ago, I did, but no matter. I only miss it a little."

Oliver ran a shaking hand over his brow. "I'm dreaming an ancient ghost."

"No, you're talking to an ancient ghost. A ghost who did you the favor of interrupting your nightmare. You can thank me anytime, you know."

"I, uh...." Oliver swallowed thickly. "Thank you."

The cottage looked completely real and not at all dreamlike. He'd left the shutters open, so just enough moonlight stole in for him to see the recent scorch marks on the hearth, the sprigs of unused moor-herb in a glass of water on the sill near the sink, his coat hanging from a hook near the door, and a transparent man perched on his chair and dressed in what appeared to be animal skins. He tried another pinch, but it didn't help.

"It's nice to see the cottage made a home again," said the man. "It's served that way, off and on, for a long time. Some of these stones formed the walls of my house."

"Your house?"

"Oh, lad, catch up, won't you? There's no reason to doubt what's so obvious, and right in front of your face too. I'm a ghost. You are my many-great-grandson, a few thousand years down the line. Look at the shape of my nose, my chin, my ears. Same as yours. Your eyes and mouth come from your other side."

Oliver rubbed his eyes, but that didn't change anything. He *felt* awake, with the stone floor hard under his blankets and his limbs heavy. Gods, was this the start of hallucinations? It hadn't occurred to him that it might be a symptom.

"So much doubt," said the ghost. "You're not a trusting man. Comes from living in the city, it does. We didn't have places like that in my day. How you lot can stand it, I'll never know."

"I couldn't stand it," Oliver muttered. "That's why I'm here."

"No, you came here because you belong here. The earth in this place makes up your very bones, boy."

"Only half of them."

The ghost wheezed a laugh. "Are you sure about that?"

"I...." Oliver fell silent. Why was he arguing with a figment in the middle of the night? He'd be twice as tired the next day. He lay back down, pulled up the covers, and turned away from the chair. But no, there were more ghosts—nearly half a dozen in a dizzying range of strange outfits, all of them grinning at him.

"Haunt me all you want, but I'm not leaving this cottage."

"Who said we want you to leave?" asked a girl of seven or eight wearing a dress of coarsely woven cloth.

"That's what ghosts do. They scare people away." Or so he'd heard in stories that he hadn't believed. Still didn't, dammit. This was nothing but the fabrication of a confused brain.

The little girl came closer and crouched beside him. She had very dirty bare feet and held a bow and arrow that were sized for her and looked quite serviceable.

"We don't want to scare *you* away. You're supposed to be here." She giggled. "You still don't believe in us. But I can prove it. Get paper and pen."

He didn't want to. But then it occurred to him that if he wrote something down, he'd have it as evidence of his own madness in the morning—in case he forgot or tried to deny it. What he'd do with that proof he didn't know, but he'd always been a man who preferred facts to supposition.

"Fine."

He stood and walked to the bureau. He'd managed to get two

drawers operational and now stored clothing in one and his few personal items in the other. Among the latter were a notebook and a pen that never needed additional ink. He had purchased it for a half-copper on Dragonford Street in Greynox, and holding it now, he wondered what damage Felix's curse might cause with it.

The little girl joined him, her feet a few inches above the floor and her movement more a floating glide than a walk. She smiled up at him, every bit a child—albeit a transparent one—with a wonderful joke.

"Tomorrow follow the top of the cliff north. When you come to a path by a broken stone wall, turn inland and walk for ten minutes. You'll see pink sprites along the way—they're very rare, you know. You'll find the stones where my village was. Look at the tallest one. You'll need to scrape away some of the dirt and things. You'll find a drawing I made. It looks like this."

Her ghostly hand wrapped around his. He couldn't feel it, exactly, although his skin went very cold, and a firm pressure guided the pen to the blank page in his open notebook. As he watched, shivering, a figure appeared: a sideways oval, four vertical lines connecting to its underside, a circle perched on the top left edge, and a squiggly line trailing behind on the right. The spectral hand lifted from his.

"That's a moor-cat. We used to see them near the edge of the village, hunting rabbits. There aren't any moor-cats anymore." She looked briefly unhappy.

"Why am I meant to do this?" asked Oliver.

The old man on the chair replied. "So you'll stop doubting, boy. Now go back to sleep. And stay out of that dream."

All the ghosts disappeared with a sound that made Oliver's ears pop.

Since he was up anyway, he drank a glass of water, pausing afterward to look through the window at the sea. Then he sighed, climbed back into his nest, and effortlessly fell asleep .

He did not go tromping around the moor when he woke up. Instead he had some breakfast and then strung a line between the cottage and the outdoor loo. Both structures already had hooks for the purpose, which was convenient. He washed his clothing and the furniture cloths, hanging the items to dry on the line. It was hard work, but he told himself he'd need to get used to it. He didn't own many outfits, so he'd need to launder often to avoid being grubby.

He was just completing this chore when Mrs. Bellflower arrived and started work on the chairs. Soon after, cheerful voices wafted over from the cliff path. Those turned out to belong to four laughing young men who'd lashed Oliver's new mattress to a wheeled cart and somehow managed to get it to the top of the cliff.

"Woulda been easier if you used a hammock instead, like we do at sea," said one of the lads, laughing.

"I've never slept in one, I'm afraid."

"Oughta give it a try, then."

Oliver had already paid for the mattress, and the men refused to take any money for delivery. They'd had too much fun in the process, they said. But they happily drank the glasses of cider he offered, flirted a little with Mrs. Bellflower—who seemed amused—and then looked down at the harbor and pointed out their boats to Oliver. Before departing, they urged Oliver to join them soon at the pubs. He could hear their jolly voices long after they'd disappeared.

"You'll be more comfortable tonight," Mrs. Bellflower announced, interrupting Oliver's brief wallow in self-pity. She jerked her chin in the direction of his bed.

"Yes. Loads better than the floor."

She began to pack up her things, stuffing thread, scissors, and needles into her satchel. "Farview should be a good place to sleep. Good air."

The previous night's weirdness, which he'd been trying not to think about, vividly returned. His notebook and pen still lay on the table. "Um... somebody mentioned the cottage is haunted."

"Felix Corbyn, no doubt." She was giving her work a final inspection and not looking his way. "He has all the stories, that one."

"Yes."

"Well, no worries. I'm sure the ghosts will introduce themselves soon enough." She said this very casually, as if mentioning some neighbors who would drop by.

Oliver gaped at her. "Introduce themselves?"

"I expect they're just like the rest of us—eager to meet the long-lost Crofter who's returned to the fold." She fastened the satchel and started for the door.

Oliver rushed to intercept her. "Your payment—"

"Paid me before I began, remember?"

"Right. But that was for one chair, and you did two."

She waved a hand. "Ah, it's nothing. Working up here's been almost like a bit of a holiday, it has. Besides, we're family. Fourth cousins twice removed, or some such." Humming, she stepped through the doorway, then tsked at some hovering imps before descending the path.

By then it was time for lunch. Oliver fried up the leftover potatoes from the night before, adding in some bits of sausage and, on a whim, a bit of moor-herb. The results were quite satisfactory. But as he was eating, he couldn't help but look at the closed notebook and then couldn't stop himself from opening it and seeing the scribbles that could, if you squinted, be interpreted as some sort of animal.

"Dammit."

The walk along the cliff was nice enough. He hadn't gone this way before, and he enjoyed the view. Birds wheeled and called, some very close by, and he wondered if they had nests along the cliff. He didn't know what species they were, but they seemed exotic compared to the pigeons and harpies of Greynox.

He told himself that it didn't mean anything when he came to a broken stone wall. The moor was littered with the remains of ancient structures. And there was certainly nothing remarkable about this one, which had probably tumbled many centuries earlier and was nearly overgrown by moss and small plants. And yes, there was a faint footpath leading inland, but footpaths crisscrossed everywhere up here. It might not even have been made by humans—this could be an imp thoroughfare for all he knew.

Oliver turned right to follow the track. Five minutes later, as he came over a gentle rise, he startled a flock of sprites. They buzzed up and around, flashing in the sunshine, before zooming by his face—teasingly, he thought—and flitting away. They were bright pink, like low clouds tinged by a setting sun. He'd never heard of pink sprites before. Well, not until the previous night.

He wasn't in the least surprised when he reached one of the collections of stones he knew to be a former village. It wasn't any more intact than the ones he'd come across already, but somehow it didn't feel abandoned. Maybe that was due to the cheery little flowers dotting the ground, or the small birds chirping, or the bees and butterflies doing their rounds. Could it really be true that his own direct ancestors had once lived in this very spot? Perhaps, but that idea set him to thinking about matters even less comfortable than ghosts, so he pushed the speculation away.

He was so bloody tired. Temptation pulled at him to lie on the soft ground and rest. Just a short nap to make up for his restless night. But he could imagine his eyes falling closed and never again opening, the moor-herb and little flowers growing around him, the earth slowly swallowing his bones. Perhaps not such a terrible fate, but he wasn't yet ready for it.

The largest stone was easy to find. It was a rough-hewn rectangle almost as high as his shoulders. He wondered whether it was native to this spot or had been brought from another place, and if the latter, how. Did his distant forebears use dragons and carts? He had no idea.

Yellow, white, and green lichens grew on the stone like spatters of paint. But if he peered closely, he could make out markings—lines and curves carved into the rock. They didn't look like anything he could identify, and he wasn't sure whether they were meant to be writing or pictures. But... yes. Just there. He gently brushed away some lichens to reveal a figure he could identify. It was, in fact, identical to the drawing on the sheet of paper he'd brought with him. And when he bent his knees for a closer inspection, he found something on the ground as well: a child-sized bow and arrow.

"All right," Oliver announced loudly, "I've stopped doubting."

It was a relief to know that at least his mind wasn't going. Or not yet, in any case.

Chapter Seven

Throughout the next four days, Oliver worked on his small repair tasks and spent his free time looking out to sea. On the last day, a steady rain made the outdoors unpleasant. He lit a couple of firestones, made tea, and tidied the cottage. When he ran out of chores, he dragged one of the octopus chairs to the biggest window and spent the rest of the day as Lyra Moon once had—but perhaps with a bit more dozing.

Over those four days, he hadn't gone to the pubs. Hadn't gone down to the village at all, and nobody came up to see him. The ghosts didn't visit again. He slept deeply and without nightmares in his new bed, and for that he was grateful.

Unless he chose to starve, he couldn't remain a hermit forever. On the fifth day, when the sun reappeared in the early afternoon, he decided to descend the cliff for provisions. He first took some time making himself presentable: washing up, shaving, combing his hair, and donning clean clothes. Then just before dinnertime, he tucked a purseful of coppers into his pocket and headed down the path.

Oliver's intention was simply to visit the grocers and then return home—or at least so he told himself. But he had to walk by the Merman to get there, and somehow he found himself going inside. The customers greeted him with a round of welcomes, as if he were one of them. Felix wasn't among the crowd, however, and Oliver tried to squelch the pang of disappointment. He was here for only dinner and ale, not Felix's company.

Tural, the blond landlord with the wooden leg, hurried to him with a broad smile. "I thought maybe you'd hated our cooking, since we didn't see you again."

"No, I've been busy."

"Well please, make yourself comfortable. An ale? Yes, I thought so. I'll be back with it in a moment."

Oliver chose the same table as last time. It was close enough to everyone else that he wouldn't appear standoffish, he hoped, and it gave him a nice view of the room at large. This time he noticed the paintings on the walls. Some were of the ocean, with and without boats, as might be expected, but a few were of snow-capped peaks. Oliver had never been to the mountains. He wondered if he'd like them.

Tural set the pint on the table. "Fish stew tonight. We always have fish stew. We also have a nice pasty tonight. But I'd recommend the crab."

"I don't...." Oliver tried not to make a face. "Crab's not a particular favorite."

"I'll bet the only crab you've had is the horrible slimy stuff they overcharge for in Greynox. Right?"

"Yeah." His father and stepmother used to serve it on special occasions, although Oliver didn't know why, since they didn't seem to enjoy it much either.

"Then you need to try Croftwell crab like my Aygun prepares it. Tell you what. If you don't like it, I'll take it away and bring you something else."

"All right."

"Good man." Tural patted him on the shoulder and limped away.

Oliver sipped his ale and relaxed, ignoring the twinge under his ribs. It had appeared the other day and wouldn't go away. It felt like rats gnawing at his bones—gently like, as if they didn't want him dead all at once or were simply working up an appetite for later.

The two men at the closest table had been talking about fishing; no great surprise there. Oliver didn't understand most of the terms, but he gathered that one of them was experiencing a mechanical problem with his boat and the other was giving advice that the first disagreed with. Then a third man entered the pub, hung up his coat and hat, and joined them. His graying hair was standing almost straight up, and after a moment, Oliver recognized him as the coachman who'd driven him from Bythington.

"Ah, look at our Jamie," said one of the fishermen as the newcomer took his seat. "He's got a newspaper, he has. Such an intellectual, our Jamie."

Jamie thudded him hard in the bicep. "You're just jealous, Tommy Bellflower, 'cause I know a thing or two about the world." With exaggerated dignity, he spread the newspaper on the table. "This came fresh from Greynox this morning, it did. A bloke left it in my coach."

Tommy blew a raspberry. "Greynox. Who gives a bloody damn what's happening there?"

"I do, 'cause I am a man of the world." While Jamie's companions cackled, Jamie peered at the print, moving his finger along as he read. "Aw, now look at that. The Queen has returned from her countryside holiday and she's acquired new specimens for the zoological gardens as well. Camels, this says. See, there's a drawing."

Tommy looked and then snorted. "That's ridiculous. No real animal looks like that. Someone's playing a joke."

The three of them discussed this for a few moments, eventually reaching the conclusion that camels might exist, but the artist who'd drawn this one had never seen one and had just made it up.

Then Jamie's expression grew serious. "Aw, now this is no good at all. There's going to be a hanging next month. Five men and a woman, this says. That's awful. I s'pose prison's just as bad or worse, but still." He shook his head slowly.

"Hanging for what?" asked the third man. Oliver hadn't caught his name, but he was quieter than the other two.

"Murder! And rioting. And property destruction. And—dunno what this one means. 'Rebellion against authorities'."

The ale suddenly tasted dry and sour. Oliver set down his glass. He wanted to walk away—no, to run—but didn't trust his legs to work properly. And although he closed his eyes, he couldn't stop hearing.

"Sounds like that lot was right busy," said Tommy. "But what did they do?"

"'Twas that nasty business at the factories. How many died? More'n a hundred, I think.

Women and children, even." He clucked his tongue. "Who'd bring children to such a thing?"

"The children worked there," Oliver whispered, his throat tight and head pounding.

"Olly, what's wrong?"

Oliver opened his eyes to find Felix sitting across from him, blocking the view of the men with the newspaper. He was dressed as usual, except today a bright red-and-yellow scarf was wrapped around his neck.

"New scarf?" Oliver's voice came out hoarser than he'd expected.

"Aye." Felix stroked a length of it. "My sister-in-law knitted it for me. I know it's a bit warm for it now, but I'll appreciate it when the weather turns cold. I... suffer a bit with the chill."

Oliver considered that for a moment. "You can't sleep too close to firestones."

"Not unless I want a conflagration. Jamie over there lets me stay in his stable during the winter. It's nice and dry, and the dragons keep the temperature a bit warmer. They grumble in their sleep, though." He flashed a quick grin, which faded. "But what's wrong with you, Olly? You looked ill just now."

"I'm tired. Hungry."

"I hope you ordered Aygun's crab. It's glorious. But don't look at me like that—I've already eaten, and I won't try to get you to pay for my dinner."

Oliver hadn't meant to appear skeptical. "Are you sure? You must have spent those five coppers by now."

"I've stayed the past two nights in one of those rooms." Felix pointed at the ceiling. "I've been helping Tural and Aygun a bit with the cleaning and such. They've fed me well."

Jamie, Tommy, and the other man were still discussing the hangings and the events that had led up to them, and Oliver didn't want to hear. He drained his glass and concentrated on Felix instead. His face had recovered from the fire, although a few red marks remained on his hands. His fingers were moving restlessly on the tabletop as if searching for something to do.

"Why didn't you just move into Farview?" Oliver asked. "Before I arrived, I mean. You could at least have had a roof over your head, and I'm sure nobody would have objected."

Felix shrugged. "Nobody down here, perhaps. But up there? It's not my house."

While Oliver was deciding how to respond to that, Tural appeared with his dinner. There were green beans with tomatoes, and more of those small hard rolls, but the centerpiece was a dish filled with what Oliver assumed were lumps of crabmeat smothered in a white sauce so hot it still bubbled around the edges.

"Try a bite or two," said Tural. "I'll replace it if it's not your fancy."

With both men watching closely, Oliver scooped a small forkful, blew on it, and popped it into his mouth. It was still hot enough that it almost hurt, yet it was also delicious. "I don't want you to replace this," he said with a laugh. "Might fight you if you tried."

"Excellent! I knew Aygun would win you over. Freshness is the key. That crab was still crawling around in the harbor at lunchtime today."

"Well, an unlucky day for him but a fortunate one for me. Thank you. Can I have another glass, please? And one for Felix?"

That seemed to please Tural. He clapped Oliver's shoulder again before leaving.

"Well, now I owe you a story," Felix said.

"Only if you want to."

"It would be a pleasure. Have you a topic in mind?"

Oliver had a great many, in fact, only some of which were fit for public airing. Some of the others were too painful to contemplate. So he settled on something he thought would be safe. "Do you know anything about moor-cats?"

Felix's eyebrows shot so high that they disappeared under his unruly fringe. "Moor-cats! I wasn't expecting you to know about them. Unless you visited the one at the National Museum in Greynox."

"I've never been." He'd thought about it a few times, but he would have felt out of place. Museums were for scholars and the wealthy, not for a man who worked as a mill guard. In addition, the huge gray National Museum was in an upscale neighborhood he rarely frequented, not far from Jayne Park.

"Oh, you should if you ever visit the city again. It's bloody marvelous. And they've a moor-cat skeleton there, with a painting next to it of what the creature looked like when it was alive."

Remembering the ghost's drawings—on paper and etched in stone—Oliver suppressed a somewhat hysterical laugh. "So they're real."

"Not anymore." Felix settled in comfortably, which Oliver now knew meant a tale was forthcoming. "We have stories about them here. Very old stories indeed about creatures that used to stalk the moors. They weren't truly cats, but they slightly resembled the small furry animals that like to purr on people's hearths and steal fish, so people called them that. They were bigger, you see. As tall as a man if they stood on hind legs. Their fur was very thick and colored light brownish green, so they blended in with the grasses if they stayed still. They howled at night. The stories say you could hear them miles and miles away. And mostly they hunted birds and small animals, but parents used to warn that moor-cats ate naughty children as well."

"Did they?"

Felix shrugged. "Dunno. But the stories also said that moor-cats were good to have around your village because they'd attack any strangers who invaded their territory. So they were guards of a sort—a bit prickly, but not unwelcome." The look he gave Oliver would have melted iron.

Oliver disguised his blush—poorly—by eating a large forkful of crab. It truly was wonderful. He could scarcely believe it was the same meat he'd picked at during family dinners.

"Anyway," Felix continued, "moor-cats disappeared centuries ago. Perhaps they were killed off when people began to keep sheep, or... I don't know. Maybe they simply died out. Most people claimed they never existed at all, that they were mere fables. One learned Noxer even wrote a paper on how the moor-cat was a symbol of our wilder natures, and that we abandoned it when we became civilized." He snorted.

"But you said there's one in the museum."

"Yes! When I was a boy, some of those university men came here—the ones who dig around in the mud. And they found not one but three moor-cat skeletons up on the moor. Ancient, of course, but intact. It was very exciting. Except for the bloke who'd written that paper, I expect. He must have been quite unhappy. But Olly, what led you to ask about moor-cats?"

"A ghost."

Felix didn't look remotely surprised. In fact, he nodded sagely as he grabbed one of Oliver's bread rolls and took a bite. "Wondered if you'd met that lot yet."

Ghosts might have made a good topic for conversation, but Tural returned with two glasses of ale and a man wearing trousers but no shirt. That was startling enough, but the large gray wings folded against his back nearly made Oliver gasp. Aygun, he presumed. The wind person. He was short and very delicately built, with hairless skin the color of milky tea. And he was smiling at Oliver as if used to being gaped at.

"Tural tells me you like my cooking." His voice was light and musical, almost like a song, with a thick but pleasant accent.

Oliver pulled himself together. "I do, very much. You've completely transformed my opinion of crabs."

"Well, they're still not very nice to be around, but they are quite tasty." Instead of holding out his hand for a shake, he bobbed his head deeply. "I'm Aygun, as you may have been told. Welcome to Croftwell. It's nice that now Tural and I aren't the only newcomers."

"I'm Oliver Webb, and thank you. But I thought you'd been here for some time."

Everyone else laughed. "We have," Aygun said. "Years. But we'll always be the man and the wind person from up north."

Tural nodded. "But don't worry. Everyone here is kind. We don't mind being a bit exotic. Brings in more business." He winked, slung an arm around Aygun's waist, and—to Oliver's absolute astonishment—dropped a kiss on his cheek. It was not a fraternal sort of kiss.

Tural and Aygun walked away, leaving Oliver open-jawed. "Did they — Are they—"

"Partners," Felix answered brightly. "I told you that."

"I thought you meant business partners."

"Well, they are. But they're also lovers." Felix took a long swallow of ale before continuing. "Look, I know how city folk can be about this sort of thing. Which is bloody stupid, because plenty of Noxers get stirred by their own sex instead of the opposite, but they force it all into hiding as if it were something shameful. Things are different here."

"Different how?" Oliver asked carefully.

"No need to hide. Probably couldn't manage it even if we tried. In case you haven't yet noticed, there are few secrets in Croftwell."

Oliver thought this over. It certainly helped explain Felix's boldness several nights earlier, when he'd come within a hairsbreadth of kissing Oliver. And it was such a tempting idea. Oliver used to envy the way opposite-sex couples could show affection so openly. They didn't have to skulk in back rooms and dim alleys, praying they didn't get arrested. And they could marry and build families together, a prospect that appealed to Oliver far more than he'd admitted to himself.

"People really don't mind?"

"No. And I've a theory about this, in fact. Nowadays most of our fisherman go out for the day and are back in their own homes by night. But a long time ago, it wasn't unusual for fishing boats to spend weeks at sea. That meant men living in close quarters for a long stretch, while back on land the women were often left to their own. Who could blame any of them for seeking some pleasure and perhaps some comfort with who they had near?"

Maybe Oliver didn't look as if he bought that theory, because Felix chuckled. "I was a printer's 'prentice in Greynox, remember. Half a dozen of us young lads shared a sleeping space about the size of your cottage loft. Don't you think we played about after lights out? Same principle."

Oliver pictured Felix naked, sprawled on a narrow cot in a dark room that smelled of paper and ink and machine grease, his head thrown back as another man sucked him off. Felix would be noisy during the act; Oliver was quite certain of that. And even while he was receiving pleasure, he'd move his hands over his partner's hair and skin.

As if he could read Oliver's mind, Felix stared at him across the table, lips curled in a wicked smile. He took a sip of ale and then quite deliberately licked away a fleck of foam. He leaned forward and lowered his voice. "What about you, Olly? What games did you play?"

It hurt to breathe, as if Oliver were a fish newly landed. He wanted... gods, he wanted so many things, a great many of them involving himself, Felix, and far fewer items of clothing. But regardless of Felix's apparent willingness and the unconcern of the villagers, Oliver couldn't have those things. He shouldn't be so greedy.

Casting about for an escape, he realized that Jamie, Tommy, and the other man had left. The newspaper remained on the table, along with their abandoned empty glasses.

"Do you think I could take that?" He pointed.

Felix blinked and turned to look. "The newspaper?"

"Yes. The coachman was reading it earlier, but I think he's done with it."

"Sure." Felix bounced up, hurried to the table, and grabbed the paper before skipping back and plopping into his seat. He slapped the paper down. "Here you are."

"Thank you."

Felix peered at the headlines. "Are you dying to learn more about the Queen's holiday? Maybe you're disappointed you missed her recent balls."

"I dance poorly." Oliver tried to keep his tone light, but the newspaper sat there like a coiled snake ready to strike. He shouldn't have asked for it. He should have tried to forget the conversation he'd overheard.

"Now there you go, looking ill again. What's wrong?" Felix set his hand on Oliver's forearm just above the wrist.

"I can't...." Deep breath in and out. "There's an article I need to read, but I don't have the courage to do so."

"I can read it to you."

Just like that, as if it were very simple. As if Felix thought nothing of offering to help a man he'd known for such a short time, an outsider with a ridiculous weakness. And Felix didn't act at all as if he believed there was anything odd or shameful about Oliver's admission. There was no pity in his eyes, simply kindness warmed by a lingering spark of desire.

Oliver felt as if he were about to fall off the cliff and, further, that he *wanted* to, even knowing what the result would be. Perhaps sometimes, if the descent was glorious enough, the eventual crash and destruction wouldn't matter so much.

"Not in here." Oliver could no longer meet Felix's gaze. "Not now."

"All right. Finish your dinner and we'll drink, and when you're ready we can go somewhere."

Drink. That was an excellent idea.

Chapter Eight

By the time they left the Merman, the hour was late and Oliver was more than a little tipsy. He didn't hold his ale as well as he used to—yet another sign of his deterioration—but for this at least he was grateful. He wanted to be muzzy-headed right now. Clarity was overrated.

He stood on the pavement, swaying a bit as though he were aboard a ship. If he turned to look at the boats in the harbor, he'd lose his balance, so he stared at Felix instead. That was certainly no hardship. He'd thought Felix pretty when he first aid eyes on him, but now that Oliver had seen some of the depths of Felix's character, he liked what he saw even better.

"Where would you like to go?" Felix asked gently. He'd drunk much less than Oliver. "Farview? I can help you up the path."

"You said you'd read me the newspaper."

"I did." Felix patted it, folded under one arm. "But perhaps you should wait until you're sober."

"I couldn't face it sober."

"All right. I'd invite you to my room, but I wouldn't have enough light to read by."

"'M sorry." And Oliver was. Probably the sorriest specimen ever to walk the streets of Croftwell. If a wave came right now and swept him away, the world would be a better place. And Oliver could be dinner for the crabs in the harbor, which seemed only fair.

Felix grasped his arm lightly. "No worries. I know a place. Come with me."

Still arm in arm, they walked slowly toward the water, which lapped peacefully at the docks. It was overcast tonight, the air scented lightly with rain, and Oliver could make out very few details in the dark. He startled, however, when a loud blowing noise came from near the boats.

"Just a dolphin," Felix said with a chuckle. "They come in some nights, I think to see what the humans are up to. Pity you can't see it. Perhaps this one came especially to make your acquaintance. Some of your ancestors used to ride them like dragons."

"My ancestors?"

"The Iceshadows. But that's a story for another night, I think."

They came to a large wooden building perched on a pier. The unlocked door opened with a creak, and Felix tugged him inside. "Careful. There's loads to trip on. Let me be your guide."

Although Felix seemed able to find his way, Oliver could see nothing in the utter blackness. Judging from the echoes of their boot-steps on the wooden floors, the space was large. The smell reminded him a bit of the cotton mills he'd occasionally visited as part of his job, but less dusty and with an overlay of mildew and salt.

"Where are we?"

"Corbyn's Sailworks, of course."

They paused for a moment, another door groaned, and Felix tugged him into what felt like a much smaller space. A moment later, a match flared and then a lantern came to life, casting a warm glow.

"Kerosene?" Oliver asked. He'd seen such lanterns only a few times, inside his former boss's house. Most people used firestones, but some of the wealthy preferred more exotic lighting.

"Aye. My dad lets me keep it here. See?" Felix lifted the lantern to better illuminate the room. It held a cot, a small table, and a single chair. There was also a chamber pot and an empty pitcher and glass. "I stay here now and then."

"No decorations. Not even octopus curtains."

Felix snorted. "No windows. I never stay for long—don't want to damage the business—but it works in a pinch."

When Oliver remained standing dumbly, Felix hung the lantern from a hook and then gently pushed him back until his knees gave and he was sitting on the cot.

"I can hear the water," Oliver said.

"Well, it's right beneath us. Don't worry, though. This building has stood since Lyra Moon's time and it's not likely to collapse under us any time soon."

Oliver hadn't been worried. He liked the sound and, for no logical reason, felt comforted by the sea's proximity. He wished he could lie down right now and let the little waves lull him to sleep. And he wished Felix would join him. They'd be quite crowded on the little cot, but Oliver didn't care. He'd finally be able to test the softness of those curls and the rasp of bristled cheeks. But he remained upright, hands laced in his lap. "I'm sorry I'm asking you to do this."

"Don't be. I like being useful."

"It's stupid."

"It's not."

They remained quiet for a minute or two, and then Oliver nodded. "I'm ready. Please."

Felix spread the newspaper out on the table and sat on the chair. "I'm guessing it's not the Queen's adventures that concern you. Which article, Olly?"

"The one with the... the hangings." It was hard to speak.

"All right." Felix cleared his throat and began to speak very clearly. After reading the headline, he continued, "Her Majesty's High Court of Greynox has sentenced five men and one woman to hang. Jack Pitman, Edward—"

"You can skip the names. Please."

Felix gave him a worried look. "All right."

HER MAJESTY'S HIGH COURT OF GREYNOX has sentenced five men and one woman to hang.

These people were tried and convicted of several counts on Tuesday for their parts in the terrible events of early April. Due to the heinous nature of the acts and the need for swift justice, the Royal Prosecutor has refused right of appeal. The executions will take place on Hangman's Hill on the thirtieth of September.

As readers will recall, the tragic events began on Oakwood Street, where unruly crowds had been gathering for weeks, disrupting the work at the nearby manufactories and impeding traffic. These crowds consisted of the unemployed, criminals, and madmen, and they were spurred into action by rabble-rousers with the goal of damaging the orderly flow of business. Authorities had several times dispersed these crowds, urging calm and lawfulness, and the Lord Mayor and the High Chancellor had publicly denounced these felonious activities. Yet agents of anarchy repeatedly whipped the crowds into a frenzy.

In late March, Lord Pentwhistle introduced legislation in the House of Lords that would increase penalties for those found guilty of loitering, provocation, and interference with legitimate trade. Instead of quelling the disturbances, these laws only served to further stoke the misconduct of the unwashed hordes.

On fifth April, a particularly large and boisterous mob gathered on Oakwood Street near Hillard's and Merryclaims' woolen mills. The horde, which was shouting at great volume, blocked traffic entirely and forced production in both mills to cease. Police officers' calls for dispersal were ignored. Several instigators, including those condemned this week, stood upon a carriage top and exhorted their followers to commit acts of trespassing, property damage, and violence.

Approximately one-half hour after the disturbance began, a flash-curse exploded, causing the immediate deaths of over one hundred participants and spectators. An additional sixty-seven deaths attributable to the curse were reported in the following days. Furthermore, substantial damage was done to both mills.

"My insurance will cover the repairs to my building and equipment," Mr. Merryclaims said during his testimony at trial. "But it will not recompense the employees who must go without pay until work can be restarted. Nor will insurance make up for the appalling loss of life."

Through intense detective operations, police inspectors were able to place responsibility for the flash-curse on the condemned, whose motive in gathering the mob seems to have been luring large numbers to their doom. It is believed that the conspirators intended to harm the hallowed foundations of our monarchy itself. They were convicted of multiple counts of murder, rioting, and property destruction in addition to rebellion against authorities.

It is to be hoped that swift justice will serve as a deterrent for any similar lawlessness that may occur in future, and that our beloved city will no longer be troubled by the pestilence of those who are ungrateful for the great benefits our manufactories provide.

Oliver sat very still on the cot, screams echoing in his head. He was thankful that Felix didn't say anything once he'd finished the article. He sat quietly, his expression uncharacteristically grim. Oliver's world was swaying, and if he closed his eyes, he could almost imagine he was on a ship riding gentle swells far out at sea.

"I've never been on a boat," he whispered, not sure if Felix would hear.

Apparently Felix did, because he nodded. "We can fix that easily enough. We can ask some of the lads to take you fishing. Or my uncle Teddy. He's mostly retired but still keeps a little boat; he'd take you out on a bit of an excursion. You could sail up the coast, maybe stop to visit Urchin Cove."

Oliver nodded absently, which was when he realized that cold tears had sprung from his eyes and were running down his cheeks. Odd, that. He didn't feel sad. Just... empty. As if the crabs he'd eaten for dinner were now eating their way back out of him. He couldn't move to wipe away the track of moisture. Tears were salty, and so was blood; every person carried a bit of the sea inside them.

Had Felix been the one to suddenly start crying, Oliver would have felt terribly awkward, and he would have either stammered something trite and inappropriate or simply fled. In the face of Oliver's tears, Felix did neither, and his face showed concern rather than pity or disgust. He remained quiet for a few moments, then stood and walked the two steps to the bed. "May I?" He gestured at the spot beside Oliver.

Breaking his paralysis just a little, Oliver nodded.

Felix sat down, close but not quite touching. And then he twisted toward Oliver and held out his arms.

Oliver fell into them.

It was a tight embrace, Felix's new scarf tickling Oliver's nose, and it felt bloody wonderful, as if no more of his strength would evaporate as long as Felix held him. Gods, when had anyone hugged him? His father had never been given to physical displays of affection, and his stepmother had mostly ignored him. The friends he went to pubs with might occasionally clap him on the back, perhaps when he'd told a good joke, but that was all the contact they had. And the men he had sex with, well, those trysts were fast and businesslike, with no extraneous touching.

Oliver eventually pulled away, sniffling and ashamed, and tried to hide behind his handkerchief. "I apologize for that."

"For what? Having emotions?"

"For showing them. It was very inconsiderate of me."

"Inconsiderate!" Felix blew a heavy breath. "A few days ago, I nearly burned down your home, but you didn't so much as look disappointed with me. And when I told you about my stupid curse, you didn't turn away. You sat there beside me, just as I'm sitting beside you now."

"You didn't blubber like an infant."

"Nor did you, Olly. And even if you do, so what? Don't you think I've sobbed myself dry when my self-pity surges? We're friends by now, I think. A friendship should be a safe place to display emotions."

"Thank you." It was a nice thought, although Oliver didn't believe in safe places.

"Do you want to talk about it or maybe something else entirely? Or we could try talking of nothing at all, but I'm not as proficient at that as you are."

Oliver didn't know what he wanted. He looked down at his feet, remembering when he'd run through a river of blood with the stench of death even thicker than Greynox's usual reek.

"I was there. On the fifth of April. I'd been there for several of the demonstrations, actually. To keep order, Mr. Hillard said. He and the other manufactory owners deployed all their guards."

"What was really going on? Why were those people so upset?"

"I'd say more desperate than upset. They worked in the factories. I don't know if you're aware what it was like inside those places...."

"I have some idea," Felix replied. "Some of the other 'prentices had family who worked in them. My colleagues considered themselves very fortunate to have a position with a printer instead."

"The mills are like small hells."

Oliver could have given details. People coughing up their lungs after inhaling clouds of fiber dust. Men and women standing at the machines sixteen hours a day, six days a week, begrudged even brief respites to eat and empty their bladders. Young children maimed and mangled; workers crammed together so closely that diseases rapidly spread. But Felix didn't need to hear all of that. Perhaps he already knew.

"The workers were asking for simple things," Oliver said. "Better wages so they wouldn't be forced to live in miserable slums. Better working conditions. Shorter workdays. Assurances that they would be cared for if they were injured at work."

"And Hillard and the others refused."

"Of course. I've been to Mr. Hillard's house many times. He's widowed, his children grown and gone, but his mansion has so many rooms that you can get lost in it. Everything inside is exquisite. He keeps a dozen dragons in his stable and three different coaches. At mealtimes, liveried staff serve him enough food to feed half of Greynox, and most of it gets thrown away. But he won't give a single copper more to his workers."

Felix chewed his lip. "Please don't take this the wrong way—I don't mean it as criticism. I'm simply curious. You say these things about Hillard, yet you worked for him."

"I did," Oliver said miserably. "Justified it to myself. I needed a roof and meals too. Told myself it was enough if I treated the workers as kindly as I could. Sometimes I'd pretend not to notice if I found a child stealing a nap behind a stack of spools or a woman pocketing a scrap-end of cloth to sew something warm for her family."

In fact, until the protests began, he'd lost no sleep over his position. He was doing a job, was all, just like everyone else. If he didn't do it, he'd end up starving on the street, and Mr. Hillard would only hire someone else. Maybe someone crueler.

"The crowd on the fifth was the biggest yet. The people standing on top of the carriages were telling them to unite, to organize. If every one of them refused to work until their demands were met, the factory owners would have to concede. Does that make sense?"

Felix nodded. "Of course. We had something a bit like that here, a long time ago. All of the fishermen refused to catch anything because —" He stopped suddenly, grinning wryly. "Sorry. Almost launched into a story there."

Oliver was almost tempted to smile back, but he needed to get the rest of the mill tale out.

"The protestors were being led in a song. Something about, oh, the power of solidarity. I don't remember the words." It had been quite beautiful, though, all those voices joined together in a vision of a better future. "I was standing at the edge of the crowd, up near the corner of Hillard's building. I expected the police would come soon and break things up as they had before, and I was glad for it. I'd been on duty since the night before and I wanted to go home and sleep."

Felix set a hand on Oliver's knee, warm and solid. He had the most elegant fingers Oliver had ever seen.

"What happened?" Felix asked quietly.

"Bang. Just... bang. It was so loud that for a few moments I was deafened, and I think I was frozen in shock. And then I could hear again, and it was nothing but screams." He took a few steadying breaths, warning the tears not to resume. "The curse causes structures —both buildings and bodies—to fail. Spectacularly. The people closest to the blast simply disintegrated, which was a mercy, really. Those farther out were... deformed. They were the ones screaming. Some of them died quickly, but others took hours. Or days."

"I can't imagine the horror of it."

"Don't try."

"Is it why you came to Croftwell?"

Oliver considered telling him the entire truth, the fine details of what had happened to him. But no, he'd burdened Felix enough. He settled for a half-truth instead. "Yes."

"I'm glad you came. The sea air heals."

Oliver also didn't tell him he'd never heal.

"Gods, I've talked so long that I'm sober again. I should go home." Oliver stood and reached for the door. Leaving the newspaper on the desk was an act of cowardice, but he couldn't bring himself to touch it.

Felix stood as well. "I'll walk you home."

"Thank you, but I'm quite capable of making it on my own."

Not that he didn't want Felix in his cottage. It was only that if Felix were there, Oliver didn't trust himself to not touch him. Kiss him. He was fairly certain Felix would be willing. But that was an entanglement Oliver couldn't afford.

"I'll guide you out of here, at least." Felix doused the lantern, leaving them in darkness. Then he took Oliver's hand and slowly led him back through the sailworks, somehow avoiding any collisions. They stood together just outside.

"Do you have a place to sleep tonight?"

Felix's smile was warm. "Yes, thanks. I can stay another night or two at the Merman without causing damage. It's quite nice. Aygun and Tural keep a good inn. You can share my bed if you want to avoid climbing the cliff."

Although Oliver shook his head no, he was happy at the idea of a place where two men could share a bed without engaging in subterfuge or worrying about censure. Or arrest.

He started to walk away, but after only a few yards, he turned back and saw Felix still near the sailworks door. "Would you do something for me?" Ask now, while he was brave enough.

"Anything."

"Do you know my mother's story?"

"No. I'm a bard, not a gossip."

Oliver chuffed something akin to a laugh. "But could you find out?"

"Of course. I'd love to, Olly."

Oliver nodded. But he had one more question before he returned to Farview.

"Why do you call me that? Everyone else calls me Oliver or Webb."

"Because you ought to be Olly to someone."

Chapter Nine

Oliver descended to the village the next morning for the provisions he had neglected the evening before. He didn't see Felix and didn't stop to chat with anyone, although he waved in what he hoped was a friendly manner. He returned home straightaway and spent the rest of the day working on his various repair projects. Well, part of the day. He took two naps as well, and spent time sitting on the bench and staring at the sea. He didn't know why; he certainly wasn't expecting the return of a long-lost lover.

When he woke up the next day, he ached all over, as if he'd been given a particularly hard beating. He eyed the enormous washtub mournfully, wishing he possessed the strength to fill it with water. He would heat it nicely with firestones and enjoy a long soak, which might help ease his pain. But even if he opted to bathe indoors—unwise due to the eventual need to empty the tub—he'd need to lug many potfuls of water between the sink and the tub. Just thinking about it made him groan.

The weather was unwelcoming: gray skies and a steady cold drizzle. Looking out the window, Oliver couldn't see past the cliff edge. Aside from quick trips to the loo and stepping outdoors to scatter crusts for the imps, he remained inside, seated in one of the comfortable octopus chairs, drinking tea.

This wasn't how he'd imagined his life winding down. He'd assumed he'd work for Hillard for years longer, continuing to squirrel away his coppers, visiting pubs, and occasionally finding a willing tryst partner. When he grew too old to be a guard, he thought he might rent a room in one of the beautiful houses near Jayne Park. Some of the well-bred families had lost a great deal of their wealth over generations and sought income however they could. He would spend his time furthering his fairly limited education by reading, and he'd stroll through Jayne Park and watch young couples paddle small boats in the lake. He would be content.

That hadn't been a grand dream; he knew that. But he'd never yearned for material possessions, and he'd never hoped for love. And now here he was, with little in the way of assets and with nobody to love. So he'd accomplished that much at least.

"Isn't Farview as nice as any room in a Greynox mansion? And isn't it better to watch the sea than a dirty little pond?"

True enough. He'd found a friend as well, which was unexpected. So he should be satisfied. He'd achieved the essence of his goals, albeit on a much shorter schedule.

But gods, he wanted more. More time. More meaning to his existence. And more of Felix.

"Greedy bastard."

When he stood to refill the kettle, a tearing pain ripped through him, as if an invisible claw had raked at his stomach. He gasped and fell to his knees, clutching his middle.

The agony gradually receded but left him so drained that he couldn't stand. He crawled to his bed and, after a few failed attempts, eventually managed to pull himself onto the mattress. Without even the strength to pull up the blankets, he fell asleep almost at once.

Although there was no light, he knew he was inside Hillard's mill. For once the great machines were still. Someone held his wrist tightly, pulling him forward. "You must see this," said his captor, his identity revealed by his voice.

"Father, no, please," Oliver begged. "I don't want to."

"You must see this."

Implacable and far too strong to brook any resistance, Oliver's father continued to tug, sometimes bumping him into a piece of machinery. The air inside the mill was so dry that adult Oliver began to wither and shrink until he was only a child again, small and terrified.

"Please!" Oliver cried. Or tried to, but no sound came out. His voice had dried up too.

His father towed him up an impossibly steep stairway and then down a hallway to a doorway dimly illuminated by a lantern. "It's supposed to be kerosene," said Oliver, who'd somehow regained the ability to speak. "Firestones react to the curse."

"Though that's not the curse that concerns you, is it, boy? It's not the curse you brought on yourself."

Oliver could see only the back of his father's head, where the bald spot continued to vanquish the fine brown hair. That view was a small mercy, perhaps. He didn't want to see his father's face and the familiar coldness in his flat brown eyes.

His father opened the door and yanked Oliver through. They stood on a small balcony hundreds of feet over Oakwood Street, which had grown much wider and the buildings that flanked it much taller. The street was packed so tightly with people that none of them could move, and they were singing a song that seemed familiar, although Oliver couldn't remember where he'd heard it. It was a lullaby, a sweet tune about a baby in a boat being rocked by the waves.

"Not what you're here for, boy," said his father. The singing stopped at once, leaving the huge crowd in eerie silence.

"I don't want to be here. Let me go!"

"Not until you see."

Oliver shook his head violently and tried to escape, but he couldn't. He was too weak. And when the sickly green cloud appeared in the sky, he couldn't even warn the people below. Who were all children, he could see now. Young ones with dirty, tear-tracked faces.

"Stop," Oliver whispered.

The green cloud dropped onto the street as a heavy fog. Shrieks and cries rang out, but they were muted by the miasma. Oliver tried to throw himself over the balcony railing—for what purpose, he didn't know—but his father held him fast. After a moment, the fog disappeared. The children were gone, but the street had become a river of blood, and the buildings were jagged cliffs. A fine spray of blood had settled on Oliver's arms and the front of his shirt.

"I saw. Now let me go."

"But that wasn't what I brought you here for. You must see this."

Oliver's father released his hand. Before Oliver could flee—either through the door or over the railing—his father turned around. And it wasn't his father. Wasn't anyone Oliver knew, in fact, although there was a certain familiarity to the features and to the hair, which was now thick and black.

"Who are you?" Oliver demanded.

The man smiled. "I think you know."

"But—"

"Oh, not again, you foolish man!"

Oliver opened his eyes. It was still daytime, although only an overcast light shone through the windows. The old-man ghost was back in Oliver's chair.

"I believe in you now," Oliver said.

"Well, then you're not completely daft. So why do you keep torturing yourself with those nightmares?"

"I don't choose my dreams." Oliver held a palm against his stomach, which still hurt.

"Of course you do. It's not as if anyone else gives them to you." The old man snorted his disdain and then looked around the room. He looked at the hearth and scrunched his toothless mouth. "We didn't have those stones when I was alive. We had to make fires with wood or peat. It was smokier and loads more work. You people have it so much easier today."

"I don't think I have it easy at all."

The ghost shrugged as if it wasn't worth arguing about.

"Why are you haunting me?" Oliver asked. "Do you want me to leave? I won't. I've nowhere else to go."

"Of course we don't! We're pleased to see family here again. We're just visiting."

Family. That was a concept Oliver had known more in principle than reality, and he certainly hadn't expected it to involve centuries-old spirits. But when he thought about it for a few minutes, he decided he rather liked the idea. It was the first time he felt as if he belonged somewhere.

"I like your visits. Especially if you interrupt those horrible dreams. But I'm not feeling well right now, so perhaps you ought to—"

"Tomorrow, go to the place where you saw the moor-cat. You'll find some yellow flowers nearby—they grow on stalks, like spears. Two or three of those flowers steeped in hot water will help ease your pain. No more than that, though! Not unless you're in a hurry to end up in my condition." The ghost cackled at his own joke.

"All right. Sir?"

The ghost laughed again. "I'm no sir."

"What shall I call you, then?"

"Granddad will do." When he smiled, his gums showed and his face folded into infinite wrinkles.

"Erm, all right." Oliver tried to think of a careful way to phrase his question but couldn't find one. "If it's not too insensitive to ask, does everyone become a ghost after death?"

That was apparently very funny. The ghost threw his head back and guffawed, slamming his hand against the armrest in glee.

"Everyone? Can you imagine that? We'd be overrun, we would. The living would be stumbling over us every minute. Nah, most people just move on, boy. We might not like it, but it's the natural way o' things. The gift of life can't last forever."

"Move on where?"

"Don't know, do I? I'm still here."

"Why, though? I don't want to sound ungrateful or cold—I'm happy you're here. But why?"

The ghost turned solemn. "It's my job, you see. Some of us are guardians. We've helped keep our home and our descendants safe for thousands of years. We can't work miracles, of course. But there's not been one successful invasion of our lands. Not one."

That wasn't true. At least a dozen different kingdoms had claimed this territory, and those were just the ones Oliver knew about. But now that he gave the matter more thought, those encroachments had been more in name than in fact. Somewhere a king or queen included this area in their list of possessions, yet aside from paying taxes to a different ruler, the locals noticed little difference. They remained here, raising their children, catching their fish, building their stone houses.

"That's a huge obligation, Granddad." It felt good to say the name. "I don't know anyone who'd be willing to work for so long."

"Of *course* you do. Anyway, it's a great honor. Our people chose us for this task because they respected us, and when we were dying they inscribed the words on our walls to create the binding. We stay as long as the stones do."

Although this was a strange concept, Oliver supposed it made sense. He nodded his understanding. But then he sighed. "I wish I knew what happens to the rest of the dead."

"Don't worry, boy. We'll make sure nothing ill becomes of you."

"No, I...." Oliver shook his head. "I was thinking about the...." He couldn't say the rest.

"About the people you saw killed in the city?"

"Yes."

"None of them suffers, boy. That's all behind them."

It was unclear how the ghost could possibly know this, but the reassurance felt good anyway. "Thank you."

The ghost stood. It was very odd to look at him and see through to the wall behind him, but when he moved toward the bed with one hand stretched out, Oliver wasn't afraid. "Rest, boy. And find those flowers tomorrow."

The ghost settled his palm on Oliver's forehead; it felt like a cool breeze. Oliver's eyelids grew heavy and then slid closed.

THE PAIN HADN'T DISAPPEARED by morning, but it had subsided to a pulling twist. Oliver could grit his teeth and endure. The rain had stopped, leaving a gray sky and muddy ground. He breakfasted, fed the imps, and set out in search of the ghost's flowers.

It wasn't a long walk—he knew that from his previous trip. But today he inched along the path, stopping often to hold his stomach and catch his breath. What should have taken him perhaps thirty minutes lasted far more than an hour, and when he reached the ghost-girl's village he sank to the soft ground, leaned back against the stone with the moor-cat, and dozed off. He dreamed of wandering the streets of Greynox in search of something important—he didn't know what—and finding the city populated only by hostile ghosts.

"Gods," he said when he jolted awake. He was cold and sore, the seat of his trousers soaked through from the damp ground. Judging by the angle of the weak sun, he'd slept for hours. It was with great difficulty that he struggled to his feet. But once upright, he took a moment to gently stroke the moor-cat and think of the small hands that had carved it so long ago. She must have been a very brave girl to become a guardian.

He found a few of the yellow flowers in a small patch nearby, just past the ruined village. The blossoms were not especially pretty and not at all showy, but droplets of moisture glistened on them like jewels. Using his pocketknife, he sliced off three of the flowers and then paused. If they were effective medicine, perhaps he should take more. But the old man had warned him that too many would kill him, and a tiny niggle in Oliver's head wondered if he might be tempted to make himself a very strong tea. It would be a simpler end than what he was facing, and almost certainly less painful. But no, he wasn't ready to give up the world just yet.

It took him so long to get back that darkness had fallen, and he walked the last bit tripping over clumps of grass and wondering whether a misstep would send him tumbling over the cliff. But he'd left a firestone lantern lit inside the cottage, and the warm light acted like a beacon, drawing him to safety. The imps, who should have been asleep already, danced around him as he crossed the final few yards.

"Fine, fine," he said with an exhausted chuckle. "Let me get inside and see what I can spare."

The imps never tried to enter the cottage, but after Oliver went inside they crowded onto the threshold, their green eyes even bigger than usual. They weren't attractive creatures, but Oliver was growing fond of their spiky orange fur and too-large ears. Besides, he likely wasn't all that attractive himself nowadays.

He spent a few minutes sorting through his meager larder, finally settling on a tin of biscuits Envina Corbyn had convinced him to purchase. Good for digestion, she'd claimed, but with his innards in their current state, digestion wasn't his major concern. Smiling at the folly of it, he opened the tin and set it just outside the door.

"Help yourself, you greedy little buggers. After all I've been feeding you lately, I expect your digestion needs some assistance."

The imps made astonished cooing sounds before grabbing pawfuls of the biscuits, stuffing some in their mouths and scampering off into the darkness with more. One of them, a smaller one who might have been a youngling, ate only a single biscuit—dropping half of it as crumbs—before creeping very slowly inside the cottage, keeping a careful eye on Oliver.

"You're a brave one," he said. "You're welcome to look around, but don't eat my dinner."

It chittered back at him as if in answer. And then instead of heading for the larder, it tiptoed over to a basket containing the scraps from Mrs. Bellflower's upholstery project. Oliver had been intending to discard them but hadn't gotten around to it. The imp pawed through the bits of fabric and tufts of stuffing, then squeaked and held up a tangled web of blue threads. The imp cast a questioning glance at Oliver.

"You're welcome to it," he said.

It made a decidedly joyful sound—very close to a child's laugh, really—and scurried away with its prize. Having finished off the biscuits, the rest of the imps followed. Oliver picked up the empty tin, groaning as he bent, then went inside and shut the door.

His clothes felt clammy and he was shivering from cold, so he set several firestones on the hearth before undressing completely and donning clean underclothes and his ragged old dressing gown. Every movement was slow and painful, as if he were ancient, but he managed to toast some bread, which he ate along with salty dried fish and the last of the tomatoes he'd bought at the grocers. Although it wasn't a big meal, it sated his minimal hunger.

By the time he finished washing up, he was ready to collapse into bed. But he'd gone to all that effort to gather those flowers, dammit, so he might as well try them. They had been crushed only a little in his coat pocket, and when he dropped them into a pot of hot water they smelled bitter and acidic, a bit like a mixture of vinegar and grass.

It tasted awful, but he drank a cup's worth.

As he choked down the last drops, sleepiness descended so rapidly that he barely made it to his bed. He fell asleep with the lanterns still lit, and he didn't dream at all.

Chapter Ten

"Thank you, Granddad," Oliver said over breakfast.

He didn't know whether the ghosts were present even when he didn't see them, but just in case, he offered his gratitude. He'd slept more soundly than he had in ages, and although the pain and weakness hadn't entirely disappeared, they'd ebbed like the outgoing tide. Perhaps his remaining time wasn't quite as brief as he'd feared.

As Oliver greeted the imps—the smallest one had used the thread to tie its fur into little tufts—an idea hit him with such force that he nearly staggered backward. For once, it was a *good* idea.

"Oh, I must take care of this at once!" he announced, and the imps seemed to agree. He made himself presentable and hurried down to the village.

Most of the boats were out, some bobbing in the harbor but the majority gone to the open sea. The waterfront was busy nonetheless. Workers were repairing one of the harbor shacks, their rhythmic hammer blows punctuating the conversations of passersby and the calls of the pasty-stand proprietress. Everyone greeted him by name, although Oliver—still new to the community—could generally respond with only a smile and "Good morning."

"How are your chairs holding up?"

Oliver turned to find Mrs. Bellflower with a basket of mussels on one arm.

"Very well," he said. "They're entirely comfortable. You're very skilled."

"Oh, it wasn't difficult. But I'd be happy to help if you decide to add more furniture. Your cottage is cozy enough now, but a few more pieces would look nice."

"I wonder if you could help me a bit now, in fact. Is there a solicitor in Croftwell?"

Her eyebrows rose, but she nodded. "Colin Davies. He went off to Greynox to study law but came back when he was done. Crofters always do."

"So I've heard. Can you direct me to him?"

"'Course."

Finding Mr. Davies's house wasn't difficult. A modest stone structure on one of the short streets running between the harbor and the cliff, it had an exuberant garden in front and a gray cat dozing on the doorstep. Not a moor-cat, of course, although it was enormous, and it gazed at Oliver as if assessing whether he might be worth eating. Apparently not—the cat closed its golden eyes and purred. Oliver stepped around it to knock on the door.

"Oh!" exclaimed the man who opened it. He was younger than Oliver had expected, quite short and round, and with a Crofter's dark hair and eyes. "Mr. Webb, I believe?"

"Erm, yes."

"Colin Davies." He chuckled as he held out his hand for a shake. "And please don't look so alarmed. You were pointed out to me the other evening at the Merman. A newcomer is a novelty here. Oh, but I'm being incredibly rude. Please come in."

Davies directed Oliver to a plush chair in a room where books threatened to spill from shelves and off tables. A black cat suddenly appeared and hopped into Oliver's lap.

"That's Charr, who believes humans are intended to be her furniture. I can shoo her away if you wish."

"No, she's fine."

For a few minutes Davies bustled about, brewing tea and then serving it along with the same sort of biscuits Oliver had given the imps. Davies seemed pleased with his visitor. He apologized several times for the disorder and cat hair, but Oliver quite liked the untidy room, and Charr's fur was soft beneath his gentle strokes. He'd begged for a cat or dog when he was a boy, but his stepmother refused to allow one, and as an adult Oliver had worked such long hours that acquiring a pet seemed unfair.

He and Davies engaged in small talk for a while, mostly about Greynox, although they hadn't frequented the same neighborhoods. Then the solicitor—who by that point had insisted that Oliver call him Colin—asked about Farview.

"I used to peek inside now and then when I was a boy. Beautiful location, of course. Are you finding it comfortable?"

"Quite. Mrs. Bellflower reupholstered some chairs for me. But in fact, Farview is what I came to speak to you about. I've need of some small legal assistance, but I'm not sure it's, erm, within my budget."

Colin dimpled. "Splendid! I'm happy to help, and my fees are quite low. They have to be in Croftwell. We've no society swells here."

"Wouldn't you have become more prosperous in Greynox?" Oliver couldn't imagine that Croftwell generated much in the way of law business.

"Ah, yes, of course. But Greynox wasn't home. I'd rather be watching my coppers here by the harbor than rolling in them in the city. But please, what can I do for you?" Perhaps as incentive, Colin poured more tea into Oliver's cup.

"It's, erm, a will, I suppose. A very simple one because I haven't much. But I'd like to ensure that when I die, Farview won't be abandoned again."

Colin nodded vigorously. "If it's just the cottage and its contents you're concerned about, it shouldn't take me more than a few minutes to draw something up. May I ask to whom you wish to bequeath it? Because if it's a close relative, a will might not even be needed."

"It's not a relative." Oliver had none that he knew of except his father, and he had no intention of handing Farview over to him. He wouldn't want it anyway. The few times he'd mentioned Croftwell in Oliver's presence, his words had not been laudatory.

"Very well." While Oliver petted Charr, Colin appeared to be calculating something in his head. Then he produced a brilliant smile. "Three coppers."

"Three! Surely you should charge more than that."

"No, no. Three is appropriate. Now wait a moment, please."

It took Colin more than a moment to prepare. He first gathered a large notebook, pen, and inkwell. Then he cleared a horizontal surface of books and papers—disturbing a third cat that Oliver hadn't even noticed, this one small and striped. It made a reproachful meow and stalked off to curl up on the hearth instead.

"Very well," Colin said, pen poised. "Let us begin with your full legal name."

"Oliver Rowe Webb."

"Rowe. Yes, of course. And the property you wish to bequeath?"

"Farview Cottage and any attached lands." Oliver had never learned how much of the moor was his, but Felix had been right: it truly didn't matter. "Also all my belongings inside the cottage. There aren't many. And my money. There's not much of that either."

Colin had been writing furiously as Oliver spoke. "Right. The cottage, the land, the contents, and the funds." He nodded as if pleased. "And to whom are you bequeathing this?"

Oliver swallowed. "Felix Corbyn."

Although Colin looked surprised, there was no censure in his expression. In fact, he beamed. "Our Felix! Oh, that's lovely. Do you mind if I ask why?"

"He's been kind to me. And he needs a home. He told me he couldn't live in the cottage because it didn't belong to him, and...." He trailed off, not knowing if he should say more.

"Yes, the ghosts object. But if you give him the property, if it's rightfully his, the ghosts will let him be."

"That's what I am hoping."

Colin wrote for a moment longer. "Well, I think that's very thoughtful of you. Not, of course, that any harm should befall a young man like yourself."

"You never know."

"Indeed. Sign here, please." Colin had brought over the pen and ink and now held the large notebook so that Oliver could sign without disturbing Charr. She remained curled into a ball, her nose tucked under a paw. Colin returned to his table and used a sharp little blade to carefully cut the page out of his book. "Excellent. Now, do you wish to keep this or do you wish me to? I have a safe storage for such things. Don't worry—it contains no cats."

Oliver liked this man very much. And his cats. "Please keep it for me. And don't tell Felix or anyone else. Until after I'm dead, of course."

"Which will be many, many years from now."

After Oliver took his leave of Colin and brushed cat hairs from his trousers, he stood outside the Merman, considering whether to go in. It was lunchtime, so he could get a bite and a pint. Or he could return home before exhaustion overcame him.

He'd been dithering for quite some time when Felix turned the corner and almost bumped into him.

"Olly! I'm glad to see you." He wore his same threadbare clothing and the new scarf, and his hair was in even more exuberant curls than usual.

"Hello, Felix. You look...." Beautiful. Tempting. Like sunshine on a gloomy day. "You look well."

"I did some work for Herbert and Tilda Loowin, these past two days. Helped them move their furniture and carry their rugs out to the garden for beating, then put everything right again. You wouldn't believe how heavy some of their things are. But I earned eight coppers and a temporary bed in their garden shed."

"Garden shed?"

"Oh, it's quite nice. Cozy."

Although Felix seemed sincere in his happiness, Oliver had to hide a frown. Felix deserved a proper home. Then Oliver pictured Felix all settled in at Farview, never worrying again about where he'd sleep, and the vision calmed him.

"Have you been well, Olly?" Felix had tilted his head, his brow creased with concern.

"Quite." He cleared his throat to free himself from the bitter taste of the lie. "I was just deciding what to do about lunch."

Felix broke into a wide smile. "Have it with me, of course. It's a beautiful day—we could have a bit of a picnic on the moor. I've something for you. Well, two somethings." His expression turned more serious. "One of them is a story."

Ah. Well, Oliver had asked him to do some digging. Besides, Oliver needed to know the truth of what he suspected. It wouldn't make any practical difference, but it might weave in some loose ends.

"A picnic sounds grand. I've never had a real one."

Felix's eyes went round. "Never had a picnic? That's a crime, that is. I'll tell you what. You change into something you won't mind getting a bit dirty, then find a good spot and spread one of those furniture cloths. I'll take care of getting the food."

"All right." Oliver dug in his pocket, pulled out two coppers, and held them out. "Will this do?"

"My treat today."

Oliver thought about eight coppers earned through two days of heavy labor. "But you only—"

"Money is like the tide for me. It comes and it goes, and there's not a thing to be done about it. A picnic will be the best thing I've purchased in ages."

Feeling ashamed at his earlier assumption that Felix was nothing but a mercenary, Oliver nodded. "All right. Thank you."

"I'll see you up top." Felix winked and trotted away.

Despite the palliative effect of last night's flowers, Oliver wasn't certain he would make it up the path. He pictured himself struggling, only halfway up, when Felix ascended with his purchases. Oliver would have to explain, which he didn't want to do. Luckily he found a sturdy tree branch lying at the bottom of the cliff. With the twigs stripped off, it made a serviceable walking stick, taking enough pressure off his body to help him bear the pain. When he reached the top, he almost tossed the branch away but stopped himself. "Might need this again," he said grimly and leaned it against the wall just outside his door.

Once in the cottage, he had to think about what to wear, which was ridiculous in many ways. For one thing, he hadn't many options.

For another, he'd never in his life given the matter much thought. And most importantly, it didn't matter. He wasn't a debutante trying to impress eligible bachelors at a ball. Snorting at his own foolishness, he settled on the oldest of his three pairs of trousers and a plain white shirt. No coat and certainly no waistcoat. His boots were muddy already, so he didn't worry about them.

If he'd possessed a large enough mirror, he might have inspected himself, so it was fortunate that all he had was a small one used for shaving.

The clean furniture cloths had been folded and stored inside the chest of drawers. He chose the scorched one on purpose, grinning, and then set out on the footpath that ran north along the cliff. During his walks to the ghosts' village, he'd spotted the perfect spot. He spread the cloth and returned to his cottage, arriving just as Felix appeared over the edge with a bag in one hand and a large cloth object folded over his arm.

"I see you've followed directions on the outfit," Felix said. "Excellent. Did you find a picnic location?"

"I did."

"Then we should go to it. But first I'll deliver the first something I promised you." Without asking for permission, Felix marched into the cottage. Oliver followed and found him spreading a green-and-gold rug in front of the armchairs.

"What's that?"

"It's a rug, Olly. I believe they have them in Greynox."

"Yes, but—"

"It belonged to Herbert and Tilda Loowin, only they were going to throw it away. It's a bit worn, it is. But I think it still looks nice enough, and see? It goes well with your octopuses." Felix waved his arms grandly.

"I.... Yes, I suppose so."

"A cottage is cozier with a rug or two and a bit of color. Farview is growing more and more to look like a home, Olly."

The ache in Oliver's chest—despite having no physical cause—matched the ongoing pain in his belly. "Thank you," he said before tears could well.

"I'm starving. I could eat an entire knucker, I could."

"You'd need a bigger bag."

Felix threw back his head and laughed. "A joke from Oliver Webb! Not a particularly witty one, but a joke nonetheless. What a rare treat!" He danced over, grabbed Oliver's hand, and dragged him outside.

As an excuse for his slow walking, Oliver pretended to admire the view. It wasn't a difficult pretense because, as always, the sea was stunning. He had the impression that if he were to remain up here for a hundred years, he'd never get tired of the panorama. The sea was such a living thing. He'd never understood that before he came to Croftwell. He'd assumed it was simply a very large version of the pond in Jayne Park, with no more personality than the contents of a washtub. In reality, though, it was more like a vast sentient creature, perhaps a god engaged in a turbulent affair with Mother Earth.

Felix put a gentle hand on Oliver's arm. "Why did you come to Croftwell?"

"I couldn't remain in Greynox any longer. It... choked me."

"But why here specifically? You could have gone anywhere. I'm sure a man like you could have found gainful employment anywhere he chose."

Oliver gave a partial truth. "But I owned a cottage here."

"I don't think that's the only reason."

"Let's go eat," Oliver said after a moment.

The cloth had been spread on the landward side of the path, up a very gentle slope and under one of the moor's few trees, a gnarled specimen with broadly spreading branches. When they arrived, Felix clearly approved. "This will do!" he said. "For a novice picnicker, you've done quite well."

It was silly, but Oliver felt warmed by the praise.

They sat down and Felix began unpacking his bag: pickles, cheese, crusty bread, hard sausage, tiny dried fish, and two of what appeared to be Aygun's currant cakes. He'd also brought bottles of cider. He spread everything out, smiling a little at the scorch marks on the cloth.

"You wanted to make sure I don't forget almost burning down your house?"

"No. I wanted to demonstrate that the cloth is still perfectly useful." Oliver chuckled. "We can even consider the burns a decorative element. Something can be flawed yet no less valuable."

Felix gaped at him, speechless for the first time since they'd met. Then he blinked rapidly and rubbed his eyes with the heels of his hands. "Before we part today, I'm going to ask if I may kiss you. I hope you'll say yes."

Oliver gaped back.

It was simple fare but quite delicious. Felix explained that everything tasted better on a picnic, a very special sort of magic that even his curse couldn't disrupt. Oliver wouldn't have traded this afternoon—or the company—for a palace feast with the Queen herself. And somehow, despite the quantity of food, they ate every bite.

Afterward, Felix contrived a makeshift pillow out of the empty bag, and Oliver lay on his back with his head cushioned and his eyes focused on blue sky through lacy foliage. Sprites flitted around them; not the rare pink ones, but these were pretty enough, like living bits of rainbow.

Felix, sitting cross-legged with his boots off, gently brushed a strand of hair from Oliver's forehead. It was the faintest touch, yet it made Oliver's entire body tingle.

"Do you want a nap or a story?" Felix asked.

He wanted a nap, truthfully. But that wasn't what Oliver *needed* most right now. "Story, please."

"I don't know the end of this one, but I think you do." Felix unwound the scarf and tucked it under Oliver's head. "There was a lass named Marina Rowe."

THERE WAS a lass named Marina Rowe. This was not in the distant past. Marina's mother had been a Moon, you see, and her father had some Moon and Iceshadow blood as well. Distant cousins marrying—not so very rare 'round here. So Marina was a Crofter through and through, with the sea in her blood and the moor in her bones.

Marina's family lived down in the village, where her father fished and her mother sewed. They had only the one child. And when Marina was a girl, she'd often come up the cliff to run on the moor and play in the old cottage, which nobody had lived in for generations. She told people that the ghosts were her friends, and I expect that was true since her family owned Farview.

She was a happy child. Independent and sturdy and strong-minded, all of which served her well when her father died at sea and her mother of a fever before Marina was quite grown. She looked after herself, she did, and the villagers didn't worry about her. She'd learned to sew from her mother and she even managed a small kitchen garden with a few chickens for eggs.

Now, Marina had always kept mostly to herself. Out of choice, not necessity. She was the type who's often most comfortable in her own company. Some of the villagers assumed she'd never marry, which was certainly her right and nobody would have plagued her about it.

But just because she didn't fancy marriage didn't mean she wanted nothing at all to do with men. Now and then she and a village lad named Peter Poole would go off for a walk on the moors. Oh, there was a bit of gossip about it—you can't avoid gossip in Croftwell. But mostly people thought the pair of them well-suited for... occasional friendly strolls. Peter was a fisherman and also an orphan, and he also kept mostly to himself.

This went on for some years. Marina was nearly thirty and content as could be. She had her home, her garden, her income, and her bits of fun with Peter Poole. She could have gone on like that forever and never complained.

Then one day Peter was caught out in a squall. The next day a fisherman found his boat broken on the rocks outside the harbor. No sign of Peter. Either he was washed away and his boat came in on its own, or he drowned when it foundered. It was a sad event, but it happens. Fishing's dangerous work. Marina mourned a bit, but she wasn't shattered by it. He was a friend, she said. They weren't in love.

Nobody knows whether Marina was aware she was pregnant before Peter died. Perhaps they both knew of the child to come, or perhaps not. I like to think Peter died pleased to know that a bit of himself would be passed down to the next generation.

In any case, Marina's condition became apparent soon enough. She was happy about it. When she went to the shops or dropped off some sewing, she'd talk about how much she was looking forward to becoming a mother. "Hadn't meant to," she said, "but I'm pleased nonetheless."

I know that in many places, people would have been scandalized by Marina's situation. But I've told you before: Crofters don't get outraged easily. And Marina was an adult who'd made her own choices and harmed no one with them. Let her have her peace, the Crofters said; she'd make a responsible parent. Besides, we always welcome children because without them, well, we'd have died out long ago.

But a few months before the baby was due, Marina announced that she was moving to Greynox. Wasn't that a shock for everyone! She said she was going to have a son and she wanted him to have choices beyond fishing. Maybe because both her father and her lover were lost to the sea. She'd find work as a seamstress in the city, she said. So she sold her house in the village and most of her things, and she packed her bag and got on the coach for Bythington.

Everyone assumed she'd return someday. Perhaps she'd live in Farview, they said. But she never came back. And nobody went up to the cottage anymore except for a few nosy tourists who got chased away by the ghosts.

That's all of the story I know.

OLIVER WAS STILL GAZING up at the leafy sky. He wasn't entirely sure how he felt, except that something had clicked into place as Felix spoke. A long-held possibility that solidified into a fact.

"He must have known," he mused.

"Who?"

"My fath—." Oliver let out a choked laugh. "The man she married in Greynox. She would have been visibly pregnant when they met, and he knew the child wasn't his."

Felix looked at him intently for a moment and then lay down

beside him. Oliver handed him the scarf so he'd have a pillow as well. A trio of sprites did acrobatics overhead.

"Do you want to tell the other half now?" Felix asked after a while. "I'd like to hear it."

"I'm not like you. Not a bard."

"Ah, but maybe it'll come as easily to you as picnicking. Give it a go." Felix took Oliver's hand, lacing their fingers together. Just that—another simple touch, but one that Oliver felt everywhere. It was like the tea from the yellow flowers, bringing him a bit of borrowed life.

"I don't really know that much. I don't remember her, and... and Mr. Webb spoke of her only rarely. He left out some important details even then."

"Tell what you wish. Remember, nothing is truer than stories."

"Right." Oliver sighed. "There was a Greynoxer named Stephen Webb."

THERE WAS a Greynoxer named Stephen Webb. He was a Noxer through and through. If his family had ever lived anywhere else, he didn't know about it. Generations of Webbs with their pale brown hair and their pale brown eyes—and their pale skin, as if they'd no memory at all of bright sunshine.

The Webbs owned one of the great warehouses along the Methes River. They prided themselves on working for a living, and although they weren't fabulously wealthy, they were comfortable. Nice houses with a servant or two, decent clothing, plenty of food in the larder. Webb children received an education, with a few even going on to university.

Stephen Webb did not go to university, but he was shrewd nonetheless. Although he was the third son, his father relied on him to help manage the warehouse, which Stephen's brothers resented a bit. Stephen devoted nearly all his waking hours to the family business, so much so that by the time he was almost forty he hadn't yet wed.

His niece, however, was engaged. Because Stephen was considered the canniest, he was the one put in charge of negotiating the various costs associated with the wedding. One expense was the dress she wanted made, a frivolous confection of taffeta and silk. The seamstress was a woman named Marina Rowe.

She was more handsome than beautiful, but he liked her forthright manner and good business sense, and so he asked her to marry him. What she saw in him, I do not know, but she accepted. They were wed quickly, without any of the fuss that the niece so enjoyed. The other Webbs were displeased over the match, and in the uproar that followed, Stephen stopped working for his father and instead took a manager position at a different warehouse. After that, his relations with the other Webbs were infrequent and strained, but he and his bride managed well enough. They bought a neat little townhouse on Varnham Street.

Marina gave birth to a boy they called Oliver Webb. He was a large baby, healthy and boisterous, with his mother's dark hair and blue eyes. Perhaps they were all very happy together. But when Oliver was two, Marina became pregnant again, and this time it didn't go well. She was bedridden for months, and in the end, both she and her daughter died. She left Oliver a document saying he had inherited a cottage called Farview, but she left him with no memories of her at all.

Stephen, continuing to work long hours, hired nannies to care for Oliver. He remarried four years later, but his new wife didn't care for children and was far more interested in her social clubs than in helping to raise someone else's son. Oliver grew up strong but alone. He'd sometimes go entire weeks without exchanging a single word with either of the senior Webbs. He became resentful. And it didn't help when he realized, at thirteen or fourteen, that other lads caught his fancy and girls did not. He knew that even a whiff of this would horrify everyone he knew.

When Oliver was younger, Stephen occasionally spoke about sending him to university to read law or medicine. But Oliver was a mediocre scholar in grammar school, and his stepmother decreed that university would be a waste of money. On Oliver's sixteenth birthday, Stephen got him a position at the warehouse he managed: moving bales of goods about, and loading and unloading carts. Oliver would often carry a shipment down to a boat docked in the river behind the warehouse, but he never stepped foot on the boats themselves. Longshoremen did that, and they got tetchy if anyone else moved onto their territory.

Shortly after Oliver turned eighteen, he and Stephen had an enormous row over the strict household rules. Stephen called him ungrateful, which was perhaps fair. Oliver called him cold and distant, no kind of a father at all. The stepmother slapped Oliver's face. Oliver packed a few belongings into a bag and left the house on Varnham Street. He never entered it again, nor did he exchange another word with Stephen or the stepmother.

Oliver could easily have found a position at one of the other warehouses, but he decided that didn't suit him. He spoke to some of the longshoremen and sailors he knew, but none of them had room to take on an unseasoned youth, not even if he was big and muscular and willing to work hard.

Oliver spent a few rough nights without a roof or a bed and with very little to eat. It was a hard lesson for a lad who'd never before wanted for basic necessities. In desperation—but not quite enough of it to return to the warehouses—he went to Hillard's mill. Hillard used the warehouse where Oliver had worked, so Oliver knew a few of HIllard's men. He presented himself to one of the guards, willing to take any job they'd give him. The chief guard took a long look at Oliver's size, asked him a few questions, and hired him on.

He stayed there for ten years. The pay wasn't bad, so by renting a simple room and not wasting too many coppers, Oliver was able to save a great deal. Those few days on the streets of Greynox had cautioned him against ever being without funds again. He expected to continue guarding until he was too feeble to manage, at which point he'd retire to a nice let room near Jayne Park.

But then... then it was April fifth.

Afterward, eventually, Oliver remembered the document his mother had left him. A cottage in a fishing village called Croftwell, far from Greynox's grim skies. He packed his few belongings and bought a train ticket for Bythington.

And there Oliver's not-very-interesting story ends.

"It's not ended," Felix said after a minute or two of silence. "It's a new chapter. A better one, I think." He gave Oliver's hand a squeeze. "Did you know that this tree we're under is a downy birch? They're good for cleansing and renewal."

Although Oliver appreciated Felix's support, he knew better. And Felix would know better too, if Oliver told him the bits he'd left out. But Oliver's fate was his own burden, not Felix's, especially since Felix had his own difficulties to contend with. Difficulties that would be partially alleviated after Oliver died, and simply recalling that made Oliver smile a little.

"I was too harsh on my fa—on my mother's husband," Oliver said. "I don't think affection was in his nature. But he was never cruel, never raised a hand to me. He gave me a home and made sure I had a job. And he never once let on that I wasn't his son, although I should have suspected. I don't look remotely like a Webb. Anyway, I should have been more understanding and appreciative."

"You were young, Olly. And it hurts terribly to not be connected to others. Everyone needs love."

"No," Oliver said after a moment's consideration. "Almost everyone wants love, but they don't *need* it. They can survive without."

"I disagree."

The sprites had fluttered away, and now a chill breeze made Oliver shiver. Felix sat up and pointed at the dark clouds forming far out to sea. "Storm coming in. Picnics are not nearly as much fun in a downpour."

Oliver rose slowly to his feet, trying not to groan, hoping he seemed merely sleepy rather than in pain. He helped Felix gather up their things and then, smiling, wrapped the scarf around Felix's neck. They walked back to the cottage at a faster rate than Oliver would have preferred, but he didn't complain.

The rain had not yet begun when they reached Farview, but the sun had disappeared and the temperature had dropped noticeably.

"I should hurry if I want to make it down to the village without getting drenched," Felix said.

"Will you be all right in that shed?"

"Aye, right as rain." Felix laughed. "That's not the best way to put it right now, is it? I'll be fine. The shed's rainproof, and I've enough blankets to stay warm."

Oliver wanted to urge him to stay, but that would be selfish. The worst thing he could do to Felix right now was encourage anything deeper than friendship between them. Not when time was so short.

Felix was staring at him in that way he had, as if Oliver were something fascinating and mysterious he'd discovered in a fishing net. Nobody had ever regarded him like that before; it was both flattering and discomfiting, and it heated Oliver's cold, empty core.

"Did you ever have a lover?" Felix asked.

"It's not like here. Men together must be secretive."

"I know. But plenty of them take lovers nonetheless. Did you?"

Bluntness was in order here, lest Felix start entertaining any romantic notions. "I fucked men now and then. Strangers, mostly. Never the same fellow twice."

Felix didn't flinch or appear shocked. "That can be a bit of fun. Did some of that myself when I 'prenticed. But you know, people like us, we're entitled to something more if we want it. Something important."

Oliver's mouth tasted bitter. "You deserve that, Felix. I can't have it, though."

"And I'd like to know why, but I expect that's another story. I hope you'll tell me when you feel up to it."

Oliver walked him to the door, wishing he could instead tug him back in and sit him in an octopus chair. Serve him some tea. Listen to him spin tales. Touch him.

Felix paused before leaving. "Oh, I haven't forgotten. May I kiss you, Olly?"

Gods, Oliver lacked the strength to refuse. He nodded dumbly. And Felix surprised him once again, stepping in for an embrace, tilting his head up and tugging Oliver's down, and pressing their lips together sweetly, softly. Tenderly.

There was nothing the slightest bit chaste about this kiss, but it was no lustful strike nor a motion done in jest. Felix kissed as if Oliver were a delicious treat he wished to savor and as if nothing else in the world was as important. He cupped Oliver's face gently in his palms, those long fingers splayed across Oliver's skin. It was all Oliver could do to keep his knees from buckling.

Eventually Felix stepped back, his lashes damp and face flushed. "Do you know why I did that?"

"Erm...."

"Not because you're handsome, although you are. I kissed you because you're kind to me and accept me for who I am. I kissed you because you make me happy."

He left without waiting for Oliver's reply.

Chapter Eleven

Felix had been right about the storm. Although it had blown itself out by the following morning, another followed fast on its heels, and that one stuck around. Oliver got drenched just going to the loo, and making his way down the slippery cliff path was out of the question even if he used a walking stick. Not even the imps showed; they were undoubtedly tucked deeply into their burrows, dreaming about the crusts and rinds they weren't getting.

Oliver did very little but gaze out the window. He managed to get the rest of the drawers open in the wooden bureau, but the effort required a nap that lasted for hours. Preparing food exhausted him, which worked well enough because so did eating it. The pain in his stomach increased a little more every hour until it was a ravening beast so fierce he could barely think. He had to hold walls and furniture for support when he walked, and even then he sometimes fell. It took him longer and longer to get up again.

He remembered an old woman who'd lived two houses down from the Webb residence on Varnham Street. Every afternoon, if the weather wasn't too foul, she'd go for a walk accompanied by her nurse. It was painful to watch her excruciatingly slow progress down the pavement. Hunched over, face drawn, she'd get as far as the cross street before turning around and inching her way back home. Oliver used to think he'd never get that old—and he'd been right. Yet even still, here he was, very much like her.

The only things that comforted him were gazing at the sea—when the clouds were high enough to give a clear view—and thinking about Felix. Oliver had kissed men, but never like that. He'd never before felt as if the person he was with wanted him specifically, rather than any available and reasonably acceptable partner. He realized it was quite possible that he appealed to Felix mostly because he was here and somebody new. But that was all right since Felix would never have the chance to get bored with him.

It wasn't just Felix's kiss that sustained Oliver, but also the way he'd held Oliver's hand and brushed a strand of hair from his face. And his stories! Oliver could imagine the details even now. His ancestor sitting in this very cottage, Aymar Iceshadow's ship appearing on the horizon. Oliver's pregnant mother content in her home and looking forward to having a child.

Even the story about his own parentage was strangely soothing. Oliver now had a better understanding of why Stephen had never held him close, and yet Oliver also appreciated that Stephen had never told him he wasn't his real son. Oliver's childhood would have been even more miserable had he known that. Being aware of it now, however, was a good thing. In one of Oliver's better hours, he managed to gather paper and pen and write a short note to Stephen, thanking him for all he'd done and apologizing for his rash youth. He didn't even know if Stephen still lived, but if so, perhaps Felix could find a way to get the note to him.

Later, curled up in a ball on his bed, Oliver pictured Felix moving into Farview and making it his permanent home. Perhaps sometimes he'd remember Oliver and think fondly of him. That was a pleasant notion.

The days passed in a haze of pain and fatigue, and Oliver gave serious consideration to staggering outside in the rain, lying down on the moor, and waiting for the last of his life to slip away. That would be preferable to leaving his corpse to pollute Felix's new home. But whether through cowardice or the last dregs of self-preservation, Oliver couldn't make himself walk out the door. So he waited. None of the ghosts made an appearance, or if they did, he was too far gone to notice.

And then one morning he opened his eyes and the sun was shining in the windows as brightly as he'd ever seen. When he dragged himself to the window and looked out, the sea sparkled as if it were made of diamonds. Oliver looked down at his body, which had gone gaunt and pale, and decided he might have one final journey left in him. It was worth the effort, anyway. He laboriously dressed, emptied the stinking chamberpot, and greeted the imps, who chattered at him like long-lost friends.

"I'm sorry! I'm sorry!" he said with a chuckle before scattering the last of his food for them. They ran off with all of it, the gleeful little scoundrels.

He took his walking stick, but even still, his progress along the footpath was torturously slow. The pain became its own entity, as if he were carrying a monster along with him. He could no longer remember what it felt like to be strong and healthy, even though he'd been both not so many months past. He had to pause often, yet he didn't dare sit down because he'd never get up again. He leaned on his stick instead, drawing some small strength from the sea below him.

Despite everything, he smiled when he reached the spot where he and Felix had picnicked. "Thank you, gods, for granting me that one excellent day." Even the Queen herself might have never enjoyed such simple perfection as an outdoor meal with a beautiful and engaging companion.

After what felt like months, he reached the broken stone wall and turned inland. The best way to keep going, he learned, was to promise ten more steps. And when that count was done, ten more. Ten seemed a reasonable enough goal.

Although he would have liked to pause at the ghost girl's carving, he didn't dare. He inched onward to the little stand of yellow flowers—and there he filled his pocket with florets. A dozen or more, he guessed, although his brain was too bleary to keep count. Then he turned around to begin his journey back.

The moor was almost entirely flat in this area, with nothing more than a few low, gentle swells. But it felt as if he were struggling up a steep hill—up the cliff itself, perhaps—with a body made of lead. Every step brought a fresh blast of agony. But he kept going, more out of pure stubbornness than anything else.

One more. One more. One more.

He could see Farview in the distance, its rounded stone shape snug against the edge of the moor. A bit of smoke puffed from the chimney; apparently he'd left the firestones lit in the hearth. Although he hadn't lived there long, the cottage had nestled into his heart in a way that neither his childhood home on Varnham Street nor any of his rented rooms ever had. Farview had grown beloved.

His knees gave, and when he tried to use the stick to get back to his feet, it broke. And Oliver just couldn't. Couldn't stand, couldn't crawl, couldn't try. He'd wasted his life in solitude in the seething masses of Greynox; he'd served nobody who deserved it and barely even himself; he'd done nothing of value. But he'd had this brief period of grace, a chance to watch the sea and to know the truth of his past, and precious hours with a man who became a true friend. He was grateful for that.

He made an attempt to roll onto his back but lacked the strength, and even the slight movement he managed made him cry out in agony. Fine. He'd meet his end embracing the moor that had been home to his ancestors.

Darkness gathered around him and the night insects began to call. The air grew chill, but he didn't feel cold. Perhaps he was feverish.

Oliver turned his head to face the water and waited to die.

"You have to see, Olly!"

He was back inside Hillard's, the machinery idle but the dust as heavy as ever. The air was a weight on his shoulders. He was alone in the mill. No. Someone was calling him. He spun around several times until he finally saw the ghost girl clutching her bow and arrow and looking at him with a depth of sorrow no child should feel. Not even a dead one.

"You have to see," she repeated.

"But I have. In a hundred nightmares since April fifth, I've seen it over and over."

"You didn't." She lifted her chin. "You have to see *now*."

"Is this a dream or delirium? Or... the afterlife?" Gods, what if he was doomed to relive that day forever and ever, hearing the screams and seeing the blood. Helping no one.

"This is here and now, but it won't last for long. Hurry!" She ran over, took his hand, and began to tug him toward the stairs. She was much stronger than she looked. But then again, he was very weak, his final heartbeats ticking away on the moor.

"I thought I envied the ones who died immediately. They never knew what happened. It was too fast for them to be in pain. But now I'm so glad I had these last months."

"Death is nothing like anyone living can imagine. You needn't fear it. And I don't remember what it's like to be alive. It was a dream I had a long time ago."

They'd reached the stairs by then. She pulled insistently, up one creaky step after another, her ghostly hand very small and hot in his.

"You must be very brave," Oliver said, "to have become a guardian."

She smiled brightly at him but didn't relent.

At the top of the stairway, she led him down the hall until they reached an imposing door.

"Mr. Hillard's office," Oliver said. He knew it well, the large space with a window looking down at the mill floor so Hillard could watch his employees without having to walk among them. "But he wasn't here on the fifth. He was up north on business."

"We're not here to see him," the ghost replied dismissively. The door, which was always kept locked, opened without her touching it, and she yanked Oliver inside. It was exactly as he'd last seen it. A massive desk with piles of paper on top, a chest of drawers that housed fabric samples, a cabinet that held liquor. A throne-like chair for

Hillard and two spindly ones for guests. And two windows, one facing out onto the street and the other inward.

No, it wasn't exactly as it had been. Now there was a door in the exterior wall. And a moor-cat sat in front of it.

At least, Oliver assumed it was a moor-cat. It was as big as a large dog, with thick tawny-green fur and small, rounded ears. Its tail was disproportionately long and its feet oversized; the sharp claws dug into the rug. Most astonishing, however, were its eyes: the same yellow as the flowers Oliver had picked, with long vertical pupils. The creature seemed alert but not alarmed.

"She's a guardian too," the ghost said.

"Is she what you wanted me to see?"

The girl laughed, the sound bright in the gloomy room. "Why would I bring you all the way here for that? You could have seen her back home, if you'd looked properly." As she spoke, the moor-cat stood and stretched, very much like a small house cat after a good nap. Then it gave one long leap and landed atop the desk, where it sat again, its tail trailing over the edge.

The door it had been guarding swung inward.

"No," Oliver moaned. But the ghost and the moor-cat waited, and how could he be a coward in the face of their courage? With his hands clenched into tight fists, Oliver walked through the doorway and onto a small balcony.

Down below, the huge crowd had gathered. A man and woman stood atop a carriage, shouting out the many ways the mill owners mistreated their workers. The throng yelled back. If Oliver looked at their faces, he saw anger and strength and hope. After days of demonstrations and rapidly growing support, it seemed as if they might finally earn some concessions from their employers. They were asking so little in the grand scheme of things, yet that little could dramatically improve so many lives.

And then Oliver gasped, catching sight of someone familiar almost beneath his feet: a tall, muscular man with black hair and blue eyes, wearing the navy-and-black uniform of a Hillard's guard. The man stood at the edge of the crowd, pressed back against a brick wall, his arms crossed and his expression one of intense concentration.

"That's me," he whispered.

"I know." The ghost made the face children make when they believe that adults are being stupid. "You're skinnier now, but I can tell it's you."

"I thought myself very strong then. But I was too weak to do anything to help."

"Maybe it's not too late now."

He barked a bitter laugh. "It's too late for anything." Then he sighed. "I've seen. Can we go now? Before—"

"Not yet."

Fine. He'd pay his penance and watch it again. The chanting and the singing continued. Some of the smaller children, perched on adults' shoulders to get a better view, were the most enthusiastic of all. Despite their tender age, despite what should have been a time of innocence, they knew the pain of backbreaking work and the misery of unrelenting poverty. They wanted a future better than that. They wanted—

Movement caught Oliver's attention. It was another man, young and lean, dressed in the same guard uniform. Oliver couldn't remember his name. He'd been hired only about a week before the fifth, when Hillard decided on extra guards due to the protests.

Like Oliver, the guard was keeping a watchful eye on the crowd, but he was also moving slowly. Stealthily, Oliver thought, as if he hoped to pass unnoticed. He pressed into the mass of people, which was strictly against instructions. Oliver could just make out his dark blond head inching closer to the center.

The guard lifted his hands above his head, cupped together as if they cradled something. Oliver couldn't see what.

"Oh n—"

The flash blinded him and the boom was deafening. When he found his senses again, he was back inside Hillard's office. He could hear the heart-piercing screams despite the closed door. The moor-cat hopped off the desk to stand beside the girl, both of them facing Oliver.

"You saw," she said.

Oliver was crying. He tried to dash the tears from his eyes. "I should have known. I should have bloody well known."

"Maybe it's not too late."

"They're dead!" he shouted before continuing more quietly. "And me too, or close enough."

"The six people convicted for doing this haven't been hung yet."

"Gods, more deaths."

"Maybe it's not too late."

And at that moment, the moor-cat sprang at him.

Chapter Twelve

"Olly! Gods, Olly!"

At first Oliver thought the imps were crying his name, which was silly. But they were all he could see, their orange fur bright against the soft browns and greens of the moor grass. They were close enough to brush against his face.

But no, imps couldn't speak, and when a hand impatiently pushed some of them away, he saw Felix staring down at him, face white and eyes huge.

"Olly!"

Oliver made a croaking sound.

"Holy Salacia and Neptune, you're alive! Are you—" Felix pushed at Oliver's shoulder and hip, rolling him onto his back. Then he started patting and lifting Oliver's clothes as if checking for injuries. He looked frantic. "What's wrong? Are you hurt?"

Strangely, Oliver felt perfectly calm. The pain was there, sharp as always, and he was so weak that he couldn't lift his head. But the sky was blue, Felix was here, and Oliver wasn't dead yet.

"Flowers," he rasped.

Felix shook his head. "What?"

"Flowers. Pocket. Tea." Oliver didn't know if they were still fresh enough to work, but it was the only advice he had. Otherwise he could remain here and become one with the moor. Perhaps someday in the far future, those university men would dig up his bones and he'd end up in a museum too. The idea made him smile.

But Felix wasn't smiling—he appeared on the verge of tears, in fact, and was breathing so heavily that Oliver feared he might pass out. Whether he understood what Oliver was trying to tell him or if it was just luck, Felix's hand slipped into Oliver's coat pocket and came out clutching several yellow florets. He stared at them in astonishment.

"Ogrewort? How— Doesn't matter." He looked back and forth between Oliver and some point in the distance, chewing his lip hard enough to make a spot of blood appear. Apparently having reached a decision, he jumped to his feet. "I'll be right— I'm sorry, Olly, I don't know what else— For the gods' sake, don't die!" With a wail of distress, he took off running at an astonishing rate.

The imps remained, with a few of the braver ones coming close enough to snuggle up against Oliver. "No food," he whispered, but they didn't seem to care about that. One of them, the small one with blue threads woven through its fur, sat near the crook of Oliver's neck and made quiet chirring sounds, somewhat like a cat's purr. The creature patted his cheek gently, taking care not to scratch him with its dagger-like claws. Oliver felt faintly ridiculous. If anyone had told him six months ago that he'd meet his end on a moor, flat on his back with imps providing comfort, he would have escorted that person to the madhouse.

He might have grayed out; he wasn't sure. The next thing he was aware of was Felix cradling Oliver's head in his lap and jamming a cup against Oliver's lips. "Drink this, blast you! Please, Olly."

It still tasted horrible, but Oliver's mouth was bone-dry, so he swallowed obediently. Some of the tea ran down his cheeks and onto his neck, but most of it got into him. He started feeling slightly better almost immediately—far too fast for the flowers to have taken effect. Must be the power of suggestion.

"Olly, I can't carry you. I'll... I'll go get help, and—"

"No."

"But I can't just—"

"Stay. Give me time."

Although Felix was gnawing at his lip again, he obeyed. He set the cup down and smoothed Oliver's hair away from his face. Oh, those clever fingers! "I should fetch someone."

"Won't help."

"I want to know how you found ogrewort flowers in August. They bloom in early spring. And I want to know... the bits of your story you haven't told me. And Olly, I want...." Felix swallowed loudly. "I want *you*. Please."

Oliver couldn't make that promise. But he could smile at Felix's upside-down face and say, "You're astonishing."

Felix merely shook his head slowly.

They remained that way for some time, Oliver oddly content, until he realized that his clothing was soaked, with a particularly nasty dampness to his trousers. And he reeked. Lovely. He'd managed to piss himself like a Greynox alley drunkard. Yet Felix, who'd surely noticed, didn't seem repulsed.

"Might stand with help," Oliver said.

Felix looked entirely doubtful, as well he might, but Oliver gave him an encouraging smile, and Felix slid out from underneath him, taking care not to let Oliver's head smash against the ground. Oliver ended up on his feet—more from Felix lifting him than from his own efforts—and had to lean against Felix to stay upright. Although Felix was thin, he was strong, and they made their slow way back to the cottage with Oliver's arm slung over his shoulders and the imps dancing around them like a strange little honor guard.

Good gods, Oliver *hurt*, but he swallowed his groans. Felix didn't need to hear him complaining when Felix was exerting so much effort to help.

Somehow they made it back. Felix dragged him to the bed, stripped off Oliver's clothing with maximum efficiency and no hints of repugnance, and covered him with the blankets. "The doctor in Urchin Cove—"

"Can't help. I told you."

"You're very ill, Olly."

"I know."

Felix tensed his jaw but stopped arguing. “Rest. I’ll… manage.” He added under his breath, “Unless I burn your house down.”

“You won’t.”

Oliver didn’t know that, of course, but he lacked the strength to worry about it. He allowed his eyes to fall closed and drifted off as Felix muttered something about Oliver owing him a story.

Time passed in a blur. Oliver was surrounded by a haze interrupted by brief moments of clarity, like the sun’s ray’s breaking through heavy clouds. Felix gave him water and tea—nice tea with honey, not the stuff with the ogrewort. He fed him as well, spooning broth into his mouth and urging him to take little morsels of soft bread from his fingers. And Felix cleaned him, washing him with damp cloths, combing his hair, even helping him use the chamberpot. Oliver would have been embarrassed about the last bit if Felix hadn’t been so matter-of-fact. “Everyone pisses, Olly, don’t they. No use being prudish.”

Surely Felix must have left occasionally. For one thing, Oliver knew the larder had been nearly empty, and yet somehow they were eating. But he was never aware of Felix’s absences—just his presence, solid and comforting. Felix spoke often, usually stories about people Oliver didn’t know, and the words washed over him like warm wavelets.

When the fog cleared more substantially, the first thing Oliver noticed was the assortment of new items on a nearby shelf. “Shells?”

Felix, sitting on the bed beside him, had been working a tangle out of Oliver’s hair. He paused to see what Oliver was looking at. “Yes, shells. And some sea-polished stones and bit of bottle glass.”

“Why?”

“There’s a lovely little bay north of here, just south of Urchin Cove. The inlet is so narrow it’s almost hidden if you’re out at sea. There are some holiday homes there, but visitors rarely come, so it’s private.” He sighed. “I should have taken you there.”

Oliver felt as if he might start purring beneath Felix’s touch. “But the shells?”

“When there’s a big storm, things end up on that beach. My uncle

Teddy sometimes collects them to sell to tourists. I don't think he makes many coppers out of it, but it gives him an excuse to take his boat out, and it gets him out of the house, so he and Aunt Dahlia are both satisfied. And you know what? If you're well enough to listen to me natter, you're well enough to eat. Hang on."

To Oliver's disappointment, Felix stood and walked to the kitchen, where he quickly assembled a small plate and returned. "Can you sit up, do you think? It'll make this easier."

Oliver needed help, so Felix arranged pillows behind him and then spent a few moments fussing with blankets like a nervous nursemaid.

"The shells?" Oliver prompted.

Felix popped a morsel of boiled egg into Oliver's mouth. "The morning after the storms ended—four days ago now—I went with Uncle Teddy to that bay. I've a better eye for treasures than he does, and he pays me a bit to help out. We collected a fair catch of 'em. I kept a few for brightening up your cottage, I did. Figured if you're not going to take it on yourself to decorate, I'd lend a hand."

"They're pretty."

"Not worth much. But nice to look at."

There were more pieces of egg, followed by a bite of something green and soggy that tasted like the sea.

"I could feed myself."

"Take advantage of being treated like royalty while it lasts, yer majesty."

Felix fed him more of the green stuff, and then his expression grew serious.

"I meant to bring you the shells right away. But we didn't get back until dinnertime, and then Aunt Dahlia offered to feed me. The next day I got some work helping to paint Fernica Moon's garden shed—she keeps it bright red—so I didn't come up then either. Then I *did* come up the next morning, and the imps were nearly hysterical, but who pays much attention to imps? Your door was open. I came inside. It smelled like... like sickness, Olly. And you weren't here." He looked away, his chin working.

"How did you find me?"

"Was the imps, wasn't it? They led me right to you. Good gods, how long were you lying there?"

Oliver, distracted by how glad he was to have fed the imps so generously, took a moment to calculate. "I think... two nights?"

Felix blanched. "Two bloody nights? If I'd brought the shells right away.... But you were sick even before that, weren't you? Sick during the storm, and I left you here all alone."

Oliver grabbed Felix's hand. "Nothing that happened to me was your fault. I'm not your responsibility."

"You bloody well are! I am your neighbor. Your friend. I care about you, Oliver Webb."

That was exactly what Oliver had meant to avoid, and yet it had happened anyway. He and Felix shared feelings for each other. Bloody hell.

"Well, you rescued me," Oliver pointed out. "I'm alive now because of you."

"And the imps. What were you doing strolling along the moor when you were ill?"

"I'd gone to get the flowers—the ogrewort. I couldn't quite make it back."

Felix's face was drawn. "Gone where?"

"It's... near some ruins."

"How did you know they were there? They shouldn't be, this time of year."

Oliver shrugged. "The ghosts told me."

That didn't seem to bring Felix much comfort. "And did they tell you that taking more than a few flowers will kill you? Because you had more than a few in your pocket."

"They told me," Oliver admitted.

Felix regarded him silently for a long minute. Oliver thought Felix was angry, but then he realized that he saw hurt in his eyes. Blast it all. Oliver should have learned from his experiences with Stephen Webb that pulling away from someone to keep a secret only makes things worse.

"You should rest now," Felix announced.

"I'm feeling stronger, though."

"How long will the effects of the ogrewort last?"

Abashed, Oliver turned away. "I'm not sure. A few days, perhaps."

Without saying anything else, Felix readjusted the pillows so Oliver could lie flat. The bedding smelled nice, he realized. Like lavender. It certainly hadn't smelled that way when he'd left Farview, and he wondered how Felix had managed to clean the sheets with Oliver in them and without Oliver noticing. He didn't ask.

He dozed, vaguely aware that Felix was moving about and performing small chores. Oliver no longer had the heavy haze of illness, however, and after an hour he came fully awake. Felix was sitting in one of the octopus chairs, facing the bed rather than the window, and he was fast asleep. Oliver watched him for a long time, his heart almost too warm and too heavy to bear.

When Felix blinked awake and saw Oliver staring, he smiled and stretched. "Hungry?"

"No."

"I can make sandwiches when you're ready. I've been avoiding using the fire more than necessary. So far the firestones haven't reacted to my curse."

Oliver remembered something one of the ghosts had said. "The people who used to live here—our ancestors—they used peat for fires. No magic there."

Felix stopped in mid-stretch. "Do you know how to do that?"

"No. But we could learn. I'll ask the ghosts when they appear again."

"Why would you do that when you have perfectly good firestones?"

So you'll know how when Farview is yours. Though Oliver didn't say that out loud, of course. He gave a different truth instead. "So you don't have to worry about a disaster."

"You know how to charm in the strangest, best ways." Felix rubbed his hands together. "How would you fancy a bath?" He gestured toward the washtub.

"That's a lot of work."

"Not for you, yer majesty. You just sit tight and watch your servant labor away."

Oliver did just that, watching Felix bring bucket after bucket of water from the pump, until the tub was so full it was going to overflow when he got into it. Satisfied with his efforts, Felix set down the bucket.

"You'd best do the heating bit. I'm apt to boil it or turn it to ice. Let me help you over."

Naked as the day he was born and leaning heavily on Felix, Oliver slowly crossed the floor. He did need the assistance, but he was surprised at how well his legs held up. He tossed a firestone into the tub and even managed to remain standing until the water had become as warm as he could bear. Then he fished the stone out and, using Felix's arms to steady himself, climbed in.

"Oh," he moaned as soon as he was seated.

"Nice, is it?"

"I'm glad I let you talk me into it." The warm water felt lovely, easing the aches in his joints and making his skin feel more supple.

"If I were king, I'd have a bath every day, I would. Twice on Sundays." Felix walked to the washstand and returned with a flannel and a cake of soap. Oliver reached for them, but Felix grinned wickedly and shook his head. "Part of my job, yer majesty."

He knelt beside the tub and began to wash Oliver's neck and chest. It felt so lovely that Oliver let another moan escape—which Felix answered with a throaty chuckle. "Enjoying that?"

"Gods, yes."

Felix moved lower, to Oliver's stomach, which was only a little sore today. He swiped the cloth in small, slow circles as if he had all day to complete this task and wanted to do nothing else. Oliver didn't know where to look—at the bright vista outside his window or at the beautiful man tending to him.

"Whiskers," he murmured.

"What?" Felix looked amused.

"I haven't shaved in... I don't know how long. I must look a mess."

"You look like Neptune. Well, you would if you hadn't lost so much weight lately. We'll fix that. But I'll shave you later if you'd like."

Oliver was going to agree, but just then Felix moved the cloth even lower, then paused, watching Oliver's face for permission. Oliver knew he should refuse, but even as he was telling himself so, he was nodding. "Please."

And good gods, he was hard already, which was neither appropriate for a bath nor likely, given his delicate health. Nonetheless, he was. Felix had abandoned the flannel completely and was using his fingers—those fingers!—to smooth soap on Oliver's shaft and over his aching bollocks.

"Felix...."

"Am I doing anything you don't want me to?"

"No."

"And I want to do it as well, don't I? And you seem healthy enough to give it a go. So why not?" Felix stopped his hand and regarded Oliver with head tilted, as if he really wanted to know.

"I... I haven't told you my whole story."

"Ah." Felix sat back on his heels, allowing his wrist to rest on the edge of the tub. "Well, I knew that already, didn't I? Let me ask you something. These untold bits—do they involve you harming anyone?"

"What? No!"

"Didn't think so. You don't at all seem the type. If I continue what I was just doing, will anyone be harmed?"

Oliver had to think about that for a moment. "You, perhaps."

"Is your tallywag magical and likely to kill me if my curse kicks in?"

Despite all the more serious emotions swirling through him, Oliver guffawed so deeply that it hurt. "It's a serviceable enough organ but nobody's ever called it magic."

"Looks more than serviceable to me, sir, but maybe that's just the water's magnifying effects. Anyway, I'm willing to take my chances."

"I don't want to hurt you, Felix."

Felix's face eyes went soft and shiny. "There you are with the sweet talk. Let me show you something." He let the cloth and soap fall into the tub, where they landed over Oliver's feet. Then, still kneeling, he unfastened the top buttons of at least three layers of shirts and pulled the whole lot of them over his head, leaving his arms and torso bare. He dropped the clothes on the floor and waited.

Felix had only a few curls of dark hair on his chest. They did nothing to obscure the large tattoo inscribed over his left breast: an intricately worked anchor, with the attached chain trailing down his sternum, curving around his ribs, and disappearing over his right side. Oliver had seen tattoos before, mostly on the arms of sailors and longshoremen, but they tended to be much simpler than this.

"It's gorgeous."

Looking down at himself, Felix grinned. "Yeah, pretty enough work, isn't it? I had it done here in Croftwell before I went to Greynox. It was like carrying a bit of home with me. Some nights at the printers, when I missed Croftwell so much I could barely breathe, I'd look at this and it'd help a bit." He stroked the lines of the ink.

"I can understand that. But—"

"It's a lesson, Oliver Webb. Because let me tell you, getting this thing put on me bloody well *hurt*. Hours and hours of lying still while George Loowin poked me with needles over and over and *over*. But I endured it because I knew I'd need a reminder of where I'm from. And I've been glad ever since that I did it. You have to pay a price for important things. If you're lucky, the things are worth what you paid."

Despite the jab of pain he knew it would bring to his stomach, Oliver leaned forward so he could run a wet finger along the length of the anchor. Felix shivered, and not, Oliver thought, from the droplets that inched down his skin. "You think this would be worth it?"

In answer, Felix gently pushed him back and then plunged his own hand into the bath. Oliver's erection, which had flagged only slightly, immediately returned in full force. Perhaps his prick was, in fact, magic. Or enchanted. The truth of it, Oliver had to admit, was that all of him *was* enchanted by this entirely remarkable man. They hadn't known each other long; they hadn't spent all that much time together. Yet Oliver was certain that even if he were granted a thousand years of life, he'd never grow tired of watching the sea or being close to Felix Corbyn.

"What are you thinking?" Felix asked softly.

"That I've never had sex in a tub."

"Should have made you get a *really* big tub so I could climb in there with you." Felix's mouth hitched into a half smile. "Anyhow, a tub makes a poor substitute for a private beach on a warm day, but it'll have to do."

Oliver imagined that: he and Felix alone and naked, the sand soft beneath their feet, wavelets teasing their toes. The smells of salt and skin—which weren't so different—and the feel of Felix in his arms.

Felix's chuckle was filthy in exactly the right sort of way. "Oh, you like that, do you? Makes sense for the son of Crofters and water fae."

Water fae? Oliver wanted to ask about that, but now wasn't the time. It had been so long since he'd felt pleasure from his body rather than weakness and pain, and Felix was so very deft, and—

Felix took his hand away, which made Oliver open his eyes. But when Oliver realized Felix's intentions, he groaned loudly. Felix was unbuttoning his trousers and pushing them over his narrow hips, baring himself to midthigh. He wrapped a hand around his own rigid cock and gave it a few leisurely tugs. "Better," he said, watching Oliver through his lashes.

"Also more than serviceable, I see." Oliver was proud of himself for managing speech.

"On land and at sea."

Oliver couldn't touch Felix without considerable effort and discomfort, so he reached for himself instead. But Felix tsked, scooted a hair closer to the tub, and grasped Oliver with his free hand. In a display of admirable ambidexterity, he wanked them both, keeping up exactly the right pressure and rhythm to make Oliver whimper.

"Watch me, love," Felix purred. "I'm imagining this is you stroking me. I'm imagining we're on that beach and you're on top of me, and I've handfuls of your arse, and you're holding our pricks together. L-lovely." His eyes briefly rolled up and he shuddered. "Like I've caught a sea god."

Oliver was most definitely not a god, but when he tried to speak, nothing came out but a low, hungry moan. He'd engaged in more intimate acts than this, and certainly ones where he had a more active role, but he'd never felt so lost in sensation. So connected to the man touching him.

His climax came like an unexpected wave, stealing his breath and drowning him in bliss. He never wanted to surface again.

But of course he had to, still gasping and ready to flush with shame at the quickness of it. But Felix had collapsed into an untidy heap on the floor, his trousers tangled around his feet, and he was gazing at Oliver with wide, sparkling eyes. His own spend glistened pearl-like on his chest, some of it adorning the anchor chain. He looked slightly dazed, which was a match for how Oliver felt.

"Aye," Felix said, voice a tad wobbly, "that was something, wasn't it?"

Oliver nodded. It had been a bloody long time since he'd had sex—or wanted to—and Felix was delicious. But that didn't explain why he felt so overcome after nothing more than a few twisty tugs. Perhaps it had something to do with his illness.

After several steadying breaths and a quick wipe at his chest with Oliver's flannel, Felix got to his feet and refastened his trousers. He didn't bother with his shirts. "I think it's time to get you out of that tub. Sorry I didn't get to washing your hair." He grinned. "Next time."

He helped Oliver out of the water.

Oliver was able to stand by himself as Felix dried him off and needed nothing more than a steadying arm to return to bed. He fell back on the mattress, bringing Felix down with him so they could kiss. It was more fervent than their first one. Not exploratory, but rather the sort of kiss exchanged by two passionate, established lovers who couldn't get enough of each other.

Felix rose up a bit when they parted. "I want to think this means you're on the mend, but I see what's in your eyes, Olly."

"I'm sorry."

"I know." Felix stroked Oliver's cheek. "Not your fault, I expect."

He gave himself a little shake and brightened his expression.

"Now, how about some food?"

Chapter Thirteen

Oliver dozed a bit after dinner and then was pleased to make it to the loo with Felix's help. It was still warm out, and getting dressed wasn't worth the bother. They passed the imps, who were apparently unfazed by Oliver's nudity.

"I ought to thank them," Oliver said after emerging from the loo.

"I've been feeding the little beggars plenty, don't worry."

Still, after they reached the cottage, Oliver grabbed a large hunk of cheese and an entire sausage and tossed them out the door, much to the imps' delight. He made it back to bed on his own and sat on the edge.

"You've been spending a lot on feeding me," he said to Felix.

"Not so much. When I told Envina you were ill, she gave me all sorts of things."

"Why would she do that?"

Felix rolled his eyes. "Crofters care for one another, don't they?"

In an attempt to hide his surge of emotion, Oliver cleared his throat. "When and how did you tell Envina anything?"

"Not long after I brought you back here. You were out cold. I didn't want to leave you alone, but you had no food at all, and it was clear you hadn't eaten properly for days. I ran down and back up. Didn't take long."

"I've been so much trouble."

"Stop it. It's nice caring for someone else for a change. Usually I'm the one relying on others' help. And anyway, I haven't had to go down since. Everyone keeps sending up baskets of supplies. I think it's all some sort of conspiracy involving the imps."

"People have been coming up?" Oliver swung his legs onto the bed and pulled up the blankets. The sun was setting and the air was growing chill.

"They don't want to disturb you, so they've been leaving things outside. Food, cider, blankets, clothing. Even a walking stick or two."

Generous and considerate. What had Oliver ever done to deserve these good people? As he made himself comfortable, he saw Felix pick up a blanket from the floor and give it a shake, then settle into an octopus chair and drape it across his lap. He twisted himself into a position possible only because he was thin.

"I brought the candle too," he said through a yawn. "Safer for me. It'll burn out shortly." He wiggled his shoulders as if to settle in more deeply.

Oliver sat up abruptly. "Have you been sleeping on the chairs?"

"Don't worry. Your octopuses are unharmed."

"I don't care about the bloody octopuses. Felix, get into bed."

"Aye?" Felix looked at him, wide-eyed.

"Aye."

Felix leapt out of the chair, sending the blanket tumbling and nearly tripping over it on his way to the bed. But he climbed onto the mattress with utmost care, as if the merest jostle might be fatal to Oliver. He clung to the far edge of the big bed, which left a large space between them.

"I won't bite," Oliver said.

"I know."

"And I'm not completely fragile."

"You seemed quite sturdy in the tub today. Stiff, anyway." Felix sniggered like a schoolboy at his own joke. Then he sighed. "I haven't slept with anyone since I was a 'prentice. Nobody's brave enough to try it."

"I've *never* slept with anyone. And didn't someone tell me just this afternoon that sometimes things are worth the risk?"

Felix scooted several inches closer, but they still weren't quite touching. "No, I said they were worth the price. That's a bit of a different story, isn't it?"

"Either way."

As Felix had predicted, the candle flickered and guttered out, leaving the cottage in near darkness. A bit of purple remained in the sky, the sun's light making a final appearance from beyond the horizon. Oliver liked that he could see it without moving from bed. His rented room in Greynox had accommodated only one small window, and it had a view of nothing but the brick wall on the other side of the airshaft.

"Why didn't you bring anyone to bed, Olly? I'm sure nobody's afraid of sleeping with you."

"The couple I let from wouldn't have allowed it. And the men I fucked—it wasn't that sort of thing. It was... fast. Businesslike."

Felix snorted. "Unless someone's getting paid, sex shouldn't be businesslike."

Oliver had to agree. Especially when Felix came a bit nearer, allowing their shoulders to barely brush and his clothed leg to touch Oliver's bare one. Oliver wasn't sure why Felix hadn't undressed completely, but he must have had his reasons. Anyway, it was good to hear him breathing so close by and to feel his body heat mingling with Oliver's, creating a warm cocoon.

Then Felix's voice came hesitantly. "Olly? Are you on the mend or will you get sicker again?"

"Sicker," Oliver admitted after a long pause. "Without another dose of ogrewort, I honestly don't know how I've managed this long. It's as if being with you has medicinal qualities."

"That's what happens when someone cares for you properly. But when you need me to, I can fetch more flowers. Just tell me where they are." He sounded doubtful, as if unconvinced he'd find them even with directions, but Oliver wasn't worried about that right now.

What he *was* worried about was the burden of his omissions. Felix crooked his neck, and as his soft curls tickled Oliver's shoulder, Oliver also experienced the sensation of being tugged away while desperately trying to hang on.

"Felix?"

"Hmm?"

"Will you tell me a story? I don't have a pint to offer in return, but I do have a story of my own."

He felt Felix's long, contented sigh against his skin. "What story do you fancy, love?"

The last word, which likely meant nothing, momentarily threw Oliver for a loop. He blinked hard to clear his head. "You said something about water fae."

"Caught that, did you? All right. The water fae live far and far across the sea, on a beautiful island no sailor can see unless the fae will it."

THE WATER FAE live far and far across the sea, on a beautiful island no sailor can see unless the fae will it. Now and then they might take pity on a ship that's battered by a tempest and taking on water fast. Or they might decide to tease sailors who've gone far too long without fresh food or fresh faces. But mostly the fae keep to themselves. They dance and eat and drink and sing and write poetry and make love on their island.

As long as they stay on their island, the fae don't age at all. But the problem with immortality is boredom, and when they grow bored, the water fae travel on ships with hulls that gleam like diamonds and sails as fine as spiderwebs in all the colors of the rainbow. They go out to see what's new in the world and what those mayfly humans have been up to, and they gather new treasures to enjoy back home.

Some people say the fae cause trouble to entertain themselves, and maybe they do. But then, so do many humans. I've been known to do a bit of that myself, haven't I? Anyway, I wouldn't say the fae are bad; they just don't think much about how they're affecting people. Like you don't think much about a bug you happen to step on or a crow you chase away from your garden. I *would* say the fae are honorable. They keep their promises, when they make them, and they have definite ideas about what's fair and not.

Now, once there was a water fae prince named Aymar Iceshadow. He was the queen's youngest son and her favorite, and I expect she spoiled him a bit. She also got in the way of all his love matches. No female or male fae was ever good enough for her precious son. She didn't mind if he played, but no settling down. No *love*.

It took ten or twelve centuries, but eventually Aymar grew frustrated with this. A roll in the grass with someone pretty was nice enough, but he wanted more. He knew that humans tended to settle down, and this intrigued him. He decided to study humans for a bit.

When he told the queen, she was beside herself. "Why would you want to go to their dreary lands when everything is so much better here?"

"Mother, their lands might be dreary and their lives short, but they fight so hard for what they want. I'd like to see why."

They argued for a long time over it—at least three or four decades, I reckon—but eventually the queen saw how sad Aymar was, and she gave in.

"You may take a ship," she said. "And you may visit the lands of the humans. But my son, remember that while you are there, you will age just as they do. Promise me you'll return before you get old."

Aymar laughed at this. He couldn't imagine staying *that* long. Humans intrigued him, but enough to be willing to feel his body weaken and see his face grow less beautiful? Of course not! So he made the promise easily.

Aymar boarded his shining ship and set out across the ocean. He and his crew had adventures along the way, of course. They escaped Scylla and Charybdis and fought a kraken. They swam and sang with the Sirens. They saw sea turtles as big as islands and fish that turned to birds when they leapt out of the water. But those are different stories, and they weren't Aymar's true goal, were they?

Now, I don't know why Aymar chose to make shore in Croftwell. It's an attractive little town with a pretty harbor, but Urchin Cove's not much different. So maybe it was just luck, or perhaps the winds happened to blow him this way. Maybe whichever god sent Lyra Moon those dreams about a blue-eyed lad felt obligated to live up to the promise. Whatever the reason, Aymar Iceshadow arrived.

And once he did, he told his crew to go back home. He'd summon them, he said, when he was ready to return. How, I don't know, but he was a fae prince, so surely he had some means. I think perhaps he could speak into a shell here and talk to the queen via a shell back home. Maybe you could try that yourself, love, with the shells I brought you.

However it worked, Aymar said goodbye to his crew, hopped into a jollyboat, and came into the harbor.

And, well, I've already told you what happened here. He and Lyra Moon met and fell in love. They had children, one of which was your mother's direct ancestor. And although our lives here are dull compared to the faes' world, Aymar was happy. For years he gave no thought at all to what he'd promised the queen.

One day, though, he looked in the mirror and saw that his yellow hair had gone white, and creases had formed at the corners of his eyes. You know, left to his own, I don't think he would have minded getting old and finally dying. But the fae keep their promises, don't they? He had to go back.

He begged Lyra to come with him, but you know how that went. Lyra loved him deeply, but she also loved Croftwell and her children. She couldn't leave. He couldn't stay. They cried together. He pledged that somehow he'd return. Lyra built this cottage up on the cliff so she could watch for him.

Aymar sailed straight home. But the queen took one look at him and became furious. "You stayed away too long! My beautiful young son is gone forever, replaced by... this. A creature of middle age."

"But I did come back, Mother, even though leaving hurt so much that my heart still bleeds. I'm still strong. I can still do many things. I learned among the humans that someone can be lovable even if they don't look perfect."

The queen's wrath had been raised, however, and a fae queen's anger is a terrible thing. She ordered him to get back on the ship and never return. So he did.

Now, at first he didn't mind the banishment. He could go back to his beloved in Croftwell, free of any obligations to the fae. But it's one thing to sail aboard a fae ship when you've a crew and are eager for adventures. It's quite another when you're by yourself with a destination in mind.

Aymar couldn't find his way back to Croftwell.

For years and years, he crossed the seas, beset by many troubles. The worst of which was knowing that Lyra grew older each day. Every night he went to bed sobbing, knowing he'd lost more precious hours with her. Some days he gazed out at the endless expanse of water and was tempted to give up the struggle. He could jump into the sea and let the fishes have him.

But the fae are stubborn—a trait some of their human offspring carry as well—and Aymar didn't give up. He kept on sailing, feeling his body grow more frail and weak, his memories of Lyra and their children fading around the edges but never entirely losing their glow.

I don't know this for a fact, mind you, but I like to think that some god took pity on Aymar and Lyra and decided to reunite them. Whatever the cause, a mighty storm brewed, and those winds blew Aymar in his poor battered ship straight to Croftwell. He didn't even know if his beloved still lived. But as soon as the lull came, he got into his jollyboat and came into the harbor. And there, of course, was his Lyra, waiting for him.

They sailed off together.

What became of them after that, I don't know. But Lyra was a Crofter, and they always return, so maybe she'll be back someday. Whatever her fate and his, though, they've met it together.

OLIVER LAY in silence for a time, loving the feel of Felix against him. And then he finally sighed. "I can't decide whether that's a happy story or a sad one."

"Well, it's both, isn't it? Sad bits and happy, just like everybody's story."

"I don't like the sad bits."

"I don't expect anyone does. But we can make the best of the happy. I think that's the moral, if you want one. Aymar and Lyra didn't have eternity together, but they had *something* and that was lovely."

"Hmm."

Felix rolled toward Oliver and began to toy with the few hairs on Oliver's chest. There was nothing purposeful about it—he wasn't trying to arouse Oliver, who wasn't capable of another go tonight and was shocked he'd been able to manage even the one—but it was pleasant to have those fingers idly stroking and tugging at him.

"So," Oliver began, "if your story is true—"

"Told you. Nothing's truer than stories, even when they're not entirely accurate."

"Do you really think one of my ancestors was a water fae?"

"Oh, I know it. You have the blue eyes, don't you?"

Oliver snorted. "Loads of people have blue eyes."

"Not round here. Not unless they're descended from Lyra and Aymar."

It was an appealing idea: a man, who is nobody in particular and with no family to speak of, discovers magic in his lineage. Oliver didn't know if descending from a fae prince was any less likely than having conversations with ghosts who were related to him, scores of generations back. He'd come to Croftwell expecting solitude and peaceful boredom, yet he'd found a friend and a personal history and several small adventures besides.

"If I were a water fae, would that mean I'd be immune to sickness?"

"If you were on your island, sure." Felix sighed. "But you're here in Croftwell."

"Enjoying my bits of happiness." Oliver squeezed Felix closer.

The cottage was now almost entirely dark, although something bright occasionally flickered past the window, like a sprite that had swallowed a star. He didn't bother to ask Felix what it was. Although intrigued, Oliver decided he'd explored enough mysteries already and would let this one go.

Felix lay pressed against him, warm and patient, not trying to prompt Oliver. But Oliver could sense Felix's air of expectation, and besides, Oliver had made a promise. He may or may not be partly fae, but he liked to do what he'd said he would. Anyway, he was feeling surprisingly strong, and it was easier to admit things in the dark, to someone whose palm rested over your heart.

"This isn't a new story," Oliver said. "It's more a continuation of one from before."

"That's all right, then. All stories connect. Like strands in a web."

That made Oliver think of a spider waiting to pounce on her prey. Yet spiders could be beautiful—a shiny blue-and-purple one lived in the eave of the loo, and Oliver had enjoyed watching her gleam in the sun. They did a service, too, gobbling up bugs that would otherwise damage gardens. Good and bad. Happy and sad. Some of each.

"On April fifth, a flash-curse went off in front of Hillard's mill, killing scores. I was right there among them."

ON APRIL FIFTH, a flash-curse went off in front of Hillard's mill, killing scores. I was right there among them. I wasn't killed, of course. At first I was simply... stunned. I've no other word for it. My senses were dull and so was my mind, as if I wasn't entirely connected to the world anymore. Perhaps that is how ghosts feel.

I wasn't a ghost, though. I'm not exactly sure what I did next. I don't remember. I do know I didn't stop to help the wounded, which I should have done. I think I simply wandered away.

When I came back to myself, I was in my room, sitting naked on a chair, and my stomach hurt. I don't mean nausea from what I'd seen. This was an ache, as if someone had dealt me a blow. I couldn't see any injury on my body, though, not even a bruise, although my uniform was drenched in other people's blood. I thought I must have banged into something while trying to get away. Anyway, the horror of what I'd witnessed was far worse than the ache.

I threw away my uniform and never returned to Hillard's. Even thinking about going there made me shake. Well, that's not entirely true. I went back there every night in my dreams, which was more than enough.

After a few days, I decided to take a bit of time to decide what to do next. I had some coppers saved. Besides, things were uneasy in

Greynox in the days after the deaths—accusations thrown about in the press over who was responsible, laws being rushed through Parliament. The Queen herself issued a statement condemning the disorder and violence. She blamed the leaders of the protest, as did everyone else of importance.

I spent my time sitting in my room or, when I couldn't stand it anymore, walking in Jayne Park. I'm not posh enough to be welcome there—I received plenty of angry stares and a few harsh words—but I'm big enough that nobody confronted me. It gave me a bit of peace to look at the pond.

That ache, though, it didn't go away. In fact, it grew worse, so that it disturbed my sleep and I felt tired all the time. I went to a doctor eventually. He heard my story, looked me over, and shook his head. Not a thing he could do for me, he said. I wasn't ill; I was cursed.

Apparently I'd taken a hit from the flash-curse after all, without even realizing it. Most people died right away or soon after, screaming in agony, but I had only been nicked by it. Problem is, that still meant I was cursed.

I visited three wizards, and they all agreed: I'd been hit by the curse and they couldn't help me. Some curses can be countered, but some you're simply stuck with. I expect you know about that as well.

The wizards said I'd die from it eventually, but slowly. They didn't know how long. Weeks, maybe months. Less than a year.

I went to herbalists and pharmacies. Tried everything, including that heal-all I planned to use on your burns. Nothing made a bit of difference. I was, essentially, a dead man. My body just hadn't heard the news yet.

And that's when I decided to come here. I'd known about Farview since I was a child, and I was always curious to see it but had never managed to find a chance. This would be a more peaceful place than Greynox, and I wouldn't have to worry about rent, so my saved coppers would stretch farther.

So here I am, in bed with you.

"YOU CAME HERE TO DIE," Felix said, voice raspy.

"Yes."

"Is that why you've pulled away from me so hard?"

Oliver had to chuckle. "I don't feel especially away right now."

"You know what I mean."

"Yes." Impulsively, Oliver kissed the curls atop Felix's head. "I didn't want to. You caught my eye from the start. But it's not fair to you, and not even fair to me. I don't have much time left."

Felix was quiet for many minutes, but Oliver could almost hear him thinking. Finally, Felix kissed Oliver's chest. "All right. Not much time. But we'll make the most of what we have, won't we? Can't we?"

"That will make it hard on you when I'm gone."

"Too late for that, love."

Chapter Fourteen

In the morning, Oliver felt stronger, which didn't make any sense. But instead of pondering the cause, he decided to stop trying to find logic in his life at this point. The important thing was that he could walk unaided all the way to the loo and back, feed the imps with enthusiasm, and get dressed all by himself. And he could sit upright in an octopus chair, drinking tea while Felix chattered during breakfast preparations.

"I can try to find the ogrewort," Felix said as he fussed with arranging fireberries, cheese, currant cakes, and pickled fish onto two plates.

"I don't need it yet."

"But when you do."

"All right."

Felix shot him an over-the-shoulder glance. "You don't mind my staying here?"

"Mind? Gods no."

"But I might burn the place down." He waved vaguely toward the hearth.

"I'll take my chances. You're more than worth it."

That earned a bright smile. "You must have charmed men off the rooftops in Greynox."

Oliver snorted. "I found them in pubs, not on roofs, and they didn't take much charming. We were all there for the same thing."

"Does make things easier, I suppose. No guesswork involved."

As Felix set the plates on the table, Oliver levered himself out of the octopus chair and carried his cup to his place setting. Compared to the upholstered chairs, the dining chairs were hard and worn smooth from decades of use.

"Did you go to the pubs when you lived in Greynox?" Oliver asked.

"Now and then. But just the boring sort; most of the men there weren't interested in other men."

The small pickled fish looked startled to have ended up on someone's breakfast dish, so Oliver ate them first. They were nicer than the ones he used to eat in Greynox—meatier and more flavorful.

"How about since then?"

Felix looked up at him, confused. "I go to the Merman all the time, don't I? You knew that."

Oliver shifted his shoulders uncomfortably. This wasn't a conversation he'd ever had, and it was probably none of his bloody business, but he wanted to know.

"What I meant was, erm, sex. You mentioned you and the other apprentices, but—"

"But that was years ago, aye. Now and then I'll meet someone at the Merman. A tourist, usually, or sometimes a visiting fisherman. I trade him a story for drinks and a few coppers, and maybe eventually we end up in his room upstairs." Felix eyed him warily, shoulders hunched, as if expecting Oliver to react badly.

But Oliver smiled. "I'm glad you've found company now and then."

"It doesn't bother you that they paid me for my company?"

"Not as long as you were willing. Felix, I spent ten years working for a man who lived like nobility while his employees wallowed in misery. I'm ashamed of that. But you have no cause to feel shame for anything you've done to survive."

Felix reached across the table to squeeze his hand, empathy making his brown eyes glow. More than empathy—passion too, and Oliver's body responded in kind, forgetting its recent near-death status. Oliver would have happily postponed breakfast to find out exactly what he was physically capable of, but he'd reminded himself of the dream he'd experienced while dying on the moor. And the epiphany that dream had brought him.

"What's the matter?" Felix looked concerned. "Are you in pain?"

"I.... No." He didn't want to talk about this. But he was done with keeping secrets from Felix, and this one was going to fester if he didn't get it out into the clean air. "Let's eat, and then I have something to tell you."

"Another story?"

"No. It's short. But important." He heaved a heavy sigh.

Felix nodded and popped a morsel of cheese into his mouth. One thing Oliver was coming to value was that Felix understood the value of words as well as the need for occasional silences. Like now, when he didn't prod Oliver to reveal more yet also didn't dismiss the matter as inconsequential. Until Felix, nobody had ever made Oliver feel significant. It was a heady sensation.

His appetite had returned in full force. He ate everything on his plate, and when Felix brought him more fish and some preserved tomatoes, he ate those too. They both drank more tea. Oliver insisted on doing the washing up and was pleased to find himself capable, although the effort tired him.

"Post-breakfast nap?" Felix asked, eyeing him carefully.

"No. I.... Let's sit outside, shall we?"

Although it was warm, Felix brought a blanket, and after they sat on the stone bench, he spread it over Oliver's lap.

"I hate feeling like an invalid," said Oliver.

Felix leaned against him. "I was a sickly child, remember? Always needing to be fussed over."

They sat together like that, some gulls wheeling nearby and the harbor far below. Felix told a silly little tale about a fisherman who thought he could train fish to jump into his nets. It made Oliver laugh, which felt as good as sex.

Oliver concentrated on each moment and what a gift it was. The beautiful view, the fresh-scented air, the sounds of birds calling and a light breeze rustling the grass. His comfortably full stomach and the taste of fireberries still sweet-tart on his lips. Felix warm against him, charming and attentive. Oliver felt wealthy with it all. One moment like this was worth a year in Greynox.

Oh, but Greynox. It still hung heavy on his shoulders.

"Before you found me on the moor, I had a dream. Or possibly a vision—I'm not sure. One of the ghosts was there. She's a young girl but she's very strong and brave."

"I'm glad you had company."

"I did, didn't I? I hadn't thought of it that way. Anyway, she helped me remember something about April fifth. It's so strange. Bits and pieces of those events are so sharp in my mind that it's like I'm living them still, but others feel faded and unreal. Like they're a story someone told me."

"Memories lie," Felix said. "But stories—"

"Tell the truth. I know. In this vision, I saw something from that day, something I'd forgotten. Or maybe I didn't truly notice it at the time it was happening. It was all very confusing."

Felix tapped his head lightly against Oliver's. "You were caught up in horror and slammed with a curse. Of course you were confused."

"This was before that, though. *Just* before that." Oliver tipped his head back against the wall and closed his eyes, as if that might somehow make the revived memory more palatable. It didn't. "I saw the man who invoked the flash-curse."

"Was he one of the speakers on top of the carriage?"

"No. He was another of Hillard's guards."

Felix didn't respond at once, but when Oliver opened his eyes to peer at him, Felix appeared thoughtful rather than disbelieving. "Can you explain, please?"

"The official story is that the leaders of the rally attempted to destroy the mills, and most people are willing to believe that. I didn't question it myself, and I should have. The leaders would have known that they were also endangering the workers. If I was running the rebellion and wanted to damage the buildings without harming my followers, I'd do it at night—not right in the middle of a protest."

"That makes sense." Felix frowned. "But does that mean Hillard was responsible for it? He ordered it?"

"Probably. Maybe with cooperation from Merryclaims and the other owners as well."

"Why would they do it?"

Oliver thought for a moment before answering. The longer he considered it, the better the pieces fit, and the angrier he grew at himself for being blind to the truth for so long.

"Hillard and the others were troubled by the protests. It was beginning to look as if there was a real chance that the workers might get some of their demands. The owners had been pushing Parliament to do something about it, but the lords weren't listening as attentively as the owners wished. Not that the lords cared about the workers, mind you, but they also didn't care much about the manufactory owners, who may be rich but aren't nobility. The lords simply didn't see any reason to act."

Felix let out a long breath. "So Hillard gave them a reason."

"I expect so." Oliver sat up straighter. "Think about it from Hillard's viewpoint. If he uses that curse and blames the organizers, Parliament will finally prohibit future protests—which they did, in fact. Plus the ringleaders of the protest are in police custody, so they'll no longer trouble you, and the surviving workers are too terrified to try again."

"But he damaged his own mill."

Oliver shrugged. "Insurance will pay for it."

"Good gods. Is he truly so evil that he'd murder scores of innocent people just to earn more coppers?"

"He already had, in a manner of speaking. He worked them to death. This was just faster."

And Oliver was complicit.

He'd spent enough time in Hillard's presence to know what kind of man he was. Oliver heard the things his employer would say when nobody but his wealthy friends and an unremarkable guard were present. He'd seen the coldness in Hillard's eyes, a reflection of the man's icy heart. And what had Oliver done? He'd protected Hillard and his machinery and his money. He'd never done a thing to protect the men, women, and children who were chained to the yoke of that mill.

He deserved the curse. Every miserable, painful moment of it and every day it had stolen from his life.

"Olly? What is it?"

Oliver kept his gaze on the placid sea. "You need to go back to the village."

"Do you need something there?"

Oliver looked at him. "Get away from me. Stay away."

He'd meant to sound harsh, meant to scare Felix or make him angry so he'd stomp away and never return. But Oliver's voice wavered and his eyes burned with tears, giving him away.

Instead of walking away, Felix gathered him into a tight embrace. "Oh, love."

And Oliver was too weak to resist. He stayed in that hug and allowed himself to take comfort from it. He allowed Felix to pet his hair and pat his back and murmur in his ear. He even allowed Felix to brush the tears from his cheeks. And as he did so, Oliver felt a new firmness grow in his chest, a sense that although he'd been worse than useless so far, he might yet serve some purpose.

He pulled away slightly. "I must return to Greynox."

"What? No! Why?"

"Justice."

Oliver stood, allowing the blanket to drop to the ground, and strode toward the cottage door. It was too late to catch the train in Bythington today, but he could pack his bag, go down to the village, and arrange carriage transport for the morning. He should stop at the solicitor's house and give him instructions. If Oliver died while in Greynox, which seemed likely, he wanted to make sure word got back to Croftwell so that Felix could inherit Farview.

Felix darted ahead, blocking Oliver's attempt to enter the cottage. "You're not going to assassinate your former employer, are you?"

Oliver gaped. "What?"

"To get back at him for what he did."

"That's vengeance, not justice."

While Oliver certainly wouldn't weep over Hillard's eventual death, murdering him would accomplish nothing. It wouldn't even stop the atrocities at the mill; someone else would take over and treat the workers just as abominably.

Although Felix seemed slightly relieved, he didn't move out of Oliver's way. "What then?"

"Six people are going to hang for a crime they didn't commit. I need to stop that. And maybe Parliament will stop passing laws against the protests if they know the truth. Maybe they'll even arrest Hillard and anyone else who was with him."

"How are you going to do all that?"

"I'll tell the truth!" Oliver yelled. "I'll tell what I saw."

Felix responded in a maddeningly calm and even tone. "I don't want to cause offense, love. But you're, well, you're not a lord or a wealthy man. Will they listen to you?"

Of *course* they wouldn't. At best they'd ignore him; more likely they'd toss him in jail or cart him off to the asylum. Or perhaps the police would just beat him to death. They tended to be friendly with the mill owners as long as the payoffs kept coming. It was all the same to Oliver, in any case: he'd die in Greynox, the six defendants would hang, and Hillard would get richer.

"I have to do *something*," he wailed.

If Felix had tried to comfort him again, it would have been too much. Oliver would have given in to his weakness and allowed the curse to take him without further struggle. He would have lain down on the bed and never gotten up again.

But Felix lifted his chin and gave a little nod. "I have an idea," he said. "Let's go talk to my granddad."

Chapter Fifteen

They didn't go to Urchin Cove that day because certain arrangements were necessary before making the journey. Felix made them lunch—he was apparently determined that Oliver wouldn't starve—and then hurried down to the village, promising to return as soon as he could set their plan in place. That left Oliver alone in a cottage that suddenly felt far too empty, so he wandered outside.

Some sheep grazed in the distance, but they paid him no mind. The imps, however, seemed happy with his presence. When Oliver sat in the grass not far from his door, the imps settled near him, some grooming one another while the young ones scampered. The blue-threaded one, who had taken a special liking to Oliver, kept dashing over to tease him with a tickle of claws before shrieking and running off again. This seemed to impress the other young imps immensely, and also made Oliver laugh until he hurt.

Just as the imps were calming down for naps, the ghosts appeared. Both of them this time, the old man and the girl, and they were strange indeed with the sun shining through their bodies. The imps saw them too but weren't alarmed. Maybe imps saw ghosts all the time.

"You're looking much better," said the girl.

"Indeed. The imps helped rescue me."

"It never hurts to stay on the imps' good side."

Oliver had definitely learned that lesson. He leaned back on his hands. "I don't know how much longer I'll feel well. The ogrewort helps, but...."

"But it's not a cure," said the old man, nodding. "I drank a lot of the stuff myself, toward the end. I died anyway." He seemed almost cheerful about it, but a person likely would stop mourning his own demise after a couple of thousand years.

"Do you know who Felix Corbyn is?" Oliver asked.

The girl laughed as if this was the silliest question anyone had ever asked, and the old man nodded his head. "Of course, boy. We've been watching him since he was a babe. He's our family too."

"I've made arrangements. After I die, Farview cottage becomes legally his. Please don't chase him away. He belongs here."

"Aye," said the man. "I can see that. Don't fret over it—we'll welcome him as we've welcomed you."

Oliver heaved a sigh of relief. "Thank you. He's a good man. He deserves a home." Then a thought occurred to him. "Do you happen to know anything about his curse? He reacts badly with magic, you know."

"Oh, it's not a curse, boy. It's a gift."

Arguing with a ghost probably wasn't a wise idea, but Oliver shook his head. "It's done him considerable harm."

"But he's managed well enough, hasn't he? Things of value have a price. Always have, even before anyone used money." The ghost snorted. "Never could understand what you see in those little bits of metal. I'd rather have a nice hunk of meat or a good fish any day. If I could still eat, that is." He laughed, a wheezy sound that made the imps chitter back at him.

Things of value have a price. Felix had said something similar. But Oliver couldn't see any value in Felix's curse, which had served to isolate him and keep him from settling down.

"The world is such a complicated place," he sighed.

"No, the world is simple. People are complicated. But don't worry, boy. Life lasts only a moment, like that final flash of color when the sun falls into the sea. Beautiful but brief."

Oliver wasn't exactly comforted by this. He let himself lie back on the grass, gauzy clouds scudding far overhead. He'd been recumbent on the moor not long ago, but lying there dying was very different from resting and waiting for his lover to return. A lover Oliver never would have met if he hadn't been hit by that flash-curse. In fact, he'd likely never have come to Croftwell at all, never lived in a stone cottage with octopus chairs or made friends with imps and phantoms. He would have lived longer, yes, but alone and in the gloom of a miserable little room in Greynox with no view of the sea. And for all he knew, he might have died young anyway—from consumption, a fever, a footpad with a knife, falling into the Methes River while drunk, or getting run over by dragons pulling an omnibus.

"Things can turn out so different from what you expected."

The girl leaned over him. He could see the sky right through her, yet she seemed as real as any living person he'd ever met.

"We had a seer in my village" she said. "She knew everything that would happen. She said it was terrible to know."

"Do *you* know what will happen?"

"Felix will come back and you'll kiss him!"

Laughing merrily, she disappeared. When Oliver sat up, the old man was gone too. Only the imps remained, and they seemed unimpressed. Oliver lay back down.

The warm sun and gull cries lulled him sweetly, and Oliver dozed for a time. Except for those few nights in Greynox when he was eighteen, he'd never slept outside, and now he seemed to be making a habit of it. He had hazy visions of a ship with a sparkling hull.

"You're lucky your imps are well fed."

Oliver cracked his eyes open and smiled at Felix. "Oh?"

"Otherwise they might have chomped on you as you slept. You look tasty."

"I look like something you'd throw back if I was caught in your net. I've lost weight and I need a shave."

"Well, come inside then. We can take care of that, can't we?"

First Felix had to satisfy himself that Oliver hadn't nearly starved in his absence. He steered him to one of the wooden chairs and theatrically revealed the contents of the basket he'd brought up from the village.

"Look at this!" he crowed, holding up a large chunk of pale pink meat. "Just as I reached the village, Henry Bellflower docked with the loveliest muttonfish you ever did see, and he gave me this much of it, and Peony Perkins gave me some clams she'd just dug up, and I've a fresh jar of those pickles you like, and see? A honeycake straight from Aygun's oven. Not to mention a jug of Tural's best mead. We'll have a feast for dinner, we will."

"All of them just gave you these things?"

"No, they gave *you* these things. They're happy you've brought life back to Farview, love." Felix's face fell. "They don't know it's not for long."

Ah, but it would be, once Felix moved in. Not that Oliver would mention that now; the bequest would feel awkward. Let Felix discover it later, after Oliver died. It might help ease his mourning and ensure that his last memory of Oliver was a good one.

"But did you make arrangements for tomorrow?"

"Of course. Jamie will take us in the morning—that's his regular coach run. Will you be able to make it down the cliff?"

"Yes. I'm feeling good now." That was only a small stretch of the truth. He wasn't feeling miserable, and he wasn't in agony, but the usual aches and weakness suffused his body. Still, he was happy because it could have been much worse. "Thank you for taking care of it."

Felix executed a showy bow. "My pleasure, yer majesty. It's bloody lovely to be useful for a change. Now, d'you want me to fetch some ogrewort?"

"No, I'm fine."

"But tomorrow?"

"The bad spells don't hit me of a sudden. They creep up slowly. I'll be all right tomorrow."

Although Felix didn't look convinced, he didn't press the issue. Instead he smiled. "We've some time before dinner. How about a shave? And another bath?"

"Two baths in two days?"

"Get your money's worth out of that tub. Anyhow, I enjoyed the last one. Didn't you?"

Whether it was the memory of the event or Felix's current lascivious expression, Oliver didn't know, but heat immediately pooled low in his belly and his breath hitched. And then Felix licked his lips, making Oliver groan.

"You're a devil."

Felix only laughed.

The shave came first, Felix scraping the blade across Oliver's skin with exquisite care. Oliver usually shaved himself, although he'd occasionally splurged on a barber, but he'd never had somebody he knew do this act for him. It made him feel both vulnerable and cared for, and it was almost thrillingly erotic. Felix knew this and played it up, occasionally brushing against Oliver as if by accident or resting the pad of his thumb over the pulse point in Oliver's neck. Up close like this, his eyes were clear and multi-layered, like amber, and his curls seemed as lively as Medusa's snakes, if considerably less lethal.

"You should grow your hair long," Felix said as if hearing Oliver's thoughts.

"It's boring. Just black and straight."

"It should fall over your shoulders like a velvet cloak. I'd make you a crown of shells and bits of colored glass, and you would stand there—naked—looking like a sea god."

Oliver blushed, but Felix's hand on his chin meant he couldn't duck his head. "Shouldn't a sea god have fins? And gills?"

"He's a god. He can have whatever he fancies." Felix moved the blade slowly under Oliver's nose. "He can have an entire court of pretty lads who cater to his every need, and he can wear pearls in his ears and twisted into his hair, and he can have entire troupes of imps to entertain him." He pulled the razor away to inspect his work, which made it safe for Oliver to speak.

"I don't want any of those things."

"What do you want? If you had a wish—and if I wouldn't muck up the magic—what would you ask for?"

Oliver answered without hesitation. "You. Here at Farview with me, until we're both wrinkled and bald and toothless."

Felix snorted as if he didn't believe this, but the softness of his eyes said otherwise. Then he cleared his throat. "Right, then. Bath."

This was easier said than done since the tub still held the cold, soap-scummed water from yesterday. So Felix laboriously bailed it out, bucket by bucket, and dumped the water outside until the tub was light enough to push out the door. A few steps away, he tipped the tub upright with Oliver's help and sent the remainder of the contents gushing onto the moor.

Felix paused before dragging the tub back. "There's a pump outside as well."

"So?"

"Bath with a view?"

How could Oliver say no? They carried the tub to a spot Felix declared perfect, and then Oliver was instructed to rest while Felix filled it. By then Felix had stripped off everything except his trousers, which made watching him especially diverting. The imps seemed to think it was grand fun as well. They cavorted about Felix's legs, almost but never quite tripping him.

Finally the tub was full. Oliver tossed in a couple of firestones and stripped while he waited for the water to heat. It felt odd to be naked outdoors, but Felix and the imps had already seen him unclothed, and hopefully nobody else would come up onto the moor. Anyway, it was glorious to get into the tub, water halfway up his torso, and to watch the sea below.

"A washtub is like a reverse boat, isn't it?" he said. "Keeps the water in rather than out."

"It's a boat for merfolk who want to travel on land."

"I thought I was a sea god, but now suddenly I'm merfolk instead?"

Felix scooped up a double handful of water and dropped it on Oliver's head. Oliver splashed him back, and soon they were engaged in a fierce water fight, in which Oliver had the advantage since he was in the tub and already wet. They were both howling with laughter—even more so when Felix slipped on the wet grass and landed on his arse.

"Now you're clean and I'm muddy," he complained.

"We can fix that. Take off your trousers."

Grinning, Felix complied. Without a stitch of clothing, he posed for Oliver with head high and hands on hips, looking for all the world like a statue in a museum. Except for the anchor tattoo and the fact that he was flesh and blood. He was half erect, nipples contracted, and cheeks with high color, the pale skin of his body the perfect foil for the dark hair on his head and groin.

"Gorgeous," Oliver breathed.

"Skinny. And someday I'll be like you said: bald and wrinkled and—"

"And still gorgeous. You've a glow to you, Felix. Like... like a lighthouse cutting through the fog. Everything around you is dull and uninteresting in comparison. You're...." Oliver huffed something between laughter and exasperation. "I'm no poet, and you're the bard. You're a miracle, is what you are. A treasure I've found without ever expecting it."

Felix looked as if he might cry, which certainly hadn't been Oliver's intent, and then sniffled loudly. "You know, the fae can charm and seduce anyone they set their minds to. So we can blame your grandfather Aymar for all this."

"I thought you seduced me. Besides, you're standing awfully far away for an effective seduction."

Smiling, Felix dropped to his knees beside the tub. "Let's concentrate on getting clean for now."

"I'm all yours."

Felix took his sweet time, rubbing a flannel over every bit of Oliver's skin yet never pausing long in any one spot. He was tender about it, as careful with the soles of Oliver's feet as he was with his most intimate bits, and if there was a more perfect way to spend an afternoon, Oliver couldn't think of one. Even the imps seemed to have Oliver's welfare in mind, disappearing without a trace and leaving Oliver and Felix with complete privacy.

But it was the shampooing that did Oliver in. After wetting Oliver's hair with cups of water, Felix rubbed in something that smelled of mint and roses and created luxurious suds. He worked the substance into Oliver's hair with his fingertips, kneading at the scalp and gently drawing the strands out, until Oliver was so hard that he groaned.

"Felix?" he said as Felix began to rinse his hair. "Let me taste you."

Felix's hand shook, sloshing water from the cup. "You want that?"

"Desperately."

"Are you well—"

"Felix. *Please.*" Because right now he was definitely not above begging.

It took a bit of maneuvering. After trying a few other unsatisfactory positions, Felix sat on the end of the tub, feet in the water and knees spread wide. That meant Oliver had to merely lean forward to reach him. He explored with hands first, stroking Felix's thighs and cupping his bollocks as if weighing them, judging the effect of every touch by the nuances of Felix's expressive face.

Then, very delicately, he tasted. He used to be good at this. He'd always enjoyed the power of it, the ability to control another man so thoroughly with just a swipe of his tongue or relaxation of his throat. He liked the precision of it as well, even the smallest movement having a large impact. And there was also an aspect of trust, in that someone —usually a complete stranger—would allow his most delicate body part between Oliver's sharp, strong teeth.

But this was even better because it was Felix, and instead of being in the deep darkness of a nighttime alley or pub's back room, they were out in the bright sunshine. Oliver could see every detail of Felix's face and the finest nuances of his expressions. When Oliver did *this*, he could watch Felix's tongue dart out. When he did *that*, Felix's eyes rolled up. Oliver forgot about the demands of his own body as he concentrated on what he could do to—and *for*—Felix.

And not surprisingly, Felix was noisy in his enjoyment, which was also a delight. As he clutched Oliver's hair, Felix moaned, whimpered, swore, and—best of all—called out, "Olly! Gods, Olly!"

Oliver took his time, teasing Felix to the brink and pulling back again, watching the warm rosy flush sweep over Felix's body. Sometimes Oliver moved his mouth to Felix's inner thigh or hip, leaving little love-bites as proof he'd been there. But then Felix would beg piteously and Oliver would return to that delicious rampant prick, now as slippery as if he'd poured oil over it.

Ah, but he'd been close to death not long before, and his stamina was disappointingly limited. He finally swooped in for one last go.

Felix gasped, said "Oh, Olly!"—and fell backwards off the tub with a startled squawk.

Oliver clambered out of the water at once, only to discover Felix flat on his back in the grass, laughing and grabbing for him. "Have pity, Olly," Felix panted. "Don't stop now."

So Oliver lowered himself over Felix—slowly, not wanting to make any of his pains worse—and ground their erections together while kissing him ravenously. It wasn't quite enough friction to satisfy either of them, so he tried to wrap his hand around both their lengths, but Felix surprised him by rolling them over so that Oliver was nestled into the grass. Before Oliver could quite react to that, Felix had flipped around as quickly as a fish, placing them each mouth to cock.

Which was a very satisfactory place to be. Now Oliver could continue his ministrations, but with the additional pleasure of kneading Felix's ass—not to mention the overwhelming thrill of Felix swallowing him down. It was, in fact, almost too much. Oliver went blind and deaf from it all. The train to Greynox could have barreled directly at him and he couldn't have moved an inch out of the way, couldn't have done anything but lose himself in the euphoric explosions consuming his body and mind.

Felix rolled off of him and scooted around to tuck his head under Oliver's arm. They were both breathing hard.

"You just had a bath and now here you are, covered in sweat and grass and moor-herb." Felix picked a tiny leaf off Oliver's shoulder and held it for him to see.

"It was worth it."

"Gods, yes. How do you feel?"

Oliver huffed. "Don't fuss over me every minute like a nursemaid. I promise to let you know if I'm about to drop dead."

Felix tweaked one of Oliver's nipples hard enough to make him yelp. "In fact, yer majesty, I was wondering if you're in good enough shape to make us some dinner. I'd rather not risk the firestones."

After a moment of self-evaluation, Oliver nodded. "I am. I don't understand it, but I feel good."

"That's what a nice round of al fresco fucking will do for a lad."

Felix hopped up and offered Oliver a hand. "Works up an appetite too. Get on with it."

FELIX SAT in the octopus chair at what he judged to be a safe distance from the hearth, dramatically imparting instructions on how to prepare their meal. He must have done a good job of it, because they ended up with a glorious feast. The clams were sweet and salty, the muttonfish as hearty as the best roast, and the pickles added welcome acidity to the flavor palette. Aygun's honeycakes were as delicious as the ones made with currants, and the mead washed it all down admirably well.

"I'm too full to get up from the table," Oliver announced when they were finished.

"And you're too heavy for me to carry, so you'll have to manage, love. Early morning tomorrow."

Oliver nodded. "Your wizard."

"My granddad. He'll be the first to admit his talents are limited, but he's all we have. And he's a good man." Felix spoke with more than a hint of pride.

Although Oliver didn't hold much hope that the wizard could help, he smiled. "I look forward to meeting him."

"Erm... I've a question."

Intrigued at Felix's unusual reticence, Oliver raised his eyebrows.

Felix scratched his neck. "Erm, when I introduce you, I can tell him we're friends. Which is true. Or I could tell him we're lovers. Which is also true."

Oliver's immediate response was surprise and confusion, dotted with some horror. Even if he'd gotten on better with the man he called father, he couldn't imagine telling Stephen Webb that he had a male lover. But this seemed important to Felix, who'd claimed that local custom accepted same-sex relations.

"Do you *want* to tell him?" Oliver asked gently.

"Aye." Felix squirmed. "If you don't mind, I mean. We're new, I know that, and our future, well.... But even already, you're more than I ever had, Olly, and I don't want to hide us. Unless you do."

"I've never had the chance to claim anyone as a lover. I'd be fortunate indeed to do that with you."

Felix beamed, hopped up from his seat, and hurried around the table to overwhelm Oliver with an embrace. Then he helped pull Oliver to his feet and steered him toward the bed. "Get ready for sleep. I'll tidy up."

Not too much later, with Felix snuggled naked against him and the darkness over them like a warm blanket, Oliver wished he had his old strength. He'd take his time exploring Felix's body even more thoroughly than before, and he'd steal a bit of oil from the kitchen and get them both nice and slick, and then—

He groaned. He didn't have his old strength, and he needed his sleep. He also needed to stop being so greedy; he'd already been granted so much.

Felix planted a messy kiss on Oliver's cheek. "Did I tell you the story of my great-great-aunt Theona, who learned to ride whales as if they were dragons?"

"You did not."

"Ah, well. See, Theona was a wild type from the day she was born. By the time she was three, her parents gave up on governing her and simply hoped that the gods watched over her instead. And what Theona loved most of all was going fast...."

Oliver fell asleep long before Felix got to the part with the whales. He dreamed of sailing through the streets of Greynox in a washtub.

Chapter Sixteen

Dawn had barely broken when they made their way down the cliff. Oliver felt well enough to forgo a walking stick, but he still gave a small sigh of relief when he reached level ground. Although the pubs were still shuttered and the shops hadn't yet opened, the docks were already a busy place. Most of the fishing boats were making their way to the mouth of the harbor, sails bellied and white wakes behind, and the handful of remaining fishermen hurried to join them. A few called out to Felix and waved.

A man who looked remarkably like Felix, but older and rounder, waved from across the street before ducking into Corbyn's Sailworks.

"My brother Itchy," Felix explained.

"Itchy?"

"Our parents named him Richard, but nobody calls him that. Not even his wife. He doesn't like it, but he gave up complaining long ago. No point fighting something like that."

Oliver raised his eyebrows. "Was it you who first called him that?"

"Might be," Felix said with a snicker. "And it could have been worse."

They stood on the pavement for a few minutes before a pair of sleepy-looking dragons appeared around the corner, pulling a mud-splashed, creaky carriage. They were big, bulky creatures, nothing like the sleek dragons favored by the wealthy in Greynox. Oliver had heard that some of the very rich would even host dragon races at their country estates. This pair certainly didn't look as if they'd win such a competition, but they seemed capable of serving their purpose.

"Hello, Felix!" called the man in the driver's seat, who Oliver recognized from the Bythington-to-Croftwell trip as well as from one evening in the Merman.

Felix called back, "Mornin', Jamie. Lovely day for a ride to Urchin Cove, isn't it?"

"Couldn't think of one better. Climb on in. It's just you two this morning."

Oliver exchanged nods with Jamie before entering the carriage with Felix and closing the door. Jamie waited a few moments, as if making sure that nobody had a sudden impulse for travel. Then he chirruped at the dragons, who began to amble lazily up the street.

"Not the fastest transport, is it?" Oliver observed.

"Ah, but it *is* the fastest land transport to Urchin Cove—because it's the only one. Enjoy the ride. It's pretty."

He was right. After leaving Croftwell, they headed north along a road that hugged the coastline. The ocean lay to their left and cliffs and meadows alternated on their right. Flowers dotted the landscape like jewels, occasional clouds of sprites fluttered around the carriage, and birds swooped and called. With their hands entwined and resting on Oliver's leg, Felix sat close to Oliver and told stories about everything they passed.

When Felix paused—probably to formulate his next wild yarn—Oliver peered through the carriage's front window, which gave a view of Jamie's back.

"He's drinking from a flask."

"Aye."

"Probably not water."

"I'd be very surprised if it was."

Oliver snorted. "He was drunk when he took me from Bythington."

"Aye, he has a favorite pub there, he has. They give him a discount if he steers travelers their way."

"But—"

"Olly, relax. Jamie could fall asleep and we'd be fine. His dragons go this route three times a week and have done for years. They know the way. And they won't let him do anything foolish."

Slightly mollified, Oliver slumped in his seat. "If you all know he drinks, why do you keep letting him drive?"

"It's his job, isn't it? What else would he do?" Felix patted Oliver's knee. "He's a good enough sort. He's tried stopping the drink a few times, but it didn't take. We all have our curses, don't we?"

True enough.

The road turned inland for a bit, rising up a gentle slope and then sweeping down to a little town. There were boats, as in Croftwell, but the harbor was smaller and shallower, without the rock formations jutting on either side of it. There was no cliff either, and no sign of a moor. A tiny cluster of commercial buildings sat near the water, with houses radiating out behind them.

"Wooden buildings instead of stone," Oliver observed.

"Aye. If you continue a bit farther north there's woodland."

The carriage came to a gradual halt in the center of the village. Jamie hopped down to fuss at his dragons, petting them and cooing. He might be a sot, but he obviously cared for his beasts; by all indications, they adored him as well.

"Thanks, Jamie!" Felix called as they disembarked, then took Oliver's arm and dragged him inland. "They've only one pub here. We can have lunch there later. Food's not as good as the Merman, but it'll do. Or if you fancy it, we can buy some provisions and eat on the dock."

"Another picnic," Oliver said, smiling.

For now, though, their path led up a little hill to a two-story white clapboard house with a gabled roof and a wide front porch. It was surrounded by a garden so lush as to resemble a jungle, with enormous multihued flowers and tomatoes, peppers, and squash bigger than any Oliver had seen.

"I'm fairly certain Granddad uses his magic for this," Felix said, waving to indicate the abundance. "He's very proud of it all."

"It's impressive."

"Olly, I'll walk you to the door and make introductions, but then I'll need to back off. I won't go far, though. Just call if you need me."

Oliver frowned. "Back off? I don't understand."

"It's my curse, isn't it? My granddad's a *wizard*, love. Imagine the damage I could do him." Felix looked miserable.

"You can't spend time with your own grandfather?"

"A few minutes doesn't hurt. After that...." Felix shrugged. "We write to one another, though. Twice a week. My curse doesn't care about that."

"I'm sorry."

It was a reminder that Oliver wasn't the only one carrying a burden. As happy as Felix seemed, he had struggled his entire life with adversities Oliver couldn't even imagine.

"Come on, then. Can't wait for you both to meet."

Felix opened the front gate and hurried through with Oliver at his heels. The door swung open before they reached the porch, and two people rushed out. One of them was a short, plump woman with a cloud of curly white hair and a pink-and-orange apron over her dress. The other—the wizard, presumably—was tall, thin, and bald, with a gray beard halfway down his chest. He had on slightly muddy trousers and a patched blue shirt with the sleeves rolled up. They were both smiling broadly.

"Felix!" cried the woman. She ran forward and threw herself at Felix with enough force that he *oof*ed and fell back a step.

"It's good to see you, Gran." He embraced her, but then she pulled back and pinched his cheek.

"Too thin. Has nobody been feedin' you, my boy?"

"I'm eating fine, I am. Gran, I want to introduce you properly."

The wizard had held back on the porch, although he retained his smile. Now he and his wife both turned toward Oliver expectantly. Oliver caught his breath. He'd never met a lover's family before.

"Olly, this is Enoch and Eselde Andox, my maternal grandparents. Gram, Grandad, this is Oliver Webb. My man." He said the last part loudly, chin raised.

Oliver expected to be struck down at once with a deadly spell, or at least slapped by Mrs. Andox. What he didn't expect was for her to turn and throw herself at him, tugging his head down so she could kiss his cheeks. Then she held him at arms' length to examine him.

"Ooh, he's lovely, Felix. Also too thin. But such a handsome face. He looks like a Moon, don't he, Enoch? Them eyes. But I don't know the name Webb and I haven't heard of him before, so he can't be a Crofter, can he? But he *has* to be, with them looks. That chin's exactly like Randall Moon's now, ain't it?" She squeezed the chin in question.

Well, now Oliver knew where Felix had inherited his verbosity. Oliver liked her already.

Felix came over and gently pried her away from Oliver. "Let him breathe, Gran. I'll tell you all about him. But he has some things to discuss with Granddad, so could we go for a walk while they talk business?"

She looked torn. Clearly, she was desperate to interrogate Oliver, but once her grandson wrapped his arm around hers, his appeal won.

"Fine. But you'll tell me all about him, you hear?"

"Every detail."

Thinking of what some of those details might include, Oliver ducked his head to hide a blush. Before he knew it, Felix and Mrs. Andox were gone, both of them chatting avidly, and Oliver was stranded in the garden under the wizard's sharp gaze.

"C'mon in," said Mr. Andox, cocking his head toward the door.

Oliver realized he hadn't uttered a single word since being introduced. "Thank you. Erm, nice to meet you, sir."

The wizard chuckled. "It's Enoch, son. And may I call you Oliver?"

"Of course."

Oliver stepped onto the porch and then into the house, where Enoch led him through a narrow foyer into a parlor edged with laden bookshelves and stuffed with furniture, colorful throw rugs, and vases of flowers.

"Sit down, sit down," Enoch said, waving at an overstuffed chair. "I'll get us some tea."

"You needn't—"

But Enoch was already gone, leaving Oliver to look around. Now he saw that the shelves were filled with more than books. There were seashells, ancient-looking glass bottles, bits of carved wood, small metal and porcelain figurines, animal bones, and other items he couldn't identify. The whole lot was slightly dusty, as if housecleaning wasn't anyone's priority, yet the chaos somehow made for a welcoming and comfortable setting.

Enoch returned more quickly than Oliver expected; maybe he'd used magic to hurry the tea along. He carried a large tray with tea things and plates of food, which he set atop some books on a low table. After pouring and a bit of fussing, he brought Oliver a steaming cup and a dish with slices of cucumber, tomato, and honeyroot, a chunk of crumbly cheese, and some purple berries that Oliver didn't recognize. "All from my garden," Enoch said proudly. "Except the cheese, of course. Can't grow that on a tree. I've some lovely biscuits there on the tray for later."

"You didn't have to go to all this fuss for me."

"Ah, no fuss, no fuss at all. Besides, it isn't every day my grandson brings his man to meet me."

Oliver winced and took a deep breath. "You don't.... It doesn't bother you?"

Enoch looked steadily at him. "Will you treat him well, son?"

"Yes! Gods, yes. He's special, isn't he?"

"He is indeed." Enoch smiled. "As long as you see that and act accordingly, that's all I need to know. He's been lonely for a long time and he deserves something more."

"He deserves everything. He's... he's such a good person." *Good* was a weak word, but Oliver hoped his emotions showed in his voice.

And maybe they did, because Enoch looked satisfied and took a sip of tea.

"Was the missus right about you being a Moon? She's rarely wrong about these things."

"She's right. My mother was Marina Rowe, but from what I understand she was descended from the Moons. Felix has been thorough in tracing my lineage for me."

"I'll bet he has. But you're not from Croftwell. That's a Greynox accent, if I'm not mistaken."

Oliver had taken a bite of tomato while Enoch spoke, and now he paused a moment to enjoy. Every tomato he'd eaten in Greynox was a pale, tasteless imposter. This was easily the most delicious vegetable he'd ever tasted. But he was here for a purpose, and it wasn't feasting.

"Yes, sir, I've spent my whole life in Greynox. But my mother—she passed when I was very young—left me Farview cottage in Croftwell, and I've recently moved there." He decided to risk a bit more. "Felix is staying there with me."

"Is he, now?" Enoch looked speculative. "And how are you getting on?"

"Beautifully. I, erm, I was very ill, but he cared for me. Saved my life, most likely. And now I'm feeling much better, but I like having him there. I like it very much, in fact."

"Saved your life? Hmm. You don't find his gift difficult?"

It was interesting that Enoch had used the same term as the ghost—gift—rather than calling it a curse. But Oliver wanted to answer the question because he sensed it was important.

"We had one minor mishap with firestones, but that's all. It's not difficult at all. And when it gets cold, I understand it's possible to warm the cottage with peat instead." Oliver would be dead by then, but that wasn't the point.

"So it is. Can I get you more tomatoes, son?"

Oliver hadn't realized he'd eaten them all. He felt his cheeks warm as he nodded. "They're delicious."

Enoch got up long enough to refill Oliver's plate and cup, then sat again. He wasn't eating, but he seemed pleased that Oliver was. Enoch wasn't talkative like his wife and grandson, and Oliver had the impression that very few things escaped his notice and scrutiny. It was a bit disconcerting, even though Oliver had nothing to hide. He was very glad that Felix had been straightforward with his grandfather about their relationship, which Enoch would surely have discerned on his own.

"If I might ask, Oliver, what prompted your move to Croftwell? Few Noxers would choose to relocate to the end of the world, especially young people such as yourself."

"Oh, I like Croftwell very well. And the sea. Although I didn't know that until I got here. The reason... well, actually it's related to that business Felix mentioned."

"The business you came here to speak to me about."

"Yes. Erm, if you don't mind."

"Of course not. Please, how can I help?" Enoch leaned back in his chair, and for just one moment, Oliver clearly saw his resemblance to Felix. It was something about the brightness of his eyes.

Gods, where to begin? Oliver wished Felix was here, because he'd do a much better job at this. But Felix couldn't be here, and besides, it was Oliver's story to tell. He swallowed more tea as he organized his thoughts. Then he finally began.

"For ten years, I was a guard at Hillard's woolen mill on Oakwood Street in Greynox...."

WHILE HE SPOKE, Oliver ate a garden's worth of vegetables and half a tin of biscuits, and he drank enough tea to fill his washtub. But he had a lot to say, and Enoch had a lot of questions. Oliver ended up giving his entire life history in addition to describing the events at the mill, and he also discussed much of what had transpired in Croftwell, including the ghosts and his vision about the true cause of the flash-curse. The only thing he omitted was the impact of the curse on him personally. He knew from his previous visits to other wizards that Enoch couldn't solve that problem, and Oliver wanted the focus to remain elsewhere. Besides, if Enoch knew that Oliver was dying, he might worry about Felix—and Oliver already worried enough in that regard.

Finally, his throat sore from so many words, Oliver sighed. "And that's my story. It's not as good as one of Felix's."

"I don't know about that. Mysterious parentage, evil plots, water fae, ghosts, bequests... that's all quite exciting."

Oliver had become comfortable in Enoch's presence, and now he chuckled. "Perhaps so, but he contributed the background for most of the exciting bits."

Enoch's warm smile spoke volumes of his love for his grandson. "He has a true gift for it, hasn't he? But tell me, son, how can I help you?"

"I'm not sure that you can. It's a rather hopeless situation. But Felix said I should try."

"Try what?"

"Six innocent people are to be hanged. I want to stop that. And because everyone's blaming the workers for what happened, it will be impossible for them to protest again. They'll have no way to fight their terrible employment conditions. I'd like to help them by revealing the truth."

"Ah." Enoch stroked his beard thoughtfully. "I require a bit of time to think. If you need to use the loo in the interim...."

"Yes, please," Oliver said with some desperation. All that tea was sloshing round inside him.

"Out the kitchen door. Can't miss it."

Oliver hoped he didn't look too undignified as he hurried down the corridor, through the cluttered kitchen, and out into the back garden, which was even more verdant than the front. In addition to more flowers and vegetables, here there were also berry bushes and fruit trees, an arbor covered in vines, and a small rock pool containing colorful fish. And, thankfully, there was the loo, covered in purple flowers as big as a dinner plates.

Afterward, he washed his hands at an outdoor pump and paused to take in the scenery. Because they were on a hill, he could just glimpse the sea through the greenery. What a beautiful place. He still preferred Farview, but he'd rather live in this house than the royal palace itself.

When he returned to the parlor, Enoch stood at a tall table, writing something on a piece of paper. He gave Oliver a small smile. "You understand, I think, that what you're asking for may not be possible. People such as us hold little sway in Greynox, where so many value power and wealth over kindness, justice, or happiness." He sighed.

"I do know. But I have to try."

"Oh, Felix did choose well, didn't he? Good lad. Do you know what my father used to say? A sprite cannot move a mountain. But a thousand sprites can move a very large stone indeed."

Although Oliver wasn't sure he understood it, he nodded sagely. "Is there anything at all you can suggest for me?"

"Yes. To begin with, friends will help. I've written down the name and address of two very fine men who live in Greynox. They've accomplished some remarkable things in the past and will make good allies." He handed over the paper.

"Thank you." Oliver slipped it into his pocket. It would be nice to have a couple of people on his side.

Enoch crossed the room and removed something from a shelf, then carried it over and pressed it into Oliver's palm. It was made of a dull metal—not heavy enough to be lead—and was roughly the size and shape of Oliver's thumb, but with odd little marks inscribed on it. They reminded him of the scratchings on the moor stones.

"This little talisman has some interesting properties, but they're limited, and it can be used only once by a particular person. It's a funny little thing, isn't it? Only one in the world. It's reputed to find its way to someone who needs it, but I discovered it years ago and never found any use for it, so I don't know whether to believe that bit."

"What does it do?" Holding it gave Oliver's hand an odd tickling sensation, as if a hundred tiny invisible insects were crawling over him. It wasn't pleasant.

"It... amplifies a memory, and allows others to see what's in your mind. Just a snippet, though, you understand? Take this to someone who has the power you need. A member of Parliament, perhaps, or a prosecutor. My friends can help you with that. Then, when that person is standing quite close, activate the talisman and concentrate very hard on the memory you want him to see. It'll be only a few minutes, so choose wisely."

Oliver nodded. "The moment the guard used the flash-curse."

"Yes, excellent, excellent. You evoke that memory and your witness will see it as if it's playing out in front of his eyes. It proves the truth of your story, see?"

Nothing is truer than stories.

"All right. Then what?"

Enoch shrugged. "Then you hope your witness will act. By that point the talisman will be useless. Throw it into a moving body of water as soon as you can—a river or the sea."

"How do I activate it?"

"You call a name of power."

Oliver blinked. "What name?"

"I've no idea."

"But—"

"When you're ready to use it, think hard. The name will come to you. It's probably one you know."

This was all very strange. But a great deal of Oliver's life had been strange lately, and he wasn't in any position to question the wizard who was trying to assist him. "If I throw it away, you won't have it anymore."

"It wouldn't do me any good, save as an ornament, and I've plenty of those." Enoch gestured at the room in general.

"As for payment… I have some coppers left, but magic like this must be very expensive."

Enoch shook his head slowly and set a hand on Oliver's shoulder. "It's a gift. One I'm very pleased to give my grandson's friend."

Dammit all, but Oliver was close to crying again. He didn't deserve the generosity he'd received from Felix, Enoch, and the Crofters in general. "Thank you," he said, sniffing.

"Tuck it away safe, now. And don't worry about any effects Felix might have on it. It's quite inert until you activate it. I do suggest making sure he's well away when you use it, however."

That was no problem—Felix wouldn't even be in Greynox. Oliver gingerly put the talisman into the watch pocket of his trousers, grateful that the tickling feeling stopped at once. Some forms of magic were certainly convenient, such as firestones and heal-all ointment—but he didn't much fancy the rest of it.

Enoch clapped Oliver's back. "I'm guessing that Felix is eager to be reunited with you, and the missus is champing at the bit, wanting to know every last thing you've said and done while you were here. May I tell her?"

"Of course."

They walked out onto the porch. Sure enough, Felix and his grandmother stood outside the gate, deep in conversation, but they stopped when they noticed Oliver and Enoch.

"Finally!" she said, a hand held dramatically to her chest. "Thought I'd be deep in my grave afore you two were done."

"Gran!" Felix protested, laughing, but she waved him away.

Oliver turned to Enoch. "Thank you again, sir. And I'm very glad we've met."

"As am I, as am I." Enoch gave him another friendly pat. "I hope we can see each other again soon."

Keeping a cheerful mask on, Oliver walked through the garden. Mrs. Andox grabbed him for another round of cheek kisses, so Felix must have said good things about him.

"Now, you wait here a mo, lads." She rushed into the house faster than Oliver would have expected and reappeared a moment later with a cloth sack. Just as fast, she picked some tomatoes, two peppers, and a cucumber and handed the sack to Felix. "It's not much, but I expect you won't want to be carrying about something heavy all afternoon."

"Thank you, Gran."

A few rounds of kisses, hugs, cheek-pinches, and waves ensued, along with several good-byes. Then Felix and Oliver started down the hill toward the harbor.

Chapter Seventeen

Although Oliver tried not to show it, he was exhausted. It had been a draining day already: early awakening, hobbling down the cliff path, trusting what remained of his life to Jamie and his dragons, meeting Felix's grandparents, pouring out almost the entirety of his life story. And it was only midday.

Felix took Oliver's arm as they walked down the gentle slope. "Have you decided on whether you'd prefer the pub or a picnic?"

"Your grandfather fed me so much that I won't be hungry for a week. You choose whichever you'd rather."

Felix laughed. "Gran fed me too. She took me down to the shops to show me off to her friends, and somehow I ended up eating. She's afraid I'm withering away to nothing. So would you like to explore the delights of Urchin Cove, or would you rather head home?"

"How much longer until the coach leaves?"

"Oh, Jamie's been gone for ages. I've arranged something else." Felix grinned, his eyes bright as the sun.

Curiosity and Felix's enthusiasm helped overcome some of Oliver's fatigue. "A surprise?"

Felix actually skipped a few steps, dragging Oliver with him. "Aye! I think you'll love it. Anyway, I hope so."

Whatever it was, Oliver loved it already because Felix had clearly planned it to please him. He couldn't remember anyone ever surprising him. Even when he was a child, he knew what he'd receive for his birthday and Solstice gifts: new sets of clothes, a bag of sweets from the confectionary around the corner, and some coppers that he was expected to spend on books. He'd appreciated those things well enough, but they were the same each time, and given without any fanfare. Depending on his age, either the nanny or the housekeeper had them waiting at the breakfast table in a neat, predictable stack.

This was far different.

They hurried down to the harbor, laughing breathlessly—like boys engaging in a small, delightful mischief—and they didn't stop until they reached the docks. A grizzled man in a small boat seemed to be waiting for them, smoking a pipe and doing something complicated with a knotted rope. Judging from his facial features, he had to be a Corbyn, so Oliver wasn't at all surprised when Felix introduced him as Uncle Teddy.

"Glad to finally meet ye," Teddy said. "Boy's been yammerin' on about ye for ages."

"I have not!" Felix insisted.

Teddy ignored him. "Hear ye been fixin' up Farview real nice like. 'T's a good thing. Place like that deserves some love."

"It's beautiful, sir. And I'm happy to meet you as well."

"Well, come aboard then, lads."

Belatedly, Oliver realized what Felix's plan was. "We're to return to Croftwell by boat?"

"'Aye." Felix frowned slightly. "Unless you don't want to. In that case we can—"

"It's wonderful, Felix. Thank you." And he meant it. The prospect of traveling by water had his heart racing with excitement, his aches and tiredness temporarily inconsequential. He was going to sea! And yes, he was fully aware that this was nothing but a tiny fishing boat of the sort that haunted harbors or hugged the coast; it would never venture far from land. But that didn't matter. Oliver had never so much as sat in a paddleboat in Jayne Park, and by comparison this would be a huge adventure.

Felix hopped neatly into the boat and gave Oliver a hand to steady himself as he stepped down as well. "Despite your ancestors, can't expect you to have your sea legs right away," Felix said. "Now look, we can have a seat just over here. D'you want to go home straightaway or would you fancy a detour?"

It would be wiser to return to Farview before his energy ran out. Oliver smiled. "A detour sounds lovely."

While Oliver and Felix made themselves comfortable at the front, Teddy busied himself with the boat, tightening this and loosening that. Within a few minutes he was smoking contentedly and manning the rudder as the boat pulled smoothly away from the dock.

Oliver closed his eyes. The gentle rocking motion was entirely new to him yet somehow felt shockingly familiar. It was like unexpectedly running into an old acquaintance you'd completely forgotten about.

"Are you all right, Olly?" Felix set a hand on Oliver's arm. "Don't be embarrassed if you feel a bit sick."

"I feel *wonderful*." Oliver opened his eyes and twisted around so he faced forward. A bit of salt spray misted his face, and he laughed as he licked it off his lips. "Why would anyone ever travel by land if they could do this instead?"

Felix's face was as joyful as a child's. "Aye? You truly like it?"

"It's not the best thing that's happened to me since I left Greynox"—Oliver waggled his eyebrows significantly—"but it's definitely the second best. Thank you for giving me this gift. You're an incredibly generous man." There was an irony there, of course, because Felix owned less in material goods than anyone Oliver knew. Even the miserable workers at the mill had a few possessions and a steady place to sleep at night. But what Felix gave was much more valuable than anything coppers could buy.

"It's glorious, isn't it? I wish I were strong enough to be a fisherman. My curse might not even matter very much—most of the fisherman don't use any magic at all. Or if they do, it's only a small charm to bring favorable winds or lure more fish."

Oliver glanced back at the village of Urchin Cove, quickly fading into the distance, and then ahead at the vast horizon. Several other sails were visible in the distance, while nearby, gulls and shags bobbed in the water. Even as he watched, a trio of fins cut the surface ten yards away and then three large creatures leapt in unison before diving back in with barely a splash.

"Porpoises," Felix said happily. "It's good luck to see them at the beginning of a voyage."

As they pulled out of the harbor, Teddy turned the boat and they headed southward, Oliver delighting in this vantage of the coastline view. "Will I be able to see Farview when we get near?"

"Sure, if your eyes are sharp."

Oliver thought that when they got there, he'd wave, just in case the ghosts were watching.

"Was my granddad able to offer you anything other than food?"

Oliver had become so caught up in his excitement over sailing that he'd almost forgotten the purpose of their journey. Chagrined, he nodded and told Felix about Enoch's instructions. "He wasn't entirely optimistic, but it's more of a chance than I had before."

"Who are the people he wants you to see in Greynox?"

"Erm, hang on." Oliver pulled out the paper. "Julian Massey and Kit Archer. Do you know who they are?"

Felix's eyes had grown wide. "Truly? Oh, I have a story for you! And the perfect spot to tell it."

Just then, Teddy turned the boat landward again, toward some craggy black rocks. Oliver was slightly alarmed until he realized there was a gap in those rocks—nearly hidden unless you looked from the right angle—and they were about to enter a small bay with a broad, sandy beach. A handful of wooden cottages dotted the area between the beach and the grassy dunes rising behind them.

"Is this where you and your uncle found the shells you gave me?"

"Yes. It's also where Mr. Massey was staying on holiday when he met Mr. Archer. I mentioned them to you earlier, I think. Mr. Archer was captured by pirates and escaped, only to be washed ashore here, nearly dead. Mr. Massey saved him, he did. And then their adventures really began."

Teddy seemed content to smoke his pipe and allow the boat to drift while Felix told his tale. Oliver leaned back against the gunwale and enjoyed.

"We should probably turn for home," Felix said reluctantly after concluding his story, which had been as exciting as he'd promised. "If we had more time we could swim. It's the perfect spot for it."

"I don't know how," Oliver admitted. It's not as if there were many opportunities in Greynox, where nobody would willingly enter the filthy Methes River.

"We'll come back and I'll teach you! It's private here, so we needn't worry about bathing costumes, and we can bring a picnic and search for treasures on the beach, and we can even—" He stopped abruptly, face falling. "We won't, will we? There isn't time."

Oliver's heart twisted. "I'm sorry, Felix. I'd rather be grateful for how much I do have instead of regretting what I don't." He cast a glance at Teddy, unsure how much he knew about Oliver and Felix's relationship, but Teddy appeared to have dozed off.

"I'm greedy, I am." Felix said. "And the more I have of you, the more I want."

"That's what I was afraid of. I don't want to hurt you."

"And I told you already. You're worth the pain."

They spent several quiet minutes bobbing in the gentle waves. Oliver was thinking about the price one must pay for something valuable; he suspected Felix was doing the same. It was a good lesson to keep in mind.

Teddy awoke with a startled jump. "Sharks!"

Felix laughed kindly. "You were dreaming, Uncle. Time to head home?"

"Aye. I saw a man get et by sharks once. Weren't pretty. 'Course, he was a right son of a bitch who nobody missed when he was gone. Prob'ly gave the sharks indigestion." Chuckling at his own joke, Teddy relit his pipe and began to steer them out of the bay.

This time they went much farther out—to avoid dangerous rocks, Felix explained. Oliver didn't mind. He enjoyed riding the swells and seeing the bow slice through the water as neatly as Mrs. Bellflower's sharp shears cutting fabric.

"I wonder what it's like to be so far at sea that you can't see the land at all," he mused dreamily. "To let the water and winds carry you as they will, and to look up at the night stars and feel as if you're sailing among them. It's like being a babe in a cradle, you see, but the mother who rocks you is temperamental, and you never know if she'll lull you to sleep or shake you to pieces. It's exhilarating. And when you leap into the waves and dive down, you're in another world entirely, one more fantastic than dreams ever bring, with sweet, savage beauty wherever you look and the light filtering down...."

He blinked and shook his head. "What... what was I saying?"

Felix was gaping at him. "Your eyes," he whispered.

"What?"

"Your eyes. When you were speaking just now, the blue of your eyes became nearly purple and sort of... sparkly."

"A trick of the light," Oliver said.

"No. And your voice... it was almost as if you were singing."

"I can't sing."

"You can't swim either, but you were describing it as if you could."

Oliver opened his mouth to answer but couldn't find anything to say. He had no idea where those words had come from, yet he knew to his very core that they were true. He could picture swimming deep beneath the ocean's surface as perfectly as if he did it every day. Just as he could imagine standing at the bow of a ship and shouting a joyous challenge at roaring tempest. More than that, though. He also knew that if he took control of the rudder, he could steer the boat unerringly to an island where ethereally beautiful creatures played their long lives away. In fact, he was tempted to do just that, except the journey would take weeks, and they had no supplies aboard Teddy's little boat.

"I'm going mad," he murmured. Clearly another effect of the curse.

"No."

"If I listen closely, I hear my name in the wind, as if someone is calling me. They're not saying Oliver, though. Not quite. It's something else—but I know it's me."

Felix was shaking, and not from cold. He swallowed thickly. "What's the name?"

Oliver let out a breath and gave in to the insanity. "I think it's... Ollyro."

"That's a fae name."

Somehow, Oliver wasn't surprised. At this point he'd lost his capacity to be shocked by anything. That part of him was burnt out, like an overworked motor in a factory.

"There were three Ollyros," Teddy interjected out of nowhere, sounding oddly like one of Oliver's childhood teachers. "All of 'em fae who decided to live with humans, the daft creatures. Givin' up perfection for the likes of us." He snorted and shook his head but didn't seem put off by Oliver's behavior.

Felix, on the other hand, had gone pale, his dark curls a sharp contrast against white skin. "You could call back," he said quietly.

And Oliver knew he could. A part of him wanted to very badly—to stand and shout, "It's me! I'm here!" at the top of his lungs and wait for brilliant gossamer sails to appear over the horizon.

"I am not fae," he said firmly. "I am mortal and entirely human. My name is Oliver Webb."

"Or Poole. Or Rowe. Or Ollyro. Just things people might call you. They don't change who you are."

"I'm a very ordinary man."

Felix, with the ghost of a smile, shook his head. "Nothing ordinary about you, love."

Oliver packed away the not-memories of swimming and of sailing through storms, and he shut his ears against the wind. He had business to attend to in Greynox.

"I'd like to go home now, please."

He couldn't tell the source of the sorrow in Felix's eyes, and gods, he hated to see it there. Felix's eyes should dance with mischief, glow with passion, sparkle with happiness.

"We're on our way. I reckon it'll be too dark to see your cottage, though."

Unnoticed by Oliver, the sun had slipped low. Now it hovered not far above the sea, as if considering whether to dive in. Its long rays reached far across the surface, turning the shore golden and making Oliver's eyes sting. "That's all right," he said. He turned his back to the open water and faced stubbornly inland instead.

"It'll be pretty coming into our harbor, though, won't it? You'll like it." Felix sighed and seemed about to say something more, then shut his mouth. But a moment later the corners of his lips turned up. "Fancy another story? I think we've time for it."

"I always want to hear your stories." Which was accurate, and in this case it might help calm his mind—or at least distract him.

"Good. This one is about one of my ancestors, way back. Probably one of yours too, since we're all tangled up when we poke back more than a few generations. I reckon I inherited my greediness from this one. His name was Bowyd—no family names back then, just given names—and he was a fisherman."

His name was Bowyd—no family names back then, just given names—and he was a fisherman. The people at that time didn't put out to sea in boats like we do. Not even little boats like this one. I don't think they knew how, and anyway they were too scared of the water gods. So they kept to the land, living off what they hunted on the moor or in the woods to the south. Those woods are fields now, but back then they had trees so thick you could barely walk through them. The people ate fish too, but they caught it by wading into the water and dragging nets. They'd get enough to satisfy a few hungry bellies, but nothing like the big catches we get offshore.

Bowyd wasn't much of a hunter. It was the being-quiet bit, wasn't it? He was always chattering away, scaring off everything in the woods. That's why he kept to fishing, because the fish don't care if you talk. And he was skilled at weaving nets. So skilled that he could have made them for everyone else and they'd have gladly shared their catches, but Bowyd was convinced he could catch more on his own. He'd natter on about that too, to anyone who'd listen—how his technique was the best and how it surely meant the ocean gods loved him. Nobody paid him much mind. "That's just Bowyd," they'd say. "More words in him than trees in the forest or stars in the sky."

Now, living was hard in those days. Nobody had any magic to help them out, so they relied on work and luck and the gods' favor. Sometimes the game would be too hard to find, and sometimes the winters would blow too long and cold, and people would die—old folks and children first. Even in good times, nobody had much. They lived in their little stone huts and kept only the few things they needed to survive. A blanket, a pot, a blade, a net. Those things and a full belly were all anyone asked for and all they expected.

Except Bowyd. He began to figure that since the gods loved him, he ought to have more. "I want a pile of furs to sleep on so my bones never feel the hard ground," he announced. Which was reasonable enough, I expect. You slept on the floor when you first got here, and I've lain on many, and it's not very nice, is it? But since Bowyd couldn't hunt, he'd have to trade for furs. So he took his finest net and went down to the water, and he told the sea goddess Therylla how pretty she was and how much he'd admire her if she filled his net. And she did, because gods can be a bit vain, can't they? Bowyd took his catch and traded it for an enormous pile of furs.

Now Bowyd slept ever so well, without the cold seeping into him, without aches working into his bones. He should have been content. But he wasn't.

"I want so many clothes that I can wear something different every day of the week," he said. The people laughed. They were like me: owned one set and washed it when they could. But Bowyd went down to the water with his net. At first he simply told Therylla she was pretty, but she'd heard that before and didn't fill his net. So now he told her that she was the most beautiful of all goddesses. That worked. He caught a mountain of fish and traded it to a nearby tribe for clothes made of woven wool and leather and fur and beads.

Bowyd was now the most stylish person in his village by far. He'd go strutting up and down between the huts, everything adjusted just so, imagining everyone envied him. They didn't. None of them could picture giving up perfectly good fish for all that frippery. But they were polite, I reckon, and they smiled as Bowyd swaggered past.

Our Bowyd was happy for three weeks, but by then he'd worn all his new clothing repeatedly and he wanted something more. He and his people ate off of big leaves or pieces of bark, and they drank from crude clay cups. Worked right well enough, didn't it? But Bowyd said, "I want a goblet of shining metal, finely wrought. And I want dishes as thin as leaves but strong as ironwood, with beautiful pictures painted along the edges."

"Won't make your food taste any better," his neighbors told him. "Won't make your mead last any longer."

But you won't be surprised to hear that Bowyd didn't listen. He went down to the water and tried to woo Therylla with his usual praises, but they weren't enough. He stood there in the waves with his empty net, thinking. "My Lady," he says at last, "have you noticed how nicely made my net is? The finest anywhere. You could wear it like lace in your hair, you could. When I catch my fill, I'll give you the net."

It was, in fact, a very fine net. Therylla filled it with fish, and after Bowyd had cleaned the fish and hung them to dry, he tossed the net into the sea and watched Therylla carry it away through the waves. Now he had no net, but he didn't care. As soon as his fish dried, he carted them to a neighboring tribe who gave him a silver goblet and two dishes that were snow-white with drawings of bright flowers along the edges.

Very pleased, Bowyd hurried home. He soon realized, however, that since he'd traded away all the fish, he had nothing to eat on his fine new dishes. And he had no net to catch more. He right away set to making a new net, and although he was hungry indeed by the time it was finished, he was in his pretty clothes, atop his tall pile of furs, with his beautiful goblet and dishes gleaming in the firelight.

But you know what? By the time he had that net ready, he'd lost weight and those clothes no longer fit him. He had to set them aside and wear old ones, bound up tight. But all he could think of was how he wanted strings of shining beads to dangle from his ears, and hang around his neck, and braid into his hair. Bowyd went down to the water with his new net, but offering it to Therylla did no good. He had to offer her something new this time.

"The finest net ever made," he told her. "It will be so big that when I throw it to you, it will stretch all the way to the horizon. Every knot will be perfectly tied, every twist a thing of beauty as well as function. You can wrap it around yourself like a gown."

Well, she liked that, she did. She filled his net—his ordinary but very good net—and he dried his catch and traded it to the neighbors for a hoard of beads made from glass, gems, and precious metals. He put them on and thought, "Not even a king has as much as I!"

But he didn't have time to show them off because he owed Therylla a net, and even a fool like Bowyd knows better than to break a promise to a goddess. He worked day and night, his belly growing emptier and emptier, his eyes getting weak, his fingers bleeding. But you know what he was thinking? That his hut, which was the same size as everyone else's even though he lived alone, was too small for all his possessions. He wanted a bigger one. "With twenty-eight rooms," he said. "One for every day of the month." He was so bent and weak he could hardly hear his own voice.

When the enormous net was complete, he dragged it down to the water, which wasn't easy in his state, and he tossed it in. He wasn't even thinking about fishing any longer. Therylla took the net at once.

Bowyd stood shivering in the waves, wanting *more*. But what had he to offer? His flattery was stale, his net-making skills—prodigious as they were—exhausted. He remembered then the stories of some of his distant ancestors, who are our ancestors too, and what they would do to please the gods.

"A sacrifice!" he cried. "Send me enough fish so that I can build my house, and I will give you a human life."

He should have been shocked to even consider such a thing. It was terrible, even back then. But nothing mattered to him now except his greed. Not even the lives of his relatives, of the people who'd once been his friends. He told himself he would find someone to toss into the sea. Someone nobody would miss. Someone of no value.

Therylla filled the new net with fish and tossed the lot onto the shore. It was more fish than a village could eat in a lifetime. They covered the beach, silver scales glistening in the sun even as their eyes went dull.

Word got out that Bowyd would give endless fish to whoever helped build him a new house. Tribespeople came from miles and miles away. Night and day they gathered stones, fitted them together, covered the roof with thatch. They left with all of the fish, but Bowyd had a house with twenty-eight rooms.

But was he content? He was not. He sat alone inside his enormous house and said, "I have worked hard all my life. Now I have a bigger house than anyone else, and more clothing, and finer things to eat and drink from, and a taller pile of furs, and many more beautiful beads. I am a very important man, and a man such as me shouldn't have to work. I want to own people, so that they will do my work for me. And I'll spend my days lounging on my furs in my fine clothing and beads."

Of course, he still had to pay his debt to Therylla, and he also had to think of what to offer her next. While he was considering this, his neighbors came to him.

"What have you done!" they cried. "You took all the fish from the sea, and now when we cast our nets they come back empty. We cannot rely on hunting alone. Our children cry with hunger at night!"

Bowyd didn't care. He shooed them all away.

He sat and he thought, and he was so weak that he couldn't even stand and walk down to the water. "No matter. Therylla can hear me wherever I am."

He cleared his throat. "Therylla? Give me an army of people who belong to me, who must do my bidding, who will do all of my work. And I will give you... my entire village. Not just one life but many. The largest sacrifice ever!" He held his breath and waited.

But Therylla had had enough. "Your greed will never end, not even if you possess the entire world. No more!" And she sent a mighty wave up from the sea, and that wave washed away Bowyd's entire house, his furs, clothing, dishes, goblet, and beads, and even Bowyd himself.

To be honest, the villagers were glad to be rid of him. But they were still faced with a fish shortage, plus their best net maker was now somewhere at the bottom of the sea. Then one clever woman remembered that she'd seen another tribe riding in tiny boats upon a river. "We could make bigger boats," she suggested. "Big enough to go out to sea, and we could go far enough to find fish again."

And they did, and those were the first real fishermen among us.

Full night had fallen by the end of Felix's tale, making Teddy's small boat an intimate space in the darkness. The sail and ropes creaked, water lapped gently against the hull, and the air smelled of salt and Teddy's pipe tobacco. And above them—yes, just as Oliver had imagined—a sea of stars he longed to swim in. Looking out past the boat, he couldn't tell where water ended and sky began.

But there was a difference between this and his... vision, or whatever it had been. Because now when he looked inland, he saw the lights of Croftwell sparkling, warmer than the stars and more welcoming. He even thought that one tiny light, high above the others, might be a firestone lantern he'd left burning in the window at Farview.

Even more than Oliver longed for the stars, he yearned for Croftwell. He hadn't lived there long, just a blink of an eye compared to his many years in Greynox. But as Teddy angled in toward the harbor and the friendly lights grew nearer, Oliver knew that *this* was his home.

Chapter Eighteen

Oliver knew that he should leave for Greynox in the morning, but he hadn't the strength of will. He made excuses about needing to rest after their excursion to Urchin Cove and about needing to pay a visit to Davies the solicitor first. But he wasn't fooling himself.

Felix, on the other hand, was delighted. He spent the next day fussing over Oliver as they ate the vegetables the Andoxes had given them. He gave Oliver another bath, which ended much the same way as the first two, with both of them panting and replete. Then he washed his own clothes and remained naked for the rest of the day while they dried. He told more stories.

They sat down at the table for a dinner of eggs seasoned with moor-herb and topped with cheese. "We could go down to the pub tomorrow, if you like. We need groceries anyhow, and we could stop in first for a pint." Felix grinned. "Wouldn't mind introducing you properly to my mum and dad, if you're up for it."

It wasn't the curse that made Oliver's heart twist into a knot as tight as any Bowyd tied. "I can't," he said quietly.

Felix's face fell, but only briefly.

"Too much for you. I understand. I can nip down, though, and bring us up something lovely from the Merman. Currant cakes and knucker pie."

"Felix—"

"And I could fetch you some ogrewort, and when it's done its job and you're feeling well, I'll arrange for Teddy to take us to that bay for that swimming lesson. We could—"

"Felix." That came out harsher than Oliver intended, and he softened his tone when he continued. "The ogrewort's a good idea, actually, but the rest.... I need to go to Greynox." He didn't say *while I still can*, but the words hung between them nonetheless.

Now Felix looked grim, but he nodded.

"Jamie doesn't go to Bythington tomorrow. It's his day off. He'll go the next, though, and we can catch the train from there. We'll be in Greynox by nightfall."

Wicked thorns sprouted in Oliver's gut, in his lungs and throat, and they traveled up his spine to prick at the back of his eyes. "It's not *we*. I'm going alone."

"Don't worry about the cost. I've a few coppers, and I can find a way to earn more tomorrow. I'll pay for my own tickets, and for my own bed and board once we get there."

Oliver pushed his plate away. He couldn't possibly eat any more now. "It's not the cost."

"Are you worried about my curse? I know they use magic to fuel the train, but I can sit in a car at the other end. I've done it before, I have, and everything was fine."

That potential issue hadn't even occurred to Oliver. "It's not your curse either."

Felix stared at him for a long minute, face expressionless. Then he gave a slow nod and stood. His movements were stiff as he began to gather his clothing from where Oliver had hung it near the hearth.

"What are you doing?" Oliver asked, lurching to his feet.

"I'm sorry."

"Sorry? Sorry for what?"

"Wearing out my welcome." Felix gave a tiny, wobbly smile. "I've spent more time with you than with anyone since I was a 'prentice. I forgot that I'm best in small doses."

"You're not!" Oliver ran over and grasped Felix's bare arms. "If we had a hundred years together, you wouldn't wear out your welcome. Please…." His voice broke and he cursed himself for his weakness, for what he was about to ask. "Please don't go yet. We can have two more nights and a day together. Please." He'd get on his knees if he had to.

"I don't understand. You still want to be with me?"

"More than I want air."

As Felix let out a long breath, some of the tension left his body. "Then why can't I go to Greynox? Then we'd have more time together."

Oliver wasn't like Felix, so graceful with language. He needed to find the right words. He moved slowly to an octopus chair and sat heavily, marshaling his thoughts into order. Meanwhile, Felix slowly put on his clothes. Even from halfway across the cottage, Oliver could smell his clean scent: lavender and soap and moor-herb. Once Felix was dressed, he came closer and knelt on the throw rug at Oliver's feet, arms resting on Oliver's knees, his eyes bright.

"I came here to die," Oliver said at last. "I expected to die alone. That would have been my fate in Greynox as well, but somehow this seemed less sad. At least I'd end under my own roof, without the reek and din of the city to disturb my last hours.

"And then I met you. With your stories and your hair and your fingers and your… your brightness. Like nobody I'd ever known. And you filled this spot that's been hollow all my life." Oliver held a palm against his heart. "I've had only a short time in this place, but I know two things. I love Croftwell. And Felix Corbyn, I love you."

Felix gasped and jerked back as if struck. For once he was speechless, his mouth gaping open.

Oliver gave a wan smile. "Don't worry. You don't have to say it back. I know I'm not…. If we were flotsam on that beach of yours, you'd be a pirate's lost treasure. I'd be a chunk of driftwood. Good for a fire, maybe, and then it's done."

Felix tightened his jaw. "No. Don't you dare say that about the man I love. I knew. The minute I saw you sitting there in the Merman, I *knew*. As if I were a fish and you'd hooked me good and proper, and I'd never be free. And don't tell me love can't happen that fast, because it bloody well can. I could tell you a score of stories about it, and every bloody one of them is true."

"I don't...." Oliver shook his head. "I can't imagine what someone like you would see in me, but I believe you. All your stories are true."

"What if I tell a story about us being together happily forever?" Tears had begun to track down Felix's cheeks, but his voice was steady. "Olly, I'm Bowyd, don't you see? Whatever I have of you will never be enough."

Oliver did see; he was Bowyd too. "I want you to think of me sometimes in the future. Maybe even after you've found someone else and have settled down comfortably."

"Olly—"

"And when you do, I want you to remember me here, at Farview, and not in some stinking rathole in Greynox. I want our last hours together to be when I still have some strength. When I don't look like a ghoul and when I'm not—" He almost said *screaming in agony* but spared Felix that much. "Two nights and a day, Felix. In a beautiful home with a man I love. That alone is so much more than I dreamed of. It has to be enough."

"You want to part on a dream rather than a nightmare."

"Yes. Please."

Felix shuddered. "I can't bear this."

"Of course you can. You've been faced with adversity your entire life, deprived of even simple joys such as your family's company. Yet you haven't just survived, you've thrived. You have more spirit than all of Greynox. You're the strongest person I've ever known."

They ended up in each other's arms, Felix mostly sitting on Oliver's lap and both of them crying. But Felix stopped asking to accompany him to the city, and Oliver was grateful for that.

Chapter Nineteen

A long bout of tender lovemaking that night led to a late awakening in the morning. As Oliver sat up in bed, yawning and rubbing his eyes, Felix padded naked to the window facing the sea. "Cloudy today."

"Will it storm?" Oliver shivered, remembering the last time.

"Not today, I don't think."

Oliver stretched, wincing at the persistent ache in his bones. It wasn't bad now, but he knew it would get worse. "Would you mind going to fetch some ogrewort?"

Felix turned to look at him, which gave Oliver a chance to gaze back. Felix was a vision, the grayish light silhouetting him and turning his bed-mussed curls into a halo. He had love bites on his neck and thighs. His tattoo seemed such an intrinsic part of him that Oliver could barely believe he'd been born without it. And Felix clearly enjoyed being watched. He cocked his hips and curled his lips, and his cock grew plump and began to rise.

"You'll have to save that thought for tonight, I'm afraid," Oliver said.

"Why? The ogrewort will wait."

"You wore me out last night. I need more recovery time." And that was damned frustrating. Here was a man beyond his wildest dreams, and they had only a day left together. But Oliver's failing body could manage only so much, and he ought to be grateful it had served him well last night.

"All right. Ogrewort it is. What will you do? Lie about and survey your realm, yer majesty?"

As tempting as that was, Oliver shook his head. "I've a few errands to run in the village."

Felix's shoulders slumped and his arousal fled. "You're still insisting on going to Greynox tomorrow. Alone."

"I have to. I don't *want* to—please understand that. Everything I could ever want is right here, standing in front of me. But six innocent people are going to die."

"They might anyway. I don't see how you can stop it."

"Nor do I." Oliver sighed. "But I have to try."

"Aye. Unlucky me. I had to fall in love with a good man, a moral one, instead of a selfish ratbag."

They'd confessed their love the day before. It was still new and fresh, and the very word made Oliver feel both toasty warm and icy cold.

Oliver made them breakfast while Felix dressed, and over breakfast Oliver gave him directions to the ogrewort. "It's quite easy to find, really."

"For you. Has it occurred to you that it might not be there for me?"

"Why wouldn't it?"

Felix chewed and swallowed a bite of sausage. "Because it shouldn't be there at all this late in the year. I think your ghosts put it there for you."

"I...." Oliver frowned. "Can ghosts do that? Make plants grow?"

"I don't know, do I? I'm no expert on them. But the local specters certainly favor you, and I've heard stories about ghosts moving things about. I guess it's possible."

Oliver remembered seeing the ghost girl's bow at her ruined village. He hadn't tried to touch it, but it had looked solid enough. He didn't know the rules for apparitions, though. Really, he didn't know *any* of the rules for this strange place. When it came down to it, he was a simple man, unimaginative and not especially bright. Not like Felix, who was as complicated as the little enchanted puzzles you could buy on Dragonford Street, with the tiny colored tiles that would rearrange themselves just when you'd come close to solving them.

Felix reached across the table to pat his wrist. "I'll go look for it. Don't worry. I'm sure it'll be there."

Nevertheless, as soon as Felix was on his way, Oliver addressed whatever invisible beings might be listening. "Show him to the flowers, please. He's doing this for me, and I'm going to need them."

Then Oliver finished dressing, grabbed a walking stick—this one a sturdy piece of driftwood—and started down the path to the village. The cool air wrapped around him as he walked, seeping through his clothes and chilling him. But when he shivered violently and his knees felt weak, he reminded himself of what he had to do and found the strength to continue. He left the stick at the base of the path in preparation for the climb home.

This time there were no cats outside of Colin Davies's house, but Charr and the gray cat sat inside on windowsills, watching Oliver as he walked to the door. Colin answered almost immediately, holding a book in one hand.

"Oliver! It's good to see you again. Come in, come in."

Oliver stopped just inside. "I won't be but a minute. I just need to tell you something."

"Of course. But you're welcome to stay for a bit. I could put on a pot of tea."

A pang made Oliver wince. Under other circumstances, he would have liked to stay and chat for a bit. Colin was an interesting fellow. Oliver could even imagine sitting in Colin's parlor with Felix, the three of them laughing about something in Greynox or Croftwell, a cat purring on his lap.

"Thank you," Oliver said. "But I'm afraid I can't today."

Sensing Oliver's mood, Colin nodded seriously. "Another time then. But what can I help you with?"

"I'm going to Greynox tomorrow. And the thing is... I doubt I'll be back."

Colin looked crestfallen. "Oh, I'm sorry to hear that. The whole village had hoped you'd be happy settled here."

"I am. I mean, it's not that. I've business to attend to there, and...." This next bit was difficult to say, as if every repeat made it truer. "I'm ill, Colin. I don't think I've much longer."

He thought Colin might shrink away from him, but instead he reached out and gave a gentle touch on his arm. "Oh, no. I'm so unhappy to hear that. There's nothing the doctors and wizards can do?"

"No."

"I see." Colin sighed. "Now I understand why you had me draw up your will."

"And that's why I'm here now. When I don't return.... I want to ensure nothing interferes with Felix inheriting Farview."

"Yes, I understand. On the occasion of, erm, your passing, you can have your people there send notice to me, and—"

"I have no people there."

Colin's frown was deep. "If you like, I can accompany you on your journey."

Oliver stifled a sob at such generosity. "Thank you, but I have to do this alone. Is there some way I can make sure you're notified when I die?"

Colin flinched a bit at the baldness of the word, but he also looked thoughtful. "Let me see.... Yes, that might work. Follow me, please."

They walked to the parlor, where both cats hopped off the sill and began twining around Oliver's legs. Afraid he might kick one or trip over them, he remained still while Colin went to his desk and scrawled something on a piece of paper. He slipped the paper into an envelope, sealed it, wrote on the front, and affixed a postage stamp. Then he examined his work, looking pleased.

"Here you go." He handed the envelope to Oliver and then scooped up and held the gray cat, who purred noisily.

"It's addressed to you."

"Precisely. Keep this on your person. And when, erm, the time is near, sign it and simply drop it in a postbox. If you don't get a chance to do so, it's likely someone will find it and post it for you." He swallowed loudly.

"What is it?"

"It's an interesting legal process, one that was instituted during the Periwinkle War two hundred years ago. A great many soldiers were, erm, meeting their end—"

"Dying. You can say it."

Colin gave a wan smile. "Right. A great many soldiers were dying, but due to the battle conditions, their remains were often unrecoverable. It caused a devil of a time in the courts, because without proof of their passing, their families couldn't receive death benefits. A lot of wives and children were left destitute. Then Lord Thistlebottom pushed a new law through Parliament. He'd been injured in the war himself, you see, so he was sympathetic. Under this legislation, a soldier could post a certain letter to his family before heading into battle. And if he didn't post another letter within a week, he was presumed dead."

"Oh." Oliver thought for a moment. "I'm not going into battle." Well, not exactly.

"It doesn't matter. The principle remains. I've never had a chance to use this procedure before, but it's perfectly sound." He appeared momentarily excited at the prospect but then seemed to remember *why* he was using this procedure and his face fell.

He cleared his throat. "As soon as I receive that letter, the clock begins to tick. If I don't receive another within a week—"

"You won't."

"—I'll have the power to ask the coroner to declare you, erm, dead, and then I can execute your will."

Feeling as if he'd been relieved of a heavy burden, Oliver let out a deep breath. "Perfect. Thank you. This is important to me."

"You're concerned about Felix, yes?"

Oliver wasn't going to lie about this. "Yes."

"I'm very sorry about the context, but I'm glad for that bit. We all worry about him."

They walked together to the door, Colin stooping to pick up

another cat—this one a tabby—along the way. He paused before Oliver exited. "Are you sure there's nothing I can do to help?"

Oliver patted his breast pocket, where he'd tucked the envelope. "You already have."

OLIVER'S next stop was at the docks, where, as he'd hoped, he found Felix's uncle Teddy sitting in his moored boat and puffing on a pipe.

"Oi, Oliver!" Teddy called. "Ready to head to sea again already?"

A part of Oliver wanted exactly that. The tug he'd felt yesterday hadn't entirely disappeared. But he shook his head. "Not today. Yesterday was lovely, though. Thank you."

"Anytime, anytime. I bet I can make a fisherman out of you. 'T's in yer blood, it is."

"I don't doubt it. But I was wondering about something else. Do you know anyone in the village who knows how to make a fire from peat?"

"Too good fer firestones, are ye?" Teddy narrowed his eyes shrewdly.

"I'm fine with them. But for Felix's sake, I thought peat might be safer. I think the hearth at Farview will work that way."

"Aye, I reckon it might." Teddy smiled, revealing all the gaps in his teeth. "Mighty glad to hear yer thinkin' of our Felix like that. Mighty glad."

"But the peat?"

"Horace Loowin uses peat when he's up on the moor during lambin' time. Says magic scares the sheep. Next time I see him, I'll tell him to come 'round to Farview and show you."

There. Another small weight gone. "Thank you."

"Come round soon, Oliver. I'll teach ye to rig."

Oliver nodded a lie and turned inland.

The Merman was nearly empty at this time of day—too late for lunch and too early for dinner or pints with friends. Two gray-haired women sat in the corner, laughing over a game of cards, and a sad-eyed man who looked as old as the stones on the moor nursed a glass on the other side of the room. Aygun and Tural stood together behind the bar, talking quietly. It must have been about something pleasant, since they were both smiling.

"Mr. Webb!" Tural called almost at once. "Good to see you again." He looked as if he meant it.

Oliver took a seat on one of the barstools. "It's Oliver. And I owe you a great deal for all the food you've sent up lately."

"Oh, we like to help keep our neighbors alive so they'll come back here and buy drinks." Tural laughed at his own joke, but Aygun rolled his eyes and thumped him on the arm.

"I'll take a pint now, if I may," Oliver said.

While Tural went to pull it, Aygun stood across from Oliver, looking at him intently. There was something distinctly birdlike about his gaze, and it wasn't just because of the wings furled on his back. Oliver knew almost nothing about wind people—before meeting Aygun, he hadn't been sure they truly existed—but he had the sense that Aygun could see things an ordinary person could not.

"Have you recovered?" Aygun's voice was light and musical, his accent exotic and pleasing.

"Not entirely, no. But I am feeling better." Neither of these statements was a lie.

"May I ask you a favor?"

"Of course."

"Sometimes I like to walk up to your cottage and stand at the cliff-edge. May I continue to do so?"

Oliver blinked. "Any time you like. The moor's not mine to control."

"You own that land. I don't want to intrude."

"I don't think anyone can really own the moor. And you're not intruding." Oliver was certain Felix would feel the same. He might even enjoy visitors after Oliver had gone.

"Thank you. It's not the same as flying, of course, but it reminds me of it a bit." He fluttered his wings, one of them long and beautiful, the other cruelly mangled.

And that was good, because Oliver needed another reminder that he wasn't the first person on the planet to suffer. Everyone carried a burden; the best he could do was carry his gracefully.

Tural came back with Oliver's glass and slipped an arm around Aygun's waist. They made a handsome couple.

"Can you tell me what time the coach leaves for Bythington tomorrow?" Oliver asked. Felix probably knew, but he might as well ask now.

Tural and Aygun exchanged glances, and it was Tural who answered. "Early. It's supposed to be at half six, but Jamie runs late, so it's usually closer to seven."

"And it arrives in time for a train to Greynox?"

"Yes."

Oliver took a long swallow of his ale. It tasted more bitter than usual. Maybe everything would taste bitter from now on.

"Felix," Aygun said abruptly. "He's important to us."

"To me as well."

"Even if someone is damaged or imperfect, he still has great value. Even if it means he must live differently than others are accustomed to." Aygun waved his wings again, this time with more force. The good one battered against Tural's back and head, but he ignored it.

Oliver leaned toward them. "I agree. And if you're referring specifically to Felix, I think he's completely bloody perfect as he is." He drank more of his ale.

Tural nodded. "It's funny. A disaster happens and we can hardly bear it. It changes everything, and we become convinced it's ruined our life. And perhaps it has. But sometimes that disaster is the key to unlocking a new door, and we find ourselves much better off than we were to begin with."

At this point, Oliver didn't know who Tural was talking about: Aygun with his broken wing, Tural with his wooden leg, Felix with his curse, or even Oliver with *his* curse. But it didn't matter because he agreed. In his own case, he probably never would have come to Croftwell if not for the flash-curse, would have never met and fallen in love with Felix. He would have remained a guard at Hillard's until he was too old for the work, then faded into retirement, unnoticed, unimportant, alone. His short time with Felix was worth more than decades of a shadow existence.

"I love Felix," Oliver said steadily. "Don't know how it happened, but it did. That love can't outplay everything, however much I wish it could. I've... obligations. But Felix understands them, and he knows how I feel about him, and that's the best I can do."

His hosts relaxed after his little speech. Tural even grinned. Aygun simply nodded. "Felix is the... the spirit of this village. That's not the right word, but it doesn't exist in your language. Do you understand?"

"I think I do."

After that, Oliver finished his drink. Then, at his request, Tural packed him four jars of mead, a pair of meat pies, and several currant cakes. Oliver insisted on paying for them. His coppers wouldn't have to last him much longer anyway. He took his leave, Tural and Aygun watching him as he left the pub.

OLIVER RECOVERED his stick near the bottom of the path, and it took him a long time to walk up the cliff. He reminded himself that this was the last time he'd travel the path in this direction, and despite the cold and his aches, he enjoyed the changing views as he rose.

Felix hadn't yet returned to the cottage, which gave Oliver a good chance to pack his bag without rubbing salt into Felix's wounds. He hadn't much to take—just the few items he'd brought with him from Greynox. But he did tuck one extra thing into his luggage: one of the shells Felix had brought him from the bay near Urchin Cove. It wasn't large but it was beautiful, shaped like an elongated cone and with a spiraling pattern in purple and red.

After he finished packing, Oliver sat outside on the bench. It was still chilly, but the clouds were high enough that they didn't obscure the view, which was just as beautiful in overcast as in sunshine. He would have sworn that more colors existed here than in Greynox, where everything seemed to be a shade of gray or brown. Here, though, while the sea contained grays, there were also gradations of blue and green; there were the reds, oranges, and yellows of flowers in the Croftwell gardens; there was the shaded black of the rocks at the mouth of the harbor; there were sails of bright white; and up on the moor, things grew in endless variations of green.

The people of Croftwell were more colorful as well, more full of life. Uncle Teddy with his boat and pipe, Colin Davies with his cats, Mrs. Bellflower with her needle and thread, Tural and Aygun with their friendly pub. Even drunken Jamie with his creaky coach and adoring dragons. And Felix most of all, of course.

For the first time, Oliver wondered how his life would have turned out if his mother had remained in Croftwell. According to Felix's story, she'd gone to Greynox to give her unborn child a better life, or perhaps to make sure he wouldn't be lost at sea like his father and grandfather, and he couldn't fault her for that. It wasn't as if he'd been utterly miserable in Greynox. He'd never gone hungry, he'd been given a decent education, and he never lacked for a place to sleep. He was certainly much better off than the people who were forced to work in the factories. But what if he'd spent his childhood in Farview or down in the village, and he'd run the moors and sailed boats since he was very young? What kind of man would he have become?

"There's no use wasting time on lives you didn't live when the one you have is so short." The old-man ghost and the girl had materialized a few feet away, and it was he who spoke.

Oliver wasn't surprised by their appearance. "Ghosts can read minds?"

"No. But we've been watching and listening to people for hundreds of years, boy. We've learned something about them."

"Do you know if Felix found the ogrewort?"

"He did. He'll be back with it soon."

Oliver nodded. "Did you somehow make it grow? For me?"

"Of course not," said the girl, laughing. "How would we do that? That patch of ogrewort has always been there. Our healer made me tea from that very patch. It didn't save me, but I didn't feel as ill." She pirouetted, her bow held over her head like an ornament.

"Felix said it shouldn't be blooming this time of year."

"No, but that wasn't our doing."

"Then whose?"

The ghosts exchanged glances with each other and shook their heads like disappointed teachers, making Oliver feel very dim. They didn't answer his question, and he lacked the will to pursue it. Maybe questioning the existence of the flowers would make them disappear.

"I'm leaving for Greynox tomorrow," he announced. "I'm going to do what I can to make things right."

"Good lad," said the old man.

Then a terrible thought struck Oliver. "Is there any chance I'll become a ghost too, and be stuck in Greynox?" He imagined himself haunting Oakwood Street, doomed to forever watch people work themselves to death in the mills.

The old man clucked his tongue. "Ah, ye needn't worry about *that*. Ghosts go where they belong."

"Where do I belong?" Oliver knew he sounded plaintive.

"You know the answer to that yourself, boy."

The girl danced over to him, her wild hair twining about her shoulders. She put her hand on his knee, and Oliver felt it—a small but significant weight and a heat that burned even through his trousers. "We haven't had a new guardian here in ages," she stage-whispered. Then she giggled and spun away.

Oliver was too astounded to respond, and both ghosts disappeared before he had a chance to say good-bye. "Thank you for your company and guidance," he said to the empty air. "Please take care of Felix."

"I can take care of myself, can't I?"

Oliver started and looked over to find Felix approaching with an uncharacteristically serious expression.

"Do you think the imps will watch over me like they do you?" he asked.

"Possibly. You feed them too. But I was addressing the ghosts."

"Ah, the ghosts. You've found quite a few friends, haven't you?"

"They know you're welcome here. They won't try to chase you away after I'm g—"

"Don't." Felix put up a hand to stop him. "I don't want to hear that word. I know it's going to happen, but let me pretend for a few more hours."

"All right." Oliver stood up from the bench, feeling stiff. All he'd done was walk down to the village and back up, but now his knees felt as if they were made of broken glass. He tried to hide his pain as well as he could.

Felix came closer, took Oliver's hand in his, and kissed the knuckles. "It's cold out here. Let's go inside and get some tea into you. I'll see what I can find us to eat."

"I brought us dinner from the Merman."

"Lovely! Then we could get into bed, all nice and snuggled under the blankets...."

They walked hand in hand into the cottage, Felix not commenting on Oliver's obvious limp. He also didn't say anything about the packed bag, although he couldn't have missed seeing it.

"Do you want to heat the kettle or risk it with me?" he asked.

"I'll risk it."

That seemed to please Felix, who worked efficiently at filling the kettle, sparking the firestone, and then steeping the flowers in a large ceramic cup that Oliver had acquired somewhere. It had leaping porpoises painted on it. *Good luck to see them at the beginning of a voyage*, Felix had said.

As Oliver sipped the bitter liquid, Felix doused the firestone and lit candles instead. Their dancing flames made shadows play along the walls and ceiling, and they made the cottage feel safe and cozy. Oliver looked around at the big bed with the cozy blankets and fluffy pillows, the octopus-and-rose chairs, the multicolored throw rug, the shells and polished stones and sea glass on the shelves. The shining washtub was overturned near one wall, temporarily serving as a makeshift stand for a pottery jug full of blooms. Felix must have brought them up from somebody's garden, but Oliver didn't know when.

This was *home*. The knowledge made Oliver's heart ache so fiercely that it was a wonder his chest didn't crack open. But the pain was slightly soothed by his knowledge that Felix would live here.

They ate in silence, but it was a comfortable one, with shared enjoyment of good food and good company. Although Oliver always liked Felix's ease with words—both in conversation and stories—he cherished other parts of him as well, such as his warm eyes and quick smiles and the way that, even when he was quiet, Felix lit up a room better than any candle or firestone could.

The sun was hovering above the horizon when they finished.

Earlier in the day, after Oliver spoke with Uncle Teddy but before he'd gone to the Merman, he'd made brief stops at the home-goods shop and the grocer's. Now he gathered his purchases and carried them outside with Felix following, curious.

The imps came bounding over at once, chattering loudly as if to scold him for tardiness. "You're the best neighbors I've ever had," Oliver informed them. "More charming and better-mannered." Then he set down their gifts: a large tin of biscuits, a heavy wheel of cheese, and an entire loaf of bread. He also had spools of thread in red, blue, yellow, pink, and shining silver. The small imp set upon these with a squeal of delight, while the others hoisted the food, chirruped at Oliver, and hurried away. It sounded as if they were singing.

"I thought you weren't going to spoil them," said Felix, leaning in the doorway.

"That was before they saved my life. After I'm— I mean, will you...." He trailed off awkwardly.

Felix took pity on him. "I'll do my best to make sure they stay spoiled." He reached out and poked Oliver's shoulder. "Come to bed, love."

They took their time getting ready. Oliver undressed Felix first, layer by layer, until he stood naked on the rug.

"Mr. Hillard has statues in his house and gardens. They're meant to be gods and goddesses, I think. You're prettier than any of them."

Grinning, Felix grabbed Oliver's shirt and pulled their bodies together. "I'll wager none of those statues have gooseflesh like I do."

"You have a number of advantages over them." Oliver squeezed Felix's pert, round arse.

They kissed for a while, Felix pressing into Oliver's body heat, Oliver smoothing hands over Felix's shoulders and back and arse or threading his fingers through those glorious curls. Every spot of contact between them was like a spark under Oliver's skin, as if Felix's brightness could spread to him bit by bit.

Eventually Felix pushed him back a bit, but only so he could unfasten Oliver's buttons and tug off his shirts. The trousers were more difficult. Oliver had to use Felix's shoulder to balance himself, and just the gentle brush of Felix's hand over his crotch was enough to make Oliver whimper.

"I feel as if, before you, I'd never done this before," he said.

Felix's eyes sparkled. "You're quite skilled for a virgin, you are."

"It's been ages since I was a virgin. I've been fucking since I was fifteen. But not with anyone who mattered."

"You've never made love, then."

Oliver pressed his lips to the soft skin of Felix's neck. "Not until you."

"I've liked all the men I slept with. I certainly don't regret any of them. But you, Olly, you're here." Felix patted his heart. "Only you. And you're a bloody big fellow, aren't you? You take up so much space, I don't expect I'll ever have room for anyone else."

Stricken, Oliver shook his head firmly. "No, no, Felix. You'll find someone who will love you much longer than I could. Please."

"And if I don't?" Felix asked with a sad smile.

"I'll… I'll come back and haunt you until you do. I'll keep sending promising suitors your way until one of them takes." Oliver was only half kidding, because if he did become a ghost, he'd try exactly that. He'd make sure Felix was happy.

"You've ambitions to be one of the guardians, have you? I can see that." Felix rubbed his chin thoughtfully. "You've been a guard already."

"That was just a job."

"Perhaps. A big bloke like you with some education? You could have chosen a variety of professions. But you chose to become a guard."

Oliver twitched his shoulders. "Yes, but a guard for what? A greedy rantallion who'd rather kill scores than spend a few more coppers."

Felix gently took Oliver's face in his hands and spoke softly. "You were lost, love. So far from help, so far from home, and with nobody to guide you." He stood on the balls of his feet and kissed the tip of Oliver's nose. "Can we get under those blankets now?"

They didn't fall on one another in a raging blaze of passion. They took their time exploring each other's bodies, as if hours were as endless to them as grains of sand on a beach. Oliver stroked and sniffed and licked the banquet of Felix's body, and Felix did the same in return. Although Oliver was already in love with the entirety of Felix, he now also fell in love with the parts: the sprinkling of dark hairs on his chest and the neat line of them on his lower belly, the little divot of his navel, the dimples above his round buttocks, the long line of his spine, the sweet and tender skin at his nape, the clever curves of his tattoo. And gods, Oliver loved what those nimble fingers and soft lips could do to him.

Before Felix, he'd always considered fucking to be a very goal-oriented activity. One wanted to reach a climax as nicely as possible, and if he wasn't a cad, he wanted his partner to do the same. That was all. But now he realized that the journey was even better than the destination, that regardless of who reached a peak and when, the giving and taking of long, slow pleasure was a delight.

When it became almost too much, he licked his way up Felix's torso, beginning at the base of his cock and stopping for a detour at his nipples, until he reached those plump, parted lips. Then Oliver laid one ear over Felix's heart and listened to its strong beat, to the whoosh of blood so similar to the sea. Felix carried the world inside him—at least, the parts that mattered to Oliver. Felix had become his world.

"What do you want?" Oliver whispered. "I'll give you anything."

"I want to bury myself inside you. May I do that?"

Oliver moaned. "Yes. Please."

Felix had placed a small clay vessel next to the bed. It held oil that wasn't the sort they used for cooking; it was thicker and smelled of roses. Which brought to mind the flowers sitting on the overturned washtub. Oliver didn't know when or where Felix had acquired the oil, but he was certainly grateful.

Felix applied the sweet-smelling stuff to Oliver's body with infinite patience and gentleness, until Oliver felt as open as a bloom on a hot summer day and was nearly desperate with need. "Please," he panted. His heart was racing so fast that he feared it might fail, and if it weren't for the distress it would cause Felix, Oliver would have welcomed that end. What better way to leave the world than wrapped in a lover's embrace, his body united with yours?

Oliver had rarely had penetrative sex, and never in a bed with his beloved's gaze fixed firmly on his. "I know you," Felix said as he moved deeper inside, making Oliver shudder and clutch him more tightly. "You will always be a part of my story. The important part. The... oh, gods, Olly, so good!... the core of it." An apt word choice as he thrust deep into Oliver.

The bed didn't creak and the new mattress took their motions gracefully. Oliver was on a ship in a tranquil sea. Or perhaps it was an island, surrounded by turquoise waters and inhabited by beautiful creatures, none of whom were as beautiful or as precious as the man inside him.

And then he lost track of where he was, because all that was important was Felix crying, "Olly!" as a great surge of bliss washed over them both, carrying them beneath the surface until they couldn't breathe, couldn't see, could only feel.

"Olly," Felix said again, this time with a sob.

They held each other, sleepless, for a long time.

Chapter Twenty

Oliver stood just outside the door to Farview cottage, bag in one hand, stroking Felix's tousled hair with the other.

"I want to beg you to stay," Felix said. "But you wouldn't."

"No, I wouldn't."

"Then I should beg you to let me go with you."

"I won't. Let's not be cross with each other. Not now."

Felix gave a reluctant nod. "Sometimes down on the rocks I'll find a starfish with one of its legs missing. Something's had a go at it, I expect. But there's the starfish still continuing its business, crawling along and searching for lunch, a new leg already starting to grow in. I envy those starfish."

"Humans are limited, aren't we?" Oliver swiped his thumb across Felix's cheek. "I love you. I never thought I'd say that to anyone. Thank you for giving me the chance."

"I love you too, don't I? Always bloody will."

There were no more words left to say, no more stories to share. Oliver, greedy as old Bowyd, leaned in for one last, quick kiss. Then he picked up the walking stick, turned on his heel, and fled.

The sun seemed to begrudge rising this morning and didn't bother to fight the clinging gray clouds. That suited Oliver's mood perfectly.

He made his way down the path and almost abandoned the stick when he reached the bottom. But he sensed that he'd soon be needing it even on flat land, so he took it with him to High Street, where Jamie waited beside his coach and dragons. He thankfully appeared to be sober at this early hour.

"Why are all the boats still in the harbor?" Oliver asked by way of greeting.

"Storm. It'll be here by midday."

Oliver thought of Felix alone in the cottage, listening to the wind howl and the rain pelt the roof and windows. He'd be cold with no fire to warm him. Hopefully Teddy would send Horace Loowin up soon, so Felix could learn how to use peat. Summer's end wasn't far off.

"So are ya comin'?"

Oliver shook himself as he realized that Jamie had been speaking to him. "Sorry. Shall I pay you now?"

"Aye. Two coppers."

"I thought it was three."

"That was one-way, Bythington to Croftwell. Round trip is five, and you're on a return ticket. So two coppers."

Oliver handed over the coins and climbed into the carriage. He had it to himself. He patted his breast pocket and heard the reassuring crinkle of the envelope, then checked his trouser pocket for the heavy, tingly feel of the talisman. Everything that was important, plus his bag and stick. He was ready to return to Greynox.

After a few minutes of clucking to his dragons, Jamie climbed onto the coach and they rattled away.

Oliver hadn't slept much the previous night; he'd wanted to savor every minute of Felix's company. And he hadn't managed any breakfast today, despite Felix's urgings. So he ought to have been tired and hungry as the coach bounced along, but all he felt was the stinging ache of loss. Something had been torn from him, leaving a gaping, bloody hole that no amount of ogrewort tea would help. The agony was centered in his chest but radiated to that spot in his belly where pain had recently come to live, and it stretched out into his limbs and head.

He squeezed into a miserable ball at the far corner of the seat and closed his eyes to everything. He didn't know what scenery they passed. For all he knew, Jamie could have been taking him across the surface of the moon.

The trip to Bythington seemed endless. When the coach finally stopped at the train station, Oliver dismounted feeling weak and old.

"Thank you for the ride, Jamie."

"When will I be expectin' ye back?"

Oliver gave a noncommittal shrug, waved, and shuffled to the ticket counter. He bought a first-class ticket this time, cost be damned. He knew he couldn't endure the close company of merry families on their way home from holidays.

As it turned out, he had to share his compartment, but only with an older gentleman who took one look at him, sniffed disapprovingly, and reburied his face in the newspaper. Oliver made the mistake of glancing at the headline, which had to do with the six condemned protesters, and his stomach lurched. Gods, what if he couldn't save them? The only proof was via the talisman, and that seemed so flimsy compared to the power of the wealthy mill owners, the justice system, and Parliament. But it was all he had.

He remembered one of Felix's more fanciful tales, this one about a small crab that had decorated its shell with a tiny colored stone, and then another, and so on, until it had built an entire island upon itself. Felix insisted that the island was still there—a few hours offshore from Croftwell—and was the only home to a marine bird called a squagrattle, which had the ability to sing unfavorable winds into a more orderly direction. The moral of the story, as best Oliver could tell, was that even a very insignificant person could, with enough patience and foresight, achieve something great.

Feeling insignificant indeed, Oliver checked his pockets for the envelope and the talisman, then fell into a waking stupor that was not at all restful.

He felt as if he aged ten years during the trip to Greynox.

He emerged, hollowed out and bleary, from Griffin's Den station.

Greynox pressed down on him at once: the early evening rush of pedestrians, carriages, and omnibuses; the cries of street vendors and the scrape of wheels on cobblestones; the reek of filth; the looming brown and gray buildings. Although he knew these streets intimately, he felt alien and unwanted.

It would have been polite to wait until morning before calling on Massey and Archer. But Oliver was learning not to take time for granted. Better to get it over with, even if he was being rather rude.

The distance to their house wasn't far, just a bit over a mile, but he took a cab instead of walking. The driver had none of Jamie's charm and, as far as Oliver could tell, wasn't particularly concerned about the welfare of his scruffy dragon.

Oliver's destination was in a nice neighborhood of the sort inhabited by moderately successful professionals. Three- and four-story houses of brick and plaster cuddled cozily, some with tidy window boxes, and the passersby wore well-made but not overly fashionable clothing. Oliver had gone to school in this neighborhood, which was slightly better than his own. It had probably been an attempt by Stephen Webb to help Oliver better himself, and for that he ought to be thankful.

He found the address Enoch had given him and knocked on the door, expecting it to be answered by an irritated housekeeper. Instead he was greeted by a tall, muscular man of perhaps forty, his sandy hair pulled back in a tail and his expression welcoming.

"Can I help you?" Not a Greynox accent, but not Crofter either. Something rural to the east, most likely.

"Erm, yes, I hope so. I'm looking for Mr. Massey and Mr. Archer. Enoch Andox sent me." He expected the door to be slammed in his face.

Instead, the man grinned. "The wizard! How is he doing? It's been a few years since— I'm sorry, how horribly rude of me. Please, do come in." As soon as Oliver entered the foyer, his host turned and bellowed, "Jule, we've a visitor the wizard sent us!"

Jule. That would be Julian Massey, Oliver recalled, picturing the slip of paper with Enoch's handwriting. Which meant he was talking with Mr. Archer.

Another man joined them almost immediately. He looked to be about the same age as his companion but much smaller, with delicate features and sharp eyes. His dark brown hair was mussed, as if he'd been running his fingers through it. He didn't look capable of helping orchestrate a battle against deadly pirates, but Felix said he had. Felix had also said these two men were lovers, which Oliver easily believed based on the fond way they looked at each other.

Oliver realized he was staring. "I'm so sorry. I'm Oliver Webb, and—"

"Are you quite well, Mr. Webb?" asked Massey, who had stepped forward and was peering up at Oliver with concern.

Gods, did he look that awful already? "I've just arrived from Croftwell," he said by way of explanation.

"And we're being terribly inhospitable. Please excuse us."

"I've interrupted you. I'll go and—"

"We won't hear of it," said Archer, taking his arm. "You've sparked our curiosity, and if we have to wait for it to be satisfied, we shall both wither and die like a garden in a drought. I'm Kit Archer, by the way. And this is Dr. Julian Massey. It's a pleasure to meet you, Mr. Webb."

They took his coat, bag, and stick and then led him into a sitting room that he liked at once. The furniture looked comfortable, and the walls and shelves were filled with pictures and objects too numerous and varied to take in. Noticing his reaction, Massey chuckled. "We've picked up a few things on our travels."

Archer nodded. "I've a knack for discovering small treasures and keeping them close."

They steered Oliver to an oversized leather armchair, and he collapsed into it with little grace. A certain amount of fussing followed, in which Oliver was offered wine or tea and opted for the latter, causing his hosts to disappear for a few minutes and then return with tea things and digestive biscuits. Somewhere along the line they also settled on first names.

"Sorry we've not more to offer," Julian said. "We just returned yesterday from a trip abroad and haven't laid in groceries yet."

"This is fine, thank you. It wasn't as if you were expecting me."

"No, but we're glad to have you here. Tell me, how do you know the wizard? You don't sound like you're from Urchin Cove."

"I'm a Noxer. But I've been staying in Croftwell these past weeks. I...." He stumbled for a moment before forging ahead. "Mr. Andox's grandson Felix is my lover."

He hadn't expected Julian and Kit to be aghast, considering their own situation. But he also hadn't expected them to look so happy.

"That's delightful!" Kit exclaimed. "The wizard's spoken of him. He thinks rather highly of his grandson."

Well, that made Oliver happy. "As he should. Felix is special."

He was comfortable in this chair with his tea and slightly stale biscuits, with these two handsome men smiling at him and a room full of interesting things to look at. He wished he had time to hear some of his hosts' stories—he knew they must have many. But they would want to get on with their evening, and Oliver's strength was flagging. He needed to get his business done, but he wasn't sure how to begin.

"Felix told me about the two of you and the pirates. I'm not sure how accurate it was—he embellishes a bit sometimes—but it's an impressive tale."

Kit had sat next to Julian on a love seat with an intricately carved wooden frame, his arm around Julian's shoulders. "My Jule is an impressive man. If you had only seen him confronting the scourge of the seas, the—"

"Darling," Julian said gently. "I don't think Oliver is here to listen to our exploits. I'm sorry, Oliver, you can take your time if you wish. But if you'll excuse my saying so, you appear exhausted, so don't worry about being blunt."

Gods, Oliver liked these two. He could imagine being friends with them, and he suspected they'd get on famously with Felix. But there wasn't time.

"In fact, I've come to beg your help. I'm trying to put something right, you see, and... and I'm afraid I don't know how. Mr. Andox recommended I speak with you."

"We'll be happy to help however we can," said Julian. He and Kit leaned forward, intent on whatever Oliver was about to say.

Oliver wished Felix were here; he'd be so much better at this.

Oliver wasn't even sure where to begin—all the pieces seemed so intertwined. After a fortifying swallow of tea, he started with his mother's move from Croftwell to Greynox.

It ended up being a longer tale than he expected, especially due to Julian and Kit's questions. Partway through the telling, they asked him to pause while they disappeared for fifteen minutes or so. Oliver took the opportunity to inspect a few of the room's fascinating items.

When they returned, they were smiling. "Please join us for dinner," Julian said.

"Oh, I couldn't put you out—"

"You're not. It's nothing fancy; just fish and chips from the shop around the corner, and the fish isn't as good as you're used to in Croftwell. But it'll do. Please join us."

Although Oliver's only food that day had been digestive biscuits, he wasn't hungry. But he still had more to tell them, and he couldn't refuse their warm and open hospitality. So he followed them into a dining room that contained a long table partly covered in papers. "I'm sorry," Julian said. "Sometimes my work spills out into this room."

"And the kitchen," added Kit. "And the sunroom. And the bedroom. It's as if his study and his surgery have some sort of creeping paper-and-book disease and are intent on infecting the rest of the house. Despite that single flaw, Dr. Julian Massey is the most talented physician in all of Greynox."

Julian blushed. "I am not. Kit, like your Felix, is prone to words of embellishment." But he looked pleased.

Kit brought them plates and bottles of cider and then distributed packets of piping hot food. Oliver discovered that he did have an appetite after all, and he told the rest of his story as they ate. He omitted his own curse as immaterial. By the time he finished, the food was gone.

They sat around the cluttered table in silence, Oliver toying with his empty bottle. Julian and Kit wore matching expressions of grim concern.

"You've endured a great deal," Julian said at last.

"But there's nothing you can do. I understand. Thank you for—"

"Wait. I didn't say that."

Kit leaned toward Oliver. "I'm firmly of the belief that one must never give up hope, no matter how impossible the situation feels. It's a philosophy that has worked well for us. And you've come all this way. Give us a few moments to think."

Oliver leaned his forehead on his hand and nodded.

"Penelope, do you think?" Julian asked Kit quietly.

"She doesn't have the influence to change the course of justice."

"No, but she *does* have the influence to attract a powerful crowd. She could convene an audience for Oliver's... demonstration."

Oliver looked up, a tiny sprig of optimism sprouting within him. "An audience?"

Kit rubbed his chin thoughtfully. "Yes, that might work."

He turned to Oliver. "Penelope Hutton is a journalist. She's quite a pioneer, really. First she managed to get hired by the *Greynox Times* despite being a woman, and then she somehow got assigned to writing about things other than who wore what and who's marrying whom. But then she quit the *Times* because she was frustrated with the manner in which they approach certain issues. Now she publishes the sort of pamphlets and broadsheets that give the aristocracy apoplexy. And she gets away with it because her father's a viscount and her husband a baron. Which makes her a baroness, of course, but she gets cross if we call her that."

Oliver had never met a member of the nobility, and he didn't have the general impression that they would care about his plight. "She could help?"

Julian answered. "Perhaps. What if she arranged a gathering?" he asked Kit. "She could invite Lord Stewtottle from the justice ministry and a few other witnesses besides. They might be able to halt the executions directly, or petition the queen for pardons, or... I don't know. I'm not a solicitor. But they could do *something*."

Oliver pictured himself standing in front of a group of men with titles as long as their arms. The sort of men who lived in huge mansions near the palace and also kept estates in the country, men who could trace their lineage back a thousand years. But then he remembered that he could trace his lineage even farther, to the people who'd lived on the moors long before this kingdom existed. And to a prince of the water fae, for that matter.

"That sounds very promising," he said. "But why would the baroness help me?"

Kit hopped up from his chair and rubbed his hands together. "Because this is exactly what she's interested in. The things she publishes are exposés on the conditions of Greynox's downtrodden. She's pushing very hard for reforms. That's how we know her, in fact. Jule devotes his practice to caring for the poor"—he paused to give Julian a proud smile—"and sometimes she interviews him. Jule sees and hears all sorts of things from his patients."

"Yes," Julian said. "I'm sure she'd be very interested in the events you witnessed. We haven't spoken to her about any of it—as I said, we've been out of the country since February—but I'd be very surprised if this hasn't been one of her concerns. Will this do for you, Oliver, do you think?"

Oliver wanted to cry with gratitude but managed to keep his eyes dry. "Yes, very well. I don't know how to thank you."

"Excellent. We'll speak to her, but in the morning if you don't mind. It's rather late."

"Oh, of course." Oliver had lost track of time completely, but the large clock on the sideboard said it was nearly ten. He had no idea he'd been talking so long. He stood. "What time would you like me to come by tomorrow?"

Julian and Kit exchanged a look. "Where are you staying tonight, Oliver?" Kit asked.

He hadn't given it much thought. His stash of coppers was running low, but he knew how to find a cheap room. "I hadn't decided yet."

"Good, because you're staying with us."

"Oh, I couldn't—"

"Of course you could. We'll be terribly offended if you don't. We've a perfectly lovely guest room upstairs that hardly ever gets used, and that's a shame and a waste. And it's a distance from our room, so you needn't worry about us keeping you awake, even if we're loud."

Julian blushed beet-red, and Oliver laughed for possibly the first time since he'd left Felix. "To hear Felix tell it, your romance is quite legendary."

"Oh, the stories I could tell you!"

"Which you won't," Julian inserted quickly. "Darling, let's get poor Oliver settled in before he collapses."

"Another time, then." Kit grinned widely.

Somehow Oliver's opportunity to refuse their offer seemed to have passed. Not that he wanted to refuse—he wasn't sure he could make it across the city in his current state. In any case, within minutes Kit was rushing upstairs to prepare the room, while Julian collected a jug of water and some peppermint candies in case Oliver might want them later. After fetching Oliver's bag, they all walked up a flight of broad stairs, down a hall, and into a room with a large window and paintings of seascapes.

"It's a bit dusty, I'm afraid," Julian said.

"It's wonderful."

"It's quite bright during the day. I have an aversion to dark, musty rooms. This one looks down at the garden, which may or may not be a disaster. We've a gardener, but I'm not sure how attentive he was in our absence."

"He's due in the morning, though," Kit added, "and he is quite decorative himself."

Julian snorted and shooed him out of the room, then turned back to Oliver. In a quieter voice than usual, he said, "Are you sure you're not ill? I'm a doctor, remember?"

As if in reaction, Oliver's gut wrenched with a painful spasm and his knees nearly gave out. He sat heavily on the mattress. "It's not.... That's not why I came here."

"I know. But healing is what I do, whenever I can. I worked hard to become a physician for exactly that purpose. It makes me feel useful," he added with a small smile.

Oliver felt obscurely guilty for being incurable. "I've seen doctors already. It's the flash-curse. It hit me as well, you see, but it's going more slowly."

Julian frowned with concern. "What about wizards?"

"Can't help either. It's all right. I've... I've made my peace with it. At least I was given enough time to know Felix."

"Not long after I met Kit, I came very close to dying. But even in that state, I knew I'd loved a good man and that I'd been a stronger person than I'd thought possible. That knowledge did a great deal to ease the sting."

Unable to speak, Oliver nodded. It was comforting to know that Julian understood and could empathize so well.

"Is it all right if I share this with Kit?"

Surprised that Julian sought permission, Oliver blinked. "I assumed you would."

"I would give my life for that man. But that doesn't mean he's entitled to every confidence."

"It's fine. It's not a secret. I just... it's not directly relevant to the issue at hand."

"Get some rest," Julian said gently. "You have heroism to perform tomorrow." He turned and left, closing the door behind him.

There was a washstand with towels in the corner of the room. Oliver shuffled over and avoided catching a glimpse of himself in the mirror. He hung his jacket on a hook, removed his shirts, and splashed some water on his face. He knew he looked disreputable, his whiskers growing in and his hair unruly, but there wasn't much he could do about that. The baroness and her audience would have to take him as he was.

Oliver removed his shoes and socks. He moved to unbutton his trousers, but first—for perhaps the tenth time that day—he compulsively checked his pocket for the talisman.

It wasn't there.

Chapter Twenty-One

A feverish search through his clothing and bag did not produce the talisman. Oliver looked again anyway, and again, until his eyes were bleary and his legs so weak that he thudded to the floor.

"Nothing I can do about it now," he whispered. He must have dropped the little metal figure somewhere along the way, and now it could be anywhere in Greynox. His carelessness had just cost the lives of six people.

Disgusted with himself, in pain, and thoroughly wrung out, he got into bed. It was a nice one, the mattress welcoming, the sheets fresh and crisp and sweet-scented. But he was in it alone.

"Gods, I'm so sorry." Oliver sat at Julian and Kit's table, slumping so heavily that he was in danger of falling off the chair. After waking, he'd searched the bedroom itself for the talisman and, when Julian came to check on him, admitted what had happened. Julian and Kit had looked through the foyer, the parlor, the dining room, and the stairway, but they hadn't found it either. "I'm such a bloody failure."

Julian hovered nearby. "You're not. You had a long journey while unwell. It could easily happen to anyone. Ask Kit how many things I've misplaced during our travels."

"Many," Kit agreed. "He gets his nose in a book and the rest of the world disappears. If I weren't so big and stubborn, I daresay he'd have misplaced me by now."

Oliver appreciated their efforts to comfort him, but there was a difference between forgetting a hat and losing the one item that might have saved lives. "I know I had it when I got off the train," he repeated for the third or fourth time. "But I might have dropped it at Griffin's Den station somehow. Or it could have escaped my pocket when I was in the cab. Or... it could be anywhere in Greynox. Worse than a needle in a haystack."

"We could visit some wizards and see if they can get us another," Kit offered.

But Oliver shook his head. "Enoch said it was unique."

They sat in heavy silence for several minutes before Oliver sighed and used the table to lever himself to his feet. "Thank you for... everything. You've been very kind." He knew he should say more. These men had gone far beyond the usual boundaries of hospitality, and he was truly grateful. But he could barely speak. He'd lost too much of himself.

As he started toward the door, Kit blocked him. "Where are you going?"

Oliver had no answer. Perhaps he ought to just throw himself in the Methes and be done with it. A quick watery death seemed better than a slow one on land.

Kit didn't move. "Please don't leave. You're welcome here as long as you like, and we'd both be miserable to see you go. If our situation were reversed and one of us had appeared at your cottage in dire straits, how would you feel if we then wandered off?"

That was an unfair blow. Of course Oliver would be unhappy, and he'd worry, and he'd blame himself for not doing more to help. He sagged so suddenly that Kit had to catch him to keep him from hitting the floor. Kit helped him out of the dining room and into a chair in the parlor. Oliver wasn't certain he'd ever get out of it again.

"I don't want to burden you," he said miserably.

"You're not," Julian replied firmly. "We're friends now, and friends help one another."

What Oliver most wanted right now was to curl up around the pain, lose himself in memories of Felix, and let the curse finish its work. But he nodded. "Then I'll ask you one thing more, if I may. I've an envelope in my coat." At least he hadn't lost that as well. "After I'm dead, please post it. It will ensure that Felix inherits Farview."

Although Julian and Felix looked unhappy, they agreed, and that was a relief. At least Oliver would accomplish that much.

"Oliver," Kit said thoughtfully, "I think you should speak to Penelope anyway."

"What's the point? I haven't any proof and she won't believe me."

"But she might. You have no motive to lie, and she is fully aware of what those bastards who own the factories are capable of. I'll wager she'll do some of her own investigating—she's good at it—and perhaps she'll find some other proof. It's at least worth a try, don't you think?"

Kit was right. Oliver had nothing to lose at this point, and it would cost the baroness no more than a little time. "All right. Thank you."

"Excellent! I'll send a message and see when she's available."

Oliver measured the pain and the extent to which his body was weakening. "I think... it had better be soon."

Gravely, Julian nodded his agreement.

"I'll go at once."

Before anyone could stop him, Kit swept out of the room. A few moments later, the front door shut quite loudly, making Julian chuckle. "Sorry. I keep waiting for him to learn patience, but I think I'm destined to be disappointed. May I get you anything? I've some heal-all in my surgery, and also poppy juice."

"Thank you, but it won't help. Nothing seems to, except ogrewort."

Julian's eyebrows rose. "Interesting. But I'm sorry—I've none of that, and I don't think I could find it. It doesn't grow anywhere near Greynox. It's not in season anyway."

"It is on the moor near Farview, apparently. The ghosts won't say who or what is responsible for that."

"Food then? Tea?" Julian squinted at him. "No, I think you'd rather rest. One moment." He hurried away, only to return a moment later with a thick quilt, which he handed to Oliver. "I've been known to fall asleep in my surgery when I've a patient recovering there. This blanket is very comfortable for naps. It was sewn by a friend in Urchin Cove."

Oliver almost expected to see octopuses and roses on the fabric, but it turned out to be a considerably more staid pattern in blues and greens. It reminded him a bit of waves, and when he spread it over himself, he felt nicely cocooned.

"I used to be strong." He let out a shuddering sigh.

"You still are."

Oliver dozed for some time. It wasn't a deep sleep, so he was dimly aware of the street noises outside, and Julian's footsteps on the wood floor, and eventually Kit's return and their quiet conversation. But he couldn't rouse himself to respond. He felt like a bit of flotsam bobbing on the sea, unable to get to shore and yet incapable of sinking beneath the surface.

Eventually he stirred, and Julian came at once. "I've some coppers left," Oliver informed him. "Enough to pay to dispose of my corpse, I believe." He'd woken up thinking that this was important.

Julian gestured dismissively. "All right, fine. Look, Penelope is up in Lathinstoke and won't be back until late tonight. Her husband—he's a good sort, I like him—promised she'll come around here first thing tomorrow. Will that do?"

Oliver figured he had at least that much time left. "Thank you."

"We'll help you up to your room so you can rest more comfortably."

His first instinct was to acquiesce. A bed would be preferable to the chair. But then he thought of something else—one more loose thread in his rapidly unraveling life. "I need to... run an errand, actually."

"I'll do it for you."

"I'm afraid this is something I must do myself." He gritted his teeth. "I need to go see Stephen Webb."

JULIAN TRIED to argue about it, at first politely and then with a good measure of exasperation. "You ought to be in bed!" he exclaimed. But Oliver still possessed enough strength to be obstinate, and he managed to get out of the chair and shuffle to the foyer where his coat and stick were.

Kit joined them partway through their disagreement, watching silently. But when Julian moved to block Oliver's way to the door, Kit intervened. "Jule, he needs this."

"He needs to be tied to the bed before he kills himself with his foolishness!"

"He's going to see the man who raised him. Need I remind you of you and your father?"

Julian slumped and massaged his forehead. "Fuck," he said very succinctly.

"Precisely. Look, I'll accompany Oliver and make sure he doesn't collapse in the street. He'll finish his business and I'll get him back here directly. Meanwhile, you can make one of your lovely restorative soups, and after we return you can feed him and tuck him in."

Oliver wasn't thrilled to be spoken of as if he weren't there, but he was also wise enough not to intervene. Not when he could see Julian giving in. Kit saw it too and sealed it with a kiss on top of Julian's head and a pat on his backside that made Julian blush.

"Thank you, my treasure," Kit said. "You can make up for it by ordering me about as much as you wish later tonight."

That turned Julian's cheeks a brighter shade of red.

But it worked. Within a few minutes Oliver was being helped into a cab by Kit. "It's not far," Oliver protested, more out of pride than anything else.

"No, but if you keel over on me, I'll have Julian to answer to, and I most definitely don't want that. Besides, this way we are contributing to the economy by paying coppers to our driver."

It was just as well. Oliver probably wouldn't have made it to Varnham Street. Every jostle of the cab had him clenching his fists and struggling not to cry out, and even though he had Kit's help dismounting, he had to spend several moments leaning on his stick before recovering enough to move forward.

The house he'd grown up in looked the same as always. The stone exterior was a tad dirtier, perhaps, but the paint on the door and window trim was in good condition.

"I don't even know whether he still lives here. Or whether he lives at all."

"There's an easy way to find out."

Easy wasn't the word Oliver would have chosen. But he lurched his way to the door and struggled up the three steps, Kit hovering at his elbow.

"Do you want me to move away?" Kit asked. "I can wait over there." He gestured at the streetlamp on the corner.

"No. Please stay."

Knocking was one of the more courageous things Oliver had ever done.

He didn't know the middle-aged housekeeper who answered the door. She looked startled, probably at his condition, and Oliver spoke quickly, before she could slam the door closed.

"Hello. I'm here to see Mr. Webb, please."

"Who's calling?"

Oliver let out a huge breath at the confirmation that Webb was there. "Just... tell him Oliver's here, please."

She peered at him skeptically and shot Kit a genuine glare, but then she nodded and gently closed the door. Oliver put his free hand against the frame to steady himself. Webb might very well refuse to speak with him. Or if he did make an appearance, it might be only to curse Oliver, to heap on a final few words of scorn. Gods, Oliver was too weak for this. Would have been too weak even if he weren't dying from a curse. But when Oliver glanced at Kit, he was reminded of Felix's stories. Kit had faced pirates; the least Oliver could do was talk to one old man.

The door opened with such suddenness that Oliver flinched back and would have fallen if not for Kit's steadying hands. And there was the man he'd known as his father. Webb had aged considerably over the past decade. His muscles had turned to fat, his hair had gone thin and white, and the lines on his face were now deeply etched crevices.

He and Oliver stared at each other for what felt like a century.

"Do you need money?" Webb asked at last. He didn't sound angry—which surprised Oliver—just wary.

"No. That's not why I'm here."

"You look ill."

"I am."

Webb's eyes flickered to Kit. "Who's that?"

"A friend. I'm... I require some assistance right now, and he's providing it." In several ways, but there was no need for Oliver to explain. "I won't stay long. I wanted to tell you something."

Webb moved back a bit, his eyes narrowing. "What?"

Deep breath. "Thank you."

That took Webb by surprise. His mouth dropped open and he sputtered something unintelligible. Oliver decided to continue.

"I know that my mother was pregnant by another man when you married her, and I know you were aware of that. But you never said anything about it to me, or to anyone else, as far as I know. You never acted as if I'm a bastard. And after Mother died, you kept me on as if I were your own. You gave me a good home, an education... everything I needed. I wish we'd had a better relationship, but I expect some of that was on me. I wasn't easy to get along with. But I am grateful for what you did for me, and I wanted you to know that."

It was a long speech and it left him winded, as if he were using up the last of his words. Still, he felt better for having said it. A bitter sore that had burned inside him was eased.

Webb said nothing for a very long time, so long that Oliver nearly turned on his heel and left. He didn't need a response; that wasn't what this visit had been about.

Then Webb cleared his throat. "I've always thought of you as my son, you know. I still do. And I did try to be a good father. I... didn't know how."

Oliver nodded.

"Do you need anything from me, Oliver?"

"Nothing more. You've given me what I needed."

They shook hands. A part of Oliver mourned that they had so little to share, yet he was also glad that they'd had this much. At least he wouldn't die with regrets.

Oliver turned around and Kit helped him down the stairs. Oliver felt Webb's gaze as he lurched to the waiting cab and, again with Kit's assistance, climbed in. But he didn't look back.

"Thank you," he whispered to Kit through gritted teeth as the cab rolled away. Lights flashed in front of his eyes, and the agony in his midsection was so severe that he couldn't sit up straight. Nevertheless, he was glad he'd made this particular journey.

On the way back, they encountered a delay due to an overturned carriage blocking traffic. Some rich person's sleek dragon was prancing around, refusing to be steadied prior to removal from its traces. It puffed little blasts of sparks, making gawkers shriek and scramble back.

"Damn fool," Kit growled. "A dragon like that isn't meant to pull a bloody city carriage."

Oliver agreed but didn't have the energy to say so. He was shaking now, although he didn't feel cold. Didn't feel anything, in fact, except the shrieking pain, as if a moor-cat was inside him and trying to claw and bite its way out. He had a vague impression of Kit taking him in his arms and holding him tightly, but all he heard was the rushing of blood in his ears and the staccato pounding of his heart.

The carriage jerked forward, making him cry out.

No. He needed to hold on just a little longer. Just until tomorrow when he could tell his story to the baroness. Not so long. He tried to slow his lungs and count out the seconds one by one. Sixty. Yes, there he was, another minute closer to his goal. He would fight for those minutes, dammit.

Then Kit was nearly carrying him out of the cab and up to the house, and Oliver was counting his seconds, and the world was growing dark and spinning away. He heard the call of a gull and the crash of waves against rocks, the creak of ropes as wind bellied a sail. He heard the soft song of wind rustling the grasses on the moor. The wind and the sea both called his name, which made him smile because they knew him.

Oliver, said the breeze.
Ollyro, said the sea.
Olly, said—
Felix?

Chapter Twenty-Two

Sensations reached Oliver piecemeal. Raised voices. The feeling of moving followed by something soft beneath him. Fingers on a pulse point, a hand holding his, a cool damp cloth on his forehead. The bitter, grassy taste of ogrewort tea. And a beloved face staring down at him, warm eyes dark with concern and curls more obstreperous than ever.

Was this the afterlife?

No, the afterlife wouldn't have the sharp smell of disinfectant. And nobody there would be softly telling him a ridiculous story about a Crofter who attempted to collect clouds.

Oliver concentrated on focusing his gaze. He might not be dead, but surely he was hallucinating. Maybe the curse had reached his brain.

"Felix?" he rasped.

"Oh, love." A long-fingered hand stroked the hair out of Oliver's face.

"How?"

"Train, of course."

Oliver's poor, muddled brain tried to make sense of that—or of anything, for that matter—and failed. No matter. The agony had ebbed and Felix was with him, and he'd enjoy that for now. Explanations could come later.

Time passed hazily, sensory impressions becoming sharp only briefly before fading away. At one point he thought someone was carrying him, and sometimes he sipped water or broth. The only real constant was Felix, who touched him and spoke to him and tended him.

When clarity finally began to dawn, Oliver had a terrible thought.

"The baroness."

He was supposed to speak with her—he remembered that—but the appointment must have passed by now.

"Have you been dreaming of royalty, love?"

Before Oliver could muster an answer, Julian spoke. "He means Penelope Hutton."

"I missed her," Oliver croaked.

Julian floated into Oliver's field of vision. "Don't worry about it. We can reschedule when you're feeling up to it. And you're doing quite a bit better today, I think."

"The ogrewort."

"Hmm." Julian's expression was inscrutable. "May I ask you something? The symptoms you experience, do they tend to wax and wane like this?"

"Ebb and flow," Oliver corrected him nonsensically. "When I have the ogrewort, I get better for a while."

Felix had placed a protective hand on Oliver's chest. "Why do you ask, Julian?"

"Curiosity. I've very little experience with curses such as this, so I've done a bit of reading. They're, erm, rarely this slow in progressing. The other victims at the mill, those who didn't perish at once, passed away within days. And I haven't found any historical references to a flash-curse doing anything but getting steadily worse."

Oliver didn't know why it mattered. Doctors worried about such things, he supposed. Perhaps Julian could get a medical journal article out of him.

"Ogrewort," he repeated.

"Yes, but it's only—" Julian stopped himself and gave a small smile.

"Never mind. I'm very pleased to see you feeling better. Let us know when you're feeling up to it, and we'll arrange for Penelope to come."

"I can—"

"Not yet," Felix interrupted. "When you can get yourself dressed and cross the room unaided, then we'll consider it. In the meantime, if you eat some real food and have a good rest, I'll tell you my latest story when you wake."

There was no use arguing, not when Felix's chin was set so stubbornly. And Oliver had the optimistic view that he had one more rally left in him. But Felix seemed to think Oliver required a bit more incentive, because he smiled and rubbed Oliver's bristled chin. "These will feel scratchy when we kiss."

"Shave them off."

"Later, perhaps. I'm going to tell you one thing now that I fancy you'll be glad to hear."

"I'm glad to hear you say anything."

"Do you see that, Julian? My man is laid out limp as old sea-fern yet he's still charming, he is." Felix grinned widely. "Olly, I have your talisman."

Oliver's heart stuttered, as did his mouth. "M-m-my.... Wh-what?"

"Your magic whatsit that my granddad gave you."

"How?"

Felix shook his head. "I'll tell you later. You have to fulfill your part of the bargain first."

Maybe taking on information more slowly was a good idea. Oliver felt as if he didn't understand anything right now. Well, except that Felix loved him—that much Oliver knew for certain. Why else would Felix be taking such attentive care of him?

Julian gave another inscrutable little smile and left to fetch some food. Meanwhile, Felix propped pillows behind Oliver so he was able to sit up, and then spent some time fussing with both the blankets and the curtains until he was satisfied. Oliver used the time to finally take in his surroundings and realized he was back in Julian and Kit's guest room, now transformed into a sickroom, complete with a cot a few feet away.

"Have you been sleeping there?" Oliver asked, pointing.

"Yes. We brought it up from Julian's surgery. You chose an excellent location to collapse, you did. He has all the right equipment, and he and Kit make wonderful hosts."

"How long has it been?"

Felix sighed. "Five days."

That was too unfathomable to comment on. How could all those hours disappear so easily? And, his mind wondered nastily, how much longer would the ogrewort's effects last?

Julian returned just long enough to leave a tray and exchange a few quiet words with Felix. Then Felix sat down and spooned a meaty porridge mixture into Oliver's mouth, as if Oliver were an infant. It tasted entirely bland, but it also felt surprisingly good to get something solid inside him. There was some lukewarm mint tea and a glass of pinkfruit juice, which must have cost someone a shocking amount of money. The minor feast was followed by a face-washing and hair-combing, courtesy of Felix. All of that quite simple activity tired Oliver enough that he didn't complain when Felix patted down the pillows and helped him lie flat. Oliver drifted off almost immediately, and while he might have been imagining things, he had the impression that Felix was singing... a lullaby?

"I'M GOING to eat you into the poorhouse."

Oliver looked at the assortment of empty dishes stacked on the side table and gave Julian and Kit a rueful look. As if the porridge had roused a beast within, he'd awakened ravenous. Felix had been entirely pleased to help shovel an inordinate amount of food down Oliver's gullet.

His hosts looked happy at the damage he'd done to their larder.

"I like cooking," Julian said. "It took me a long time to learn. My earliest efforts were appalling. Now it's nice to see people enjoying what I prepare."

Kit rubbed his own stomach. "Yes, and with more mouths to feed, some of us might be less tempted to enjoy overmuch."

Oliver guessed that they were growing tired of his litany of thank-yous, so he turned to Felix instead. "You made me a promise."

"Indeed." Felix was sitting on the edge of the bed, and now he settled in more comfortably. Julian and Kit took seats on small chairs flanking the window, looking like schoolboys eager for their bedtime story. They must have had ample opportunity to experience Felix's bard skills during Oliver's period of unconsciousness.

"This tale begins almost immediately after you left, Olly. I was sitting inside the cottage and trying not to cry. And I wasn't succeeding."

I WAS SITTING inside the cottage and trying not to cry. And I wasn't succeeding. In fact, I bawled like a baby, I did, until I felt so drained and empty it's a wonder I didn't wither and die. I tried to eat some breakfast but I had no appetite, so I went looking for the imps instead. But they were nowhere to be found on account of the incoming storm. It wasn't raining yet, but the wind had picked up and I could smell the fresh water coming in over the salt.

I went back inside the cottage and tidied a bit, and then I spent... I don't know. Hours, I expect. Sitting at the window and watching the sky darken. It fitted my mood. I couldn't help but think of Lyra Moon sitting in that very place for years and years, and I envied her because she knew her beloved would return. I knew mine wouldn't.

Before the winds got really bad, I should have fastened the shutters. But I didn't, and although the rain soon sheeted down so hard I couldn't see anything else, I didn't move from that spot.

You know, the building stones on either side of that window have those scratchings on them. I'd never paid them much mind before—you can find stones like that all over Croftwell. But as I sat there, the marks began to move. Crawling slowly, like snakes when it's cold out. Under other circumstances I would have been scared, but you'd washed all my emotions away, Olly. Let the snakes have me, I figured. What with my curse, they'd probably choke on me.

They didn't attack me, though. Stayed stuck to the wall, they did, but they rearranged into a shape. The same one that's on the stone near the ogrewort—a moor-cat, plain as day. I did something foolish then, but nobody's ever claimed I was clever. I touched the moor-cat. It wasn't anything more than a simple outline, right?

But then it wasn't. It jumped out of the stone, as real and solid as you please, with its fangs gleaming and its claws glinting.

I scrambled away but tripped over my own feet and fell behind the chair. Before the moor-cat could move or I could stand, the small octopuses on the chair came to life as well. They squirmed over to the cat, and climbed up its legs, and twisted their arms around its face. It was making the most horrible sounds. Screaming even louder than the wind.

A smart man would have run away then, even with the storm, or at least picked up a weapon of some kind. I could only watch, sitting there and gaping like a fish on a hook.

Then the girl appeared. Not from the stone wall—she just poofed from thin air, and I could see right through her. She marched over to the moor-cat and waved her hand as if she were shooing gnats. The octopuses returned to the chair and became nothing but fabric again. The cat stopped yowling. The girl looked straight at me and said, "You need to come with me."

Now, I've sighted ghosts before. I used to come to Farview now and then before you moved in, Olly, but if I stayed more than a few hours, the shadows would shift in ways they shouldn't, and the air would grow cold as ice, and I'd hear these little snatches of words I couldn't understand. The meaning was clear, though. I didn't belong and the ghosts wanted me gone. But I'd never seen them so clearly and never had a conversation with one.

"It's nasty out there," I said to her. "Please let me stay until the storm dies down." I didn't fancy making a trip down the cliff in that wind, and there was no other shelter atop the moor.

That little lass huffed at me as if I were the stupidest creature to ever vex the world.

"You can stay here forever. Our Oliver said so. You belong. But right now you've got to come outside so I can show you something."

Quarreling with spirits is unwise. But the storm was so heavy, I'd be blind as soon as I stepped outside. "Can't it wait until later?"

"No, it only works when the weather's like this. Come on; it isn't far. We'll show you the way."

I didn't even bother with shoes and a coat. Neither would do me any good against the water and mud. I followed that ghost out into the squall, and the moor-cat crowded close against my leg.

"Grab her fur!" the girl cried.

So I did, and although I couldn't see the ghost, the cat could. I ducked my head and closed my eyes—the wind and rain so thick it was even hard to breathe— and we struggled along. It occurred to me that I could end up walking straight off the cliff-edge. I'd have to trust the ghost and the cat.

She told me true: it wasn't far. Five minutes at most, although it was a long five minutes. We stopped suddenly. I could have been anywhere at all for all I could see, and the cold was digging into my flesh. I reckoned I might be the first Crofter in a generation to drown on dry land.

"Dig here!" the girl shouted.

"What?"

"Dig!"

Nothing but to do it. I fell to my knees and started scrabbling at the soil. It was saturated but gave easily, so that was good. But my hands cramped and my fingernails tore, and as far as I could tell, I was doing nothing but making a muddy little pond. I was ready to give up when my fingers touched something hard.

It was a bone. Bones, in fact. I'll wager they're a match for the ones in the National Museum. Which might have been interesting, but unearthing long-dead moor-cats wasn't my priority at the time.

"Found your bones." I had to shout to be heard. "Bring me back to the cottage." I couldn't possibly have found my own way, you see.

"Dig more," the girl said.

I don't pretend to know anything about ghosts or what they want and why. People are hard enough to suss out when they're alive, aren't they? But the lass was stuck on the idea and the moor-cat was watching. So I dug.

This time when I touched something solid, it wasn't a bone. It was wood and rectangular. A box, I realized.

"Carry it back," the girl ordered.

It was bloody heavy, I'll tell you that, and I had to clutch it under one arm so I could hold the cat's fur with my other hand. The walk back was even worse, with the wind directly in my face, but I was eager to know what was in that box, so I slogged as fast as I could.

Oh, it felt lovely to return to the cottage! Even without a fire, and with nothing but candles for light, it felt right snug compared to the outdoors.

I was soaked to the skin. I stripped—the girl paid no attention—and wrapped myself in one of Olly's lovely thick blankets, and then I inspected the box. After I wiped away the dirt, it was a plain thing. No markings, the wood crudely hewn, and with a rusty little lock holding it closed.

"I hope you're not going to make me go back out in this weather to get the key," I said.

The moor-cat lifted a paw and broke the lock with one good swipe. Handy creature it turned out to be. Inside the box was an old fabric bag, half-rotted, and inside that... oh, Olly. Silver coins, not even tarnished. Gold as well. Jewels.

I turned to the girl. "Someone's missing this. Who do I return it to?"

She laughed. "The last owner has been dead for over four hundred years. He doesn't need it anymore. It's yours now."

Normally, I would have been overjoyed. This was a treasure beyond all my dreams. But it all seemed dull and worthless, no more value than the muck I'd removed it from.

"Money means nothing to me now. I've lost my Olly."

She gave me another of those looks. "Not yet, silly man. You can use some of these shiny things to pay your way."

"Pay my way where?"

"To the city, of course."

I shook my head. "Olly doesn't want me there."

"Of course he does. He wants that more than anything. And you have to bring him what he needs."

She pointed at the shelf right over the bed, where I'd arranged those things from the beach near Urchin Cove. *Your* beach, Julian and Kit. A few nice shells and pretty stones. And there, next to a chunk of smooth driftwood, was Olly's talisman.

LOOKING PLEASED WITH HIMSELF, Felix took a drink of Oliver's water.

Oliver shook his head. "I had that talisman in my pocket when I left Farview. It was still there when I got off the train—I checked. How did it get onto that shelf?"

"Damned if I know," Felix said with a shrug. "And I'd swear it wasn't on the shelf before the storm hit. I'd tidied up around the bed and never saw it."

"Could it be the ghosts' doing?" Kit asked.

Nobody knew the answer to that. But it raised another question, which Oliver voiced. "Whether it was the ghosts or... something else... the issue is why. Why take the talisman from me, and why insist that Felix return it?"

Felix nodded. "I wondered that too. The girl and the cat disappeared as soon as they showed me the talisman, so I couldn't ask. I was stuck inside the cottage all night, worrying over it. Luckily the storm ended before dawn. I hurried down and bribed Jamie with one of those silver coins to go to Bythington instead of Urchin Cove that morning. And the whole ride there, and the entire time in that train, I fretted. At least I had a good idea where to look for you when I arrived."

Oliver frowned, thinking of bright, joyful Felix miserable and troubled because of him. And because of the interference of spirits. Maybe the long-dead grew bored and messed about with the living to entertain themselves. Well, that was fine for them, but he didn't want them bothering Felix.

Julian spoke next. "Felix arrived twenty minutes after the two of you left. We were looking forward to surprising you with the talisman when you returned. But when you got back...."

"I thought you were dead," Felix growled.

Oliver patted his hand. "Not quite. Where did the ogrewort come from?"

"Extra from the other day. I was hoping it was still fresh enough, in case you needed it. Which you bloody well did."

"But I imagine it's no good now." Which meant there were no more chances for Oliver to temporarily feel better. He needed to speak with the baroness while he still could.

"I don't think the ogrewort—" Julian began. Then he winced and shook his head, and Kit gave him a questioning look that he waved away. "Felix, may I ask you something?"

"Anything you like."

"Are you a healer?"

Felix burst into laughter. "Me? I'm just helping Olly out a bit. Nothing magic about that, I can assure you."

"Are you certain? I thought your grandfather once mentioned something about you having abilities."

"You heard that wrong, mate. I've the exact opposite of abilities, I do. It's a curse—unrelated to Olly's curse. I was born with mine. Magic goes wrong near me. It's why I've been staying away from your firestones. I nearly caught Olly's cottage on fire." Felix seemed almost cheerful about it, the way an acquaintance of Oliver's used to make jokes about his own missing eye. *An unfortunate circumstance*, they both seemed to believe, *but life goes on*.

Except when it didn't, as in Oliver's case. And he had things to do.

"Can I see the baroness tomorrow? I'll be on my feet before then." Oliver wasn't lying about that. He was feeling eager to stand and move around a bit. To accomplish what he could, when he could. He had to remind himself that even with the talisman, his story might not change a thing. But now his chances had improved.

Kit stood. "I'll go arrange it right now."

Chapter Twenty-Three

"I didn't want you to see me like this."

Oliver was struggling to walk across the room. He made it to the window, hung on to a chair for a moment, and turned back to the bed, collapsing heavily onto the mattress. Naked, because putting on clothes was too much effort right now.

"It doesn't make me love you any less," said Felix.

"But I'm—"

"Stop. I'm here. Do you want me to leave?" Felix gazed steadily at him, as if issuing a dare.

Oliver sighed. "No. I want you with me. But I'm being greedy like Bowyd."

"Oh, Bowyd can go hang. Now, do you need help with the chamber pot?"

By the time Kit returned, Oliver had made several circuits of the room, sat up long enough for Felix to shave him, and had another glass of pinkfruit juice. He was recovering in bed when Kit and Julian knocked on the door.

"It's your house," Oliver said when they came in. "You don't need permission to enter."

Kit rolled his eyes dramatically. "For the hundredth time, you are not an unwelcome intruder. Neither of you are. You're our valued guests, and I daresay old men like us are delighted to have a touch of adventure back in our predictable lives."

Oliver didn't believe most of that. Julian was only a decade older than him, and Kit just a few years more than that. Neither of them was anywhere close to decrepit. And in the years since they'd left Urchin Cove, they'd had enough excitement to fill a library. But he smiled because he'd learned already that Kit tended to flowery language, and both Kit and Julian were the kindest people he'd ever met. Felix had told him that they flat refused to accept any payment from him, despite the expenses they were incurring and irrespective of Felix's newfound wealth.

"Now," Kit said, "I've been to Penelope's, and she remains quite eager to hear your story. She's been thinking about how to receive it, in fact, and she's asked two things. First, is it all right if she brings a sizable audience? They're going to be highly skeptical, but she has the clout to persuade them to come."

Everyone looked at Oliver, who shrugged. "That's fine. I'll speak to the whole bloody Parliament if I have to."

"Nothing quite so dire, I think. Just several influential parties. Her other request might be more difficult, however. She asked if she could meet you at Hillard's instead of here."

Oliver frowned, but before he could respond, Felix made an irritated sound and said, "Why? Why force Olly to go tromping all the way across the bloody city? She knows he's ill."

"I don't think she realizes how ill. And Penelope, well, she has a taste for... theater. She's not one to go quietly about her business. The bigger, more public fuss she makes, the better results she gets. I think she wants the people she invites to be able to picture the scene exactly, which will happen better if they're standing right there. And I also suspect she wants to watch Hillard's reaction, if he's there."

The mention of his old employer made Oliver shudder, but he saw the logic in what she wanted. Although he didn't want to see the mill again—he'd visited it enough in his nightmares—he would do anything he could to maximize his chances for success. "All right."

"Are you certain?" asked Felix, and Julian looked concerned as well.

"Yes."

"All right," Kit said. "Ten o'clock tomorrow morning at the mill. But I'm going with."

"As am I," Julian said. "You might need muscle or medical help. Or simply some friends."

"I'm sure it will be quite a party," Oliver said sourly.

OLIVER SPENT the entire rest of the day alternately eating, walking, and catnapping, supervised at all times by Felix.

"Shouldn't you get some rest too?" Oliver asked as he ate dinner—working the cutlery by himself this time.

"I'm not tired."

"You've all of Greynox just outside the door and you're stuck inside with me. If you want to go to a museum, or—"

"Olly, I didn't come here to be a tourist. There's no place on the planet I'd rather be than with you."

Oliver smiled around a mouthful of roast beef. "How did someone like me ever get lucky enough to meet someone like you?"

Felix ducked his head and looked away. "My family and neighbors, they're all kind to me. They make sure I get by. But until you, nobody ever considered themselves fortunate to know me." He rubbed his eyes. "It means the world to me, Olly. Knowing that you value me."

Now Oliver had to put down his fork because his throat felt tight. "Other people do too, you know. Aygun said you're the soul of Croftwell. Colin Davies told me everyone worries about you. They care, Felix. They see who you are."

Felix sniffled and poked at the perfectly good roll on his plate. Then he looked up at Oliver with a frown.

"That reminds me.... I wasn't snooping, I promise. But I had to undress you after you collapsed on us, and when I was setting out your clothing later I found an envelope in your pocket. It's addressed to Colin Davies."

Well, damnation. Oliver hadn't wanted to discuss this topic, but he also didn't want to lie or be evasive.

"Yes. I'm meant to send it to him shortly before I die. It's some old legal trick related to the Periwinkle War, and I don't fully understand it, but he does. And that's what matters. It... serves as proof of my death."

"Why does Colin Davies need that?"

"So he can execute my will."

Felix's brows flew up. "Your will!"

"Farview. That's the only important thing that I own."

"Do you reckon your father will want to live there?"

"My fath—" Oliver shook his head. "I can't imagine him stepping foot anywhere near Croftwell. I'm not leaving anything to him. It's for you, Felix. Farview will be your home. I've told the ghosts, so they know to let you stay in peace."

Felix's eyes, still damp from the emotion moments earlier, went wide and his mouth fell open. "You've left Farview to me?" he whispered.

"Of course."

"Why?" It came out as almost a wail.

"Because I love that cottage and want it to be taken care of, and I know you will. Because I love *you* and want you to have a good home and not have to sleep in shacks and garden sheds."

Felix stood and came around the little table so he could wrap Oliver in his arms. He buried his face in Oliver's hair, which muffled his words a bit. "I had a plan, I did. I was bringing things in so you'd be so comfortable, you'd never want to leave. I was trying to trap you with rugs and copper washtubs and seashells."

Oliver had to laugh. "Your evil plan worked perfectly. I didn't want to leave. I think.... I don't know this, mind you. I've no proof at all. But I think even though I die here, a part of me will always be there. Not a ghost, although I'd gladly help guard the place for eternity. Some essential bit of me will remain. Does that make sense?"

"Yes." Felix sighed against him. "Crofters always return."

"And I am a Crofter. You helped me see that."

It was the complete truth. Despite having lived in Greynox his entire life, and despite Julian and Kit's hospitality, the city had felt alien to him since he arrived. Perhaps it always had been. He'd never truly felt as if he belonged. He'd attributed that to his upbringing and his nature, but in fact, he was simply in the wrong place.

"I'll look after your cottage, Olly. I'll feed your imps and chat with your ghosts. And I'll sit at your window looking out at the sea and know that you're there with me."

"Don't sleep over there," Oliver begged. He'd managed to get himself ready for bed, which felt like a big accomplishment, and now he watched from the comfort of his pillows as Felix did the same.

Felix, ready to pull back the blankets on the cot, looked uncertain. "Are you sure?"

"This bed is not as big as the one at Farview, but it's big enough. I know I might not smell my best—"

"I've spent my life around fishermen. I can definitely handle you. But I don't want to jostle you."

"I'm not that fragile. In fact, I wouldn't mind a bit of jostling." In response to Felix's incredulous look, Oliver shrugged. "Nothing too strenuous. But I'd like to... to touch you. If you don't mind."

"Of course I don't bloody mind," Felix muttered.

He abandoned the cot and climbed onto the bed, his lean body warm and solid against Oliver's. Felix was wearing a thin nightshirt he'd borrowed from Julian, and Oliver wore nothing but knee-length cotton drawers. That left a fair opportunity for close contact, especially when Felix tucked himself under Oliver's arm.

Oliver stroked Felix's chest, fancying he could feel the inked anchor beneath the fabric. "I wish I'd had the chance for a tattoo," he said.

"What would it be?"

"A ship with sails full of wind and its name on the hull."

"What name?"

"Felix Corbyn, of course."

Felix snuggled in closer. "I'd like that. I met a sailor once—can't remember where he was from, but he was spending a few nights at the Merman. He had tattoos everywhere. Even a fish on his cock. He could make it flop about."

Oliver chuckled. "I don't think I'd want something that exotic." He yawned hugely and squeezed Felix a bit tighter.

"Then there's Melville Farnsworth, whose tattoos began to tell secrets."

"Did they, now?"

Oliver drifted to sleep over the tale.

He dreamed he was standing at the bow of a great sailing ship, scudding across a calm sea so fast that the gulls in the sky couldn't catch up. The ship's hull was as hard as stone and glittered in the sunshine, and the enormous sails were of every color imaginable. He wasn't alone; beautiful men with butter-colored hair and bright blue eyes were climbing the rigs or sweeping the deck. A few of them laughed as they dipped fishing lines over the gunwale and into the water.

"Where are we going?" Oliver asked one of the sailors passing by.

The man laughed. "What does it matter, when the journey is so delightful?" Then he pointed so Oliver would see an assembly of whales—a dozen of them at least—breaching the water and arcing back in so close to the ship that Oliver was sprayed with their splashes. The whales appeared again and again, racing along with such power and such obvious joy that Oliver had to smile. And when he looked on the other side of the ship, he gasped with surprise: merfolk were swimming alongside as well. Their green hair trailed behind them and sharp teeth glimmered like ice. One of them, a male with a turquoise-colored torso and yellow-striped tail, smiled at Oliver and sang in a language that was all vowels, then disappeared beneath the surface.

"His song won't work on you."

Oliver spun around.

A man and woman stood a few feet away. It was the woman who'd spoken, and at first glance Oliver thought she was quite ancient. But then his vision shifted and she looked hardly out of her teens. Her hair was straight and black as a raven's wing, falling well below her waist, and her eyes were the same deep brown as Felix's. She wasn't delicate—in fact, she looked accustomed to hard physical work—but she radiated tranquil power. She wore a silky emerald blouse and a pair of tan trousers tucked into tall black boots.

The man was as fair as she was dark, his long hair so blonde that it was nearly white and his eyes a hue that was almost purple. He was slender, with high cheekbones and a wide mouth curled into a smile. His skin was so white it was almost blue, like a pail of fresh milk. He wore nothing but a gauzy ruby-colored wrap around his hips; his bare feet displayed toenails painted to match the fabric.

"Welcome, Ollyro," said the man. "We've been waiting for you for a long time." His accent was like none Oliver had heard before. It had a delicate ring, like good china.

At a loss for what to do, Oliver ended up executing a clumsy bow. "Lyra Moon and Aymar Iceshadow, I'm guessing. I'm sorry. I'm not sure how to address you properly."

They laughed. "We're family," Lyra said. "Call us whatever you like."

"This isn't real. I'm asleep in Greynox right now, and you're just a dream."

Both of them came closer, and Lyra rested a hand on his arm. "You're right about part of that, lad. You're dreaming next to your lover. But that doesn't mean this isn't real. Dreams are a type of story, aren't they? The truest kind of all."

He shook his head disbelievingly. "Why am I here?"

"Because we're eager to meet you, of course. And to give you two messages."

"Listen carefully," Aymar said. "You believe that your journey is nearly over. But you're strong. How could you not be? Look whose blood flows in your veins. Believe in your strength and you may find that your adventures have barely begun."

Oliver didn't believe that. Even asleep he felt the hard knot of pain in his gut and the weakness in his limbs.

"What's the second message?" he asked stubbornly.

Aymar smiled warmly. "We're on our way."

OLIVER WOKE ABRUPTLY. The room wasn't completely dark; they hadn't closed the curtains and a streetlamp's pale yellow light stole inside. Felix was still gathered under his arm, his curls soft against

Oliver's bare skin, their legs intertwined. It was a very comfortable position.

"I'll be strong as long as I need to," Oliver whispered, so quietly that even he could barely hear. It felt as if the bed was rocking gently beneath them, and when he licked his lips, he tasted salt. He returned to the ocean of sleep.

Chapter Twenty-Four

Although Oliver awoke before the sun rose, he felt well rested. The aches were only a dull thud not worth bothering about. He remained in bed just for the pleasure of holding a sleeping Felix awhile longer but eventually extricated himself and stood at the window, watching the sky attempt to brighten. It wasn't having an easy time of it, even though the city's usual pall of smoke was thinner than average today.

Julian had been right about the gardens—they did look rather untended. But Oliver liked the untamed enthusiasm of the plants, the exuberance of the multicolored blooms, and the haphazard sprawl of the shrubbery. There was even a small family of imps bathing in the fountain. They looked fatter and cleaner than the city's usual. He suspected Julian and Kit had been feeding them.

"You won't view the sea, no matter how hard you look."

Oliver swiveled his head to smile at Felix. "I'd rather look at you anyway."

Felix got out of bed and sauntered over for a morning kiss. It was deeper and more passionate than Oliver expected—not that he was inclined to complain. Felix fit so perfectly in his embrace, as if a sculptor had created them as a set.

"I dreamt about Lyra and Aymar," Oliver said as they rested their heads on each other's shoulders.

"A good dream?"

Oliver considered for a moment. "I think so."

"I dreamt of something similar—Aymar's ship. But it was far away and blurry, like I was seeing it through heavy fog. Quite frustrating, because I wanted to board it rather urgently. You were on it, you see."

They'd been discussing a tattoo of a ship right before Oliver fell asleep, so the concordant dreams made sense. Still, his spine tingled.

"Breakfast?" he asked.

They dressed and crept downstairs as quietly as possible, but Julian was already sitting in the kitchen, looking tired over a cup of tea. "I'll put the kettle on," he offered, but Oliver waved him back down.

With Julian's permission and directions, Oliver prepared plates of toast, smoked fish, and thinly sliced ham, along with a handful of purple grapes. He brought the food and tea to the table, where he and Felix sat opposite Julian.

"You're looking very well today," Julian observed.

"That's what comes of a good bed and loads of good food. Are you always up so early?"

"No." Julian stifled a yawn. "I had a patient last night. A rag cutter, barely fourteen years old. She had a badly infected wound due to a slipped blade. I think I've saved her hand. I hope so." He looked much older than his years and infinitely weary.

Oliver said, "Your work is so badly needed, yet it must be so difficult on you."

"Sometimes. When it presses on me too hard, Kit whisks me away somewhere interesting and exotic. By the time we return, I'm ready to work some more. But there are so many of them, and I can't help them all."

"If you help even one, though, you've made a huge difference for that one. That girl last night, what would have happened to her if not for you?"

Julian sighed. "She might have died. At the least, she would have lost the hand."

Oliver had witnessed plenty of young people who'd been mangled by machinery or otherwise damaged by their employment. If unable to work, they were forced to beg or to sell their bodies—until they were murdered or died of pox or drink. If they were extremely fortunate, they might eke out a half-life as one of the gaunt, filthy scavengers who collected rubbish and sold what they could, or who stood near the outdoor markets in all sorts of weather trying to sell flowers to would-be suitors and penitent husbands.

"And you've also certainly helped us," Oliver pointed out.

Felix nodded vigorously. "From the stories I'd heard about you, I knew you and Kit were heroes. But now I know you're also profoundly good."

"Thank you." Julian took a sip of his cooling tea and sat back in his chair. "For the first half of my life, nobody expected anything of me—including myself. I get a certain satisfaction out of proving them wrong."

After they ate, Felix insisted on washing up—something that could be done without magic. Before Julian retired to his bedroom for a brief nap, he and Felix both suggested that Oliver rest up as well. But he refused. He was far too anxious about what was coming.

At half past nine, fully dressed and hair combed, Oliver checked and double-checked to ensure that the talisman was safely in his trouser pocket. Grinning wickedly, Felix stuck in his hand as well. "Yes," he said with a bit of a grope, "everything's definitely there."

They went downstairs, where Julian and Kit were waiting in the foyer. Julian still had dark circles under his eyes but hushed anyone who suggested he stay home. Kit shrugged. "No use arguing once his mind's set on something. He'll always get his way. He seduced me when I was recuperating, you know."

Julian huffed and pushed Kit's arm.

"Are you carrying a *sword?*" Oliver asked Kit. Because that was certainly what the object strapped around his hips appeared to be.

Kit patted the hilt. "Of course. Would you like one as well? I've another inside, and one of my belts would fit you well."

"I wouldn't have the faintest idea what to do with it. As a guard, I carried a cudgel and nothing more."

"Those can be quite useful. But I'm sorry, I don't have one to lend you. I've always preferred blades." He grinned at Oliver's astonishment. "I am a man of few talents, and most of the skills I do possess serve me when Jule and I are alone together. But I am an excellent swordsman with metal as well as flesh—Jule, stop blushing; these gentlemen are not innocent virgins—and so when the occasion calls for it, I proceed armed."

"Does this occasion call for it?"

Kit shrugged. "Almost certainly not. But it never hurts to be prepared."

Outside, Kit hailed a cab. It was a large one, the outside shining and the interior surprisingly clean. The driver looked quite sharp in his bottle-green coat and hat, which, whether by design or accident, coordinated well with his two healthy-looking dragons. Unfortunately, there was nothing he could do about the traffic.

"Could have walked there as fast," Oliver muttered fretfully.

Kit leaned over to pat his knee. "Penelope will be there. She's coming from even farther away and may also be delayed."

They traveled slowly through Kit and Julian's neighborhood—past its elegant, dignified houses and the squares with tranquil fountains—and into the area where Oliver had grown up. The residences there were still quite nice but not as refined, and the streets were a bit grimier. A commercial section with restaurants and shops came next, followed by an area in which people with moderate but steady incomes—clerks, schoolteachers, government workers—lived in rented rooms or flats. The next neighborhood contained workshops where craftsmen and artisans plied their trade and lived in rooms behind or above their workshops. Other storefronts sold cheap, often second-hand goods, and most residents stayed in the inexpensive lodging houses. As an adult, Oliver had lived in a similar neighborhood.

"Are you all right?" Felix whispered into Oliver's ear.

"Yes." But that was a lie. In fact, Oliver felt queasy, not from the curse but from nerves. It was taking all his will not to lean out the window and vomit.

Felix wasn't fooled. "You'll do fine, Olly." He said this more loudly, and Julian and Kit nodded their agreement.

"What if I don't? What if I fail? Gods, six people will die. And even if I'm successful, scores have died already."

"Didn't I just this morning hear someone give Julian a lecture about how making a difference to even one person is a grand accomplishment? Olly, you've made all the difference to me. Remember that."

Oliver wasn't exactly made more optimistic, but a bit of the nausea subsided.

The cab skirted most of the next section, where factory workers crowded into miserable, lightless tenements and ragpickers, costermongers, and beggars crowded the filthy pavement. Every face here was pinched and hopeless, even those of the children, and the viscous air carried unbearable stenches.

It was almost a relief to emerge near the Methes River, where dirty brick factories and mills loomed over the cobbles and filled the sky with smoke and the heavy *thud-thump* of machines. Oliver used to walk by these buildings daily, his boots stomping along while his mind was far away. Sometimes he'd imagine the quiet retirement he planned for himself, and sometimes he'd think about the nameless men he'd fucked in alleys and pubs. Every now and then, though, he'd remember that his mother had left him a cottage by the sea, and he'd wonder what it looked like, and whether he might enjoy a visit there sometime.

The machines inside Hillard's mill, usually audible from the street, were silent, but the bright red of newer, cleaner brick showed where the building had recently been patched. If the interior had been badly damaged as well, it might still be undergoing repairs. Oliver wondered how the displaced workers had been managing to pay for rent and food.

About a dozen people stood near the entrance, watching as the cab pulled to a halt. Most of them were grim-faced men in bespoke suits, but there was also a woman in her forties, her graying hair cut in a no-nonsense bob, her dress well-cut but plain, as if she valued quality but didn't much care about fashion. She hurried over to greet them.

"I was afraid Mr. Webb had taken ill again," she announced as they disembarked the cab.

"Traffic," Kit said. "It seems as if every day this wretched city becomes more difficult to traverse. But please allow me to make introductions. Penelope, Mr. Oliver Webb and Mr. Felix Corbyn. Gentlemen, Baroness Penelope Hutton."

"*Please* don't, Kit," she groaned. She held out her hand for a shake, sparing Oliver the dilemma of how to properly acknowledge a noblewoman. "You're friends of Kit and Julian, which means, by extension, you're now friends of mine. I'm Penelope and I'd like to call you Oliver and Felix, if I may."

She was, without a doubt, the most confident person Oliver had ever met. He could easily imagine her leading armies into battle or conquering new realms. This heartened him appreciably. If anyone could force the authorities to listen to his tale, it was Penelope.

"I won't bother introducing *them*," she said, waving a dismissive hand toward the men clustered just out of earshot. "The minister of justice, the police commissioner, a couple of journalist acquaintances, and some assorted members of Parliament. I daresay at least one or two of them will make a half-decent witness."

"Thank you for doing this," Oliver said.

"I'm not doing it for your sake, you understand. I'm sure you're delightful, and that's fine when inviting someone for tea, but I'm doing this on behalf of the workers."

He nodded. "So am I. And the six people who are condemned to hang."

Her smile seemed entirely genuine. "Excellent. And we can have tea some other time."

She led the four of them in a march to the waiting crowd, the members of which eyed Oliver and Felix warily. A few of them looked openly contemptuous, but that didn't bother Oliver. He wasn't trying to gain their esteem, just their ears.

"Well, out with it," demanded a bony man with bushy eyebrows that met in the middle. "We've spent long enough already in this miserable hellhole."

Penelope fixed him with a glare. "The workers spend sixteen hours a day in this hellhole, Lord Collingcombs. And they don't go home to mansions full of servants to wait on them. But Oliver, please do proceed."

Oliver stuck his hand in his pocket and was enormously relieved to feel the talisman's shape and the resulting tingle on his skin. "I think it would be better if we did this on the river side of the building."

There were fewer bystanders there to be shocked by his memory, and it would also be easier to throw the talisman into the water when he was through with it. Once activated, the less time it spent near Felix, the better.

Collingcombs and the others grumbled predictably, but Penelope lifted her chin and began to tramp along the sidewall of the building. Kit rested his hand on the sword hilt and smiled menacingly, and the group fell obediently into line.

No boat was currently moored at Hillard's dock, but several were tied up at nearby mills, their broad hulls low in the foul water. These were the small boats that plied the river, delivering goods from factories to warehouses like the one where Stephen Webb had worked. Oliver wondered whether these vessels envied their larger brethren that sailed the purer seas.

Between the back of the Hillard building and the river was a wide platform made of planking, used to temporarily store crates of fabric waiting to be loaded onto ships. Oliver had stood here for hours, ostensibly to watch over the valuable merchandise but mostly admiring the longshoremen and envying their profession. Now the space was empty save for a single Hillard's guard—a young man Oliver didn't know—who took one look at all of them and scurried inside like an imp running for cover.

Penelope nodded, Felix smiled encouragingly, and Oliver took a deep breath. He spoke loudly and clearly so there would be no mistake about what he said.

"I was a guard here for ten years. I was working on April fifth of this year. The protest was going on, and I was standing in front of this building on Oakwood Street, just a few yards from where I met you. I was watching closely. And I saw a man I knew, another man employed as one of Hillard's guards, set off the flash-curse and hurl it into the crowd. I saw people die."

As Oliver spoke, Penelope and two of the men had been scribbling frantically in notebooks. The rest of the audience wore frowns and grumbled to one another.

"That is a lie!" came a voice from near the building. A familiar voice.

Hillard himself came stomping over, flanked by the guard who'd reported their presence and by a nervous-looking assistant whose name escaped Oliver for the moment. Hillard's normally pale face had gone purple.

"How dare you! How *dare* you!" He waved his fist so threateningly in Oliver's direction that Kit took a few steps forward. He looked ready to draw his sword at the slightest provocation.

But while the guard and the assistant wavered, Hillard did not. He narrowed his eyes. "I gave you employment when you were nothing. I granted you a good salary so you didn't have to work with the scum on the machines. Because of me you never went hungry, never went without a place to lay your pathetic head. And you repay my generosity with treachery and vicious lies."

"I'm telling the truth," Oliver said, head high. "And you're responsible for nearly two hundred deaths."

Hillard swung to face the witnesses. "Did you hear that? He's allied with the agitators, spreading falsehoods in hope of ruining me completely. No doubt he was in on the scheme as well. Hang him with the others!"

Felix, standing at a distance so as not to interfere with the talisman's magic, made a small noise of distress, but Oliver wasn't afraid. Even if these people believed Hillard and condemned Oliver, he was doomed anyway. A swift death in a noose might be preferable to a longer one from the curse. It was wonderfully empowering to have nothing to lose and a great deal to gain.

A man with a hook nose and round belly spoke up. "Mr. Hillard is a successful businessman and a prominent member of the community. I see no reason why we should doubt him due to nothing more than the word of this...." He gestured at Oliver. "This... person." He said the last word as if he begrudged it.

"I have a reason," Oliver said. "I have proof."

"Your statements aren't proof of anything except your complicity," Hillard snarled.

"But I've more than that. I have this." Rather pleased with his dramatic flourish, he pulled the talisman from his pocket and held it aloft. It wasn't very impressive looking in itself, yet it emanated a crackle of force that even Hillard seemed to sense.

"What's that?" demanded the hook-nosed man.

"A device given to me by a wizard. When I invoke it, you will be able to view my memory firsthand. You'll see exactly what I witnessed on April fifth."

Well, that impressed everyone. The men gasped and spoke to one another rapidly, while Penelope continued to take notes. "I'll have questions about that device later, Oliver. Quite a lot, I think."

Still holding the talisman high, he concentrated on the instructions Enoch had given him. *Activate the talisman by calling a name.* At first his mind was such a perfect blank that he almost panicked. But then he heard something, like the breeze carrying a voice from far away. Just the faintest sounds, like beach sand shifting under bare toes or tiny crabs scuttling across rocks at the tideline. Like the moor grass springing upright after a drenching rain.

He heard the name. Enoch had been right—it was a name he knew.

"Marina Rowe," he said clearly as he focused on the moments he'd been trying so hard to forget, the seconds just before his world shifted forever.

Nothing happened. The onlookers began to shift their feet. Penelope stood with pen poised over her book.

Felix was looking at Oliver with absolute trust and conviction, as if he knew to a certainty that the talisman would work. He clearly didn't recognize that Oliver had been distracted by thoughts of his mother and fears that he'd invoked the wrong name in some sort of bizarre fantasy about being rescued by the parent he'd barely known.

Just when Hillard was opening his mouth to say something—no doubt something toxic—the talisman became so hot in Oliver's grip that he almost dropped it. His skin heated, and it felt as if tiny firestones had ignited along his spine. All sounds were sucked away with a *whoosh*. And a scene appeared in the space between him and the crowd.

Everything was instantly familiar, even though the figures were more transparent than Croftwell's ghosts. There was Oakwood Street, packed so tightly with people that it was almost impossible for them to move. Young children perched on parents' shoulders. Across the sea of people, the rusty brick walls of Merryclaims' mill rose high.

Oliver could smell the press of sweaty bodies and feel the rough brick of Hillard's mill against his back. He'd been standing here a long time and his feet ached, but the songs and speeches of the protesters made him feel hopeful. It was a huge turnout, the biggest by far, and it felt as if the mill owners would *have* to listen to the workers' demands. How could so many voices be ignored?

A movement caught his attention, no more than twenty feet away, a fellow guard with dark blond hair that curled near his collar. With just a hint of a mustache, he couldn't have been older than twenty, and his skinny frame swam in his too-large uniform. His eyes were enormous and glassy, as if he were drugged or not in his right mind. Oliver couldn't remember his name. Bill something perhaps. Or maybe it was Bob.

The young guard moved slowly into the crowd. That was forbidden—they'd been instructed to stay close to the building—and also dangerous. He could get swallowed up in a mass such as that. He inched a few more feet into the congested street, then turned around. His gaze caught Oliver's.

Without changing his deadpan expression, the boy lifted cupped hands above his head—and threw something directly at Oliver.

The world erupted into a hell of screams and blood, then the images dissipated like smoke.

Oliver collapsed to his knees, and Felix was there at once, grasping his arm and calling his name. But the talisman was scorching Oliver's hand. He staggered to his feet, pulled away from Felix, and heaved the magical object in a high arc toward the river. It landed without even a splash and sank immediately out of sight.

Everyone looked shocked. Even Julian and Kit and Felix, who'd known what to expect, had gone white. One elderly man in a gaudy red coat burst into tears and was awkwardly soothed by the man next to him, who might have been his son or grandson. Penelope had stopped taking notes.

Oliver lifted his chin. "Do you believe me now? Those six people are innocent, and you must stop their executions at once. And you must try Hillard for killing nearly two hundred men, women, and children."

For a shining moment, he was triumphant. He, Oliver Webb, had done what was necessary, and as a result, justice would be served.

Then Hillard screeched and threw something. It bounced off the planks and into the river, leaving a gaping hole only a few feet to Felix's right.

"He has more flash-curses!" someone screamed.

Well, of course he did. He was wealthy; he could afford as many of the fucking things as he wanted.

Everything unfolded slowly, like a terrible nightmare. Most of the bystanders stampeded away, a few of them stumbling in their haste and scrambling back to their feet. The guard and the assistant joined them. Four people, however, moved toward Hillard: Penelope with her pen raised like a weapon, Julian with hands clenched into fists, Kit with his sword drawn. And Felix, sweet, beloved Felix, with no weapon at all. But Hillard reached into his pocket and drew back his arm, and there was no way any of them would reach him before he threw.

Oliver roared. Just as Hillard's hand came forward, Oliver surged ahead and shoved Felix out of the way with all his might.

A split second later, the flash-curse smashed into Oliver's chest with a tremendous bang.

Although he was deafened, he didn't die at once, which was a surprise. He fell to the ground and was still aware enough to see Kit's sword come down in a wide arc and Hillard's detached head fall, the body following a moment later. The eyes stared at Oliver in complete astonishment before going sightless.

And Oliver was still alive when Felix crawled to him and cradled Oliver's head in his lap, great tears falling on Oliver's face like splashes from the distant sea.

There was pain, naturally, but Oliver had been living with pain for so long now that it hardly mattered. What was more important was that he'd accomplished his goals and Felix was unharmed. So were his new friends, who knelt beside him. Julian was tearing at Oliver's shirt, probably to get a better look at the wound. Oliver hoped it didn't look too appalling; he didn't want to distress anyone more than he already had.

Voices flowed back as the deafness from the explosion faded.

"Hold him, Felix!" Julian was saying urgently. "Hold him tight. Don't let go."

Well, Oliver approved of that, but he didn't understand why it was so important to Julian. He tried to say something—he wasn't sure what—but couldn't seem to make his mouth work properly. No matter. He'd already said the vital things.

"Felix, you need to concentrate. As hard as you possibly can."

"On what?" Felix cried.

"On Oliver. On undoing that accursed fucking curse."

"But I can't—"

"Holy Eurynome's ghost, what is *that*?"

That was Kit speaking, and whatever he saw—in the river, probably, behind Oliver where he couldn't see—made everyone gasp and freeze. Apparently Oliver wasn't quite dead enough to have lost his curiosity, because now he wanted to know what had everyone so astonished. More distant voices exclaimed in wonder and Penelope shouted, "Good gods!"

But when Oliver tried to twist around so he could see, he found that he could barely move, and anyway Felix still gripped him tight.

"Don't die, Olly. Hang on. Oh gods, you need to live to see this!"

A few moments later, Oliver did see.

Several new people had appeared around him. One woman had dark features and a face that bore a decided resemblance to Oliver's. The others weren't people, strictly speaking. They were pale and beautiful, with an unearthly glow and inhumanly graceful movements.

"Aymar," Oliver managed to croak as one of the pale creatures crouched next to him.

"You have managed quite an adventure, haven't you? Tell me, do you enjoy being cursed?" Aymar was grinning as if this were a wonderful joke.

"No."

"You've caught yourself a good one. But let's fix it, shall we? Your wizard's done quite a good job at that already, but we can speed things up. I'm eager to get back out to sea. We're going to have the devil of a time cleaning that filthy river water off my ship."

Aymar placed his hands on Oliver's chest, just below where the flash-curse had hit.

The pain disappeared. Not just the new pain but the old as well. And every single ache and twinge that Oliver had accumulated over the past months, along with every ounce of exhaustion. He felt better and stronger than he'd ever had.

Crowing in joy, Oliver pulled free of Felix's grip and sprang to his feet. He hauled Felix up and wrapped him in a bear hug so strong that Felix squeaked breathlessly. Oliver kissed him fiercely and then loosened his arms, but only so he could grasp Felix's hand instead.

"Wh-what?" Felix finally stuttered. Which was more than anyone else was able to manage.

Aymar inclined his head toward Felix. "You know who we are, lad. I am Aymar Iceshadow, prince of the water fae, and this is my lovely, brilliant wife, my Lady Lyra Moon. These are some of my crew members." He swept his arms toward the other fae. "You know our story—you've been telling it for years."

"B-but you're *here*."

"Didn't Ollyro tell you we were coming?"

Oliver could have explained. Probably should have. But he was so overcome with delight that all he could do was squeeze Felix's hand and beam. He wasn't dead. Wasn't dying. And the curses were gone.

It was Julian who gathered enough wits to speak next. He bowed quite prettily to the fae. "I'm Dr. Julian Massey, my lord and lady. This is my partner, Kit Archer."

"We've heard about you," said Lyra, grinning like a gleeful child. "That bit with the pirates in Urchin's Cove."

"Erm, yes. May I...." He paused. "I believe I understand at least some of what just happened, but not all of it. May I ask a few questions?"

"Of course," she said.

"Oliver ought to be dead twice over. He told us he'd witnessed the flash-curse in April, but I didn't realize how close it was until today. He was hit almost directly. People who were much farther away were, erm, blown to bits. But he wasn't."

Oliver blinked. In his memories of that day, time and distance had been badly distorted. He also hadn't known—until today—how close that guard had been.

"Why wasn't I killed at once?"

"Precisely," Julian said. He looked like a detective in one of the lurid novels Oliver used to occasionally read. "You were injured, and the curse was eating away at you. That's odd enough, and I don't have an explanation for that bit. But after you met Felix, your sickness came and went, which a curse shouldn't do."

"That was the ogrewort," said Felix, and Oliver nodded.

"But it wasn't! Ogrewort is an odd herb. It takes very little to cause overdose and death, yet even the maximum safe dosage has rather weak medicinal capacity. It's used to ease toothaches or reduce a low fever, not to snatch someone from death's jaws."

Felix huffed. "But it worked. Every time Olly drank ogrewort tea, he felt better."

"Who made him that tea?"

Oliver had an inkling where this was going. "Felix did. Felix made me the tea every time. And every time I went away from him, I got worse." Twice, in fact, he'd almost died. Until Felix showed up and nursed him back to health. "Is it.... It's your curse, Felix."

Felix still looked confused, but Julian smiled widely and the fae nodded like proud parents of a clever child.

"I think so," said Julian. "Felix, you think of your magic aversion as a curse, and of course it's made your life quite difficult, I understand that. But really, it's a very powerful magic of its own. You actually disrupt other magic. And a flash-curse is—"

"Magic," Felix whispered.

"All those times you were near Oliver and caring for him, you were counteracting his curse. You weren't aware of it. You merely thought you were engaging in more prosaic healing efforts. But you were unconsciously working away, unraveling the harmful magic within him. As you did just now, I might add."

Felix shuddered and fell against Oliver. "I... am going... to have a conversation with my granddad, I am."

Chuckling, Oliver wrapped an arm around him and kissed the top of his head. He didn't care who saw. "You saved me, Felix. You saved my life."

Still muffled against Oliver's shoulder, Felix made a sound somewhere between a sob and a laugh. "Seems to be some of that going round, isn't there?"

However, Julian wasn't finished solving his mystery. "I'm still a bit confused. Felix can work against the curse, but he wasn't there on April fifth. He and Oliver didn't meet until some months later. And just now, we all saw that bastard Hillard score a direct hit on Oliver, who should have disintegrated before Felix got a chance to help."

It was an interesting question, but Oliver didn't feel especially invested in the answer. He'd listen because it was like reading to the end of the book to find out who did it. But all he truly cared about was that he was now holding Felix and, as far as he could tell, could continue to do so into the foreseeable future.

"It's simple," Lyra said. "My Aymar is Ollyro's grandfather, several generations removed. Ollyro may have only a few drops of fae blood, but it's powerful stuff, and the fae are naturally immune to harmful magic."

"He's immortal?" Felix asked hopefully.

Aymar chuckled and shook his head. "I'm afraid not. He has a human span of years and most human weaknesses. But I think you'll find you can fit plenty of excitement into that."

Oliver wasn't disappointed in the least. He wouldn't have wanted immortality without Felix anyway.

"This is so fascinating!" Julian said.

Kit took Julian by the arm. "Don't start poking anyone with scalpels, my love. I think this is one scientific inquiry that you'll have to let go."

Oliver stuck his nose into Felix's soft curls. Despite several days in Greynox, Felix still smelled of the sea and a bit like moor-herb. It was an intoxicating scent, one that made Oliver feel the urgent need to take his lover somewhere private and demonstrate exactly how much he needed him. How much he valued him. How much he loved him.

But a large crowd remained, including members of the nobility, a contingent of water fae, a human ancestor who should have died a long time ago, and a corpse with its head several feet away. Not to mention the man who'd accomplished that and was currently cleaning his blade with a rag.

"Erm," Oliver said, "Hillard is dead."

Kit smiled merrily. "I hope so, for his sake. It'd be damned inconvenient to be missing one's head. Although I know a few people who might not notice the difference." He cast a glance toward the members of Parliament and had to muffle giggles entirely unsuited to a large, armed man in his forties.

"But you.... Your sword.... And the six people condemned to hang...." Given the day's events Oliver could be forgiven for his failed eloquence, but it was frustrating to be so incoherent.

Penelope pursed her lips, strode over to the cluster of men, and dragged one of them over by his elbow. He cast a wary eye on Kit and the fae, but in a visible effort at bravery, he straightened his shoulders. "Yes, Lady Hutton?"

"You are the Minister of Justice."

"I am aware of that."

"Mr. Webb has presented us with rather convincing evidence as to the true cause of the deaths on April fifth, wouldn't you say? What will you be doing about that?" She fixed him with the stare that was probably taught to blue bloods from birth, implying dire consequences if demands weren't met.

The minister shuffled his feet. "I will summarize these events to Her Majesty and Parliament immediately. I imagine there will be an extensive inquiry."

Oliver's patience was overtaxed. "I don't care about a bloody inquiry! What about those six people?"

A long pause followed, during which Kit played with the hilt of his sword more obviously than necessary.

"I give you my word," said the minister, "that they will receive full pardons."

Penelope wrote in her book. "And compensation. I'm sure they and the families of the victims will receive compensation from Mr. Hillard's estate."

Looking like a man conceding a battle, the minister nodded. "Just so."

But why not press a bit more? "And Mr. Archer?" Oliver said. "He won't be facing any troubles over... that?" He gestured at the mess that used to be his employer.

"Not at all. I saw what happened myself. Mr. Archer behaved heroically. He deserves a medal, not prosecution." The minister all but batted his lashes at Kit, who did look entirely dashing and handsome. Julian rolled his eyes as he were used to that sort of thing, and Kit almost preened.

Oliver stood on the planks behind the mill, feeling so odd that he momentarily worried he hadn't actually been cured. Then he realized the source of the sensation: relief. All his burdens and worries were gone, leaving him feeling light enough to float away like a dandelion puff. Only Felix's embrace kept him anchored.

"We can go home now," Oliver said in wonderment. "Back to Farview, where we can learn to build peat fires and feed the imps until they can barely move and have Mrs. Bellflower make us octopus curtains."

Felix looked up at him with shining eyes. "And teach you to swim and drink ale at the Merman and chat with your ghosts and spend so much time in bed we'll barely remember how to walk."

Oliver was going to add more items to their paradise itinerary—or perhaps simply drag Felix to Griffin's Den station—but Aymar stepped close. Funny how Oliver had been so overwhelmed by everything that he'd nearly forgotten the fae were there.

"I'd be delighted to offer you passage to Croftwell. With, if you fancy it, a detour to our home island. I think my mother would be quite entranced by the two of you."

"I thought she rejected you," Felix said. Somewhat more bluntly than necessary, perhaps, but he'd had a trying experience.

Aymar didn't seem to take offense. "She did. But time passes and grudges fade. Parents and children reconcile. My Lady Lyra and I live there when we're not traveling, and my mother adores her."

"The home of the water fae!" Felix breathed.

For his part, Oliver was thrilled with the prospect of a sea voyage. He could almost smell the salt air already. He turned to look at Julian and Kit, but they were already waving him toward the ship.

"There's no better way to live," Julian said. "Adventures with your beloved and then a return home together. So go. We'll see one another again, I suspect."

Felix took Oliver's hand. "And we'll have new stories to exchange. Let's go, Olly!"

Laughing, Oliver and Felix ran toward the gleaming ship.

Epilogue

The sun was already hovering over the harbor when Oliver started up the path. He settled the sack more comfortably over his shoulder and ran up the cliffside, pausing once or twice to admire a view that never grew tiresome. He reached the top just in time to encounter a gaggle of rowdy children.

"Uncle Oliver!" shouted the youngest, a girl with more than passing resemblance to a certain ghost. She threw herself at him with considerable force and wrapped herself around his legs. "We was feeding the imps! And Uncle Felix told us 'bout eels so long you had breakfast with the front end and dinner with the back. Did you really see them eels?"

"That was just a story," opined an older boy officiously.

Oliver smiled. "Ah, but stories are the truest things. Of course we saw giant eels. And whales so tiny you could hold them in your hand."

Her eyes grew wide. "Ooh, tell us 'bout them whales."

"Another time. I daresay your parents are wanting you home for dinner now."

Laughing and talking loudly, the children hurried down the path. Oliver paused a moment longer, taking in the sight of Farview cottage with the summer's last flowers blooming in the window boxes and smoke puffing from the chimney. No matter how many times he saw it

—whether he'd been gone an hour or a month—it took his breath away and made his heart sing.

But not as much as the man waiting inside.

Oliver sprinted the last few yards, burst in through the front door, and landed in Felix's welcoming embrace. He dropped the sack and gave his lover an enthusiastic and thorough kiss, with gropes thrown in for good measure.

"What did you bring us for dinner?" Felix asked when he could breathe again.

"Knucker! We found a whole pod of them an hour offshore, and a real beauty took our line. We spent almost the whole day bringing it in. I'm starving and fair done in."

"No energy left at all?" Felix said teasingly.

"Well... maybe a *bit*."

Oliver reached for another kiss—dinner could wait—but Felix danced away. "I have news for you, I do. I wasn't just sitting here all day gazing longingly out to sea."

"No, you were telling stories to children."

"That too." Felix hefted the sack and removed the paper-wrapped parcel of knucker meat and a basket of sea-fern. There were also some of Aygun's currant cakes and four pints of cider. It would be an excellent meal, along with the potatoes and carrots they already had. "Go clean yourself up and I might tell you my news."

Oliver stripped out of his brine- and water dragon–scented clothing at once. He'd wash it the next day. He cast a longing glance at the gleaming washtub, wishing he had time for a bath, but settled for efficient swipes with soap, wet cloth, and towel. Dressed in clean, comfortable clothing, he sat down at the table to watch Felix prepare dinner. Sometimes he tried to help, but Felix always shooed him away. Now that he could go near the hearth without fear of causing a conflagration, Felix enjoyed cooking very much. And, well, Oliver enjoyed watching him.

They'd been together for over two years now, and every moment remained a joyous gift. Sure, they had small squabbles now and then, as all couples did, but they were never about anything important. In fact,

Oliver suspected that Felix picked fights on purpose, just so they could enthusiastically make up.

"So are you ready to become a fisherman full-time?" asked Felix as he sliced the knucker into manageable pieces.

"No, but I do enjoy these occasional excursions. Oh, I saw your mum this morning. She says we should pay her a visit. She wants to hear about our most recent travels."

It was the third time they'd visited the island, a beautiful place where Oliver and Felix enjoyed immense popularity, most likely because they remained a novelty to the fae. It was lovely to spend a week swimming in the warm water, lolling on the beaches, or feasting while the fae sang or performed elaborate plays. But it wasn't home. Farview always called them back.

"Mum's going to have to wait," said Felix. "We'll be off to Greynox tomorrow."

Oliver blinked. "We will?"

"Julian and Kit sent us a letter. By wyvern!"

That made Oliver whistle. Wyvern post was terribly expensive, reserved primarily for nobility or extreme emergencies. "Are they all right?"

"They're fine. But they and Penelope believe that one of the factory owners is using a spell to keep workers docile. It's almost like magical enslavement, it is." He plopped the hunks of knucker into a big frying pan, sprinkled them with moor-herb, and began wrapping vegetables in sea-fern. "They think maybe my curse—"

"Your gift," Oliver corrected.

"—will help them suss out what's happening. I don't mind a bit of detective work."

Oliver frowned. "But your grandfather...."

"Oh, I know very well what granddad's worried about." He mimicked the wizard's voice, badly: "If the wrong sort find out about you, they'll want to exploit you, son. Use you as a weapon."

"You don't think his fears are justified?"

Felix fussed with the food for a few moments. Even though his back was turned, Oliver understood him well enough to know he was searching for the right words. Finally, Felix turned, tongs in hand.

"I expect they *are* justified. And I understand why he wasn't forthcoming all those years. He loves me and wants me to be safe. But I'm a grown man, I am. I can choose to take risks when I know they're worth it."

"And this one is?"

"You know how those people live, Olly. If I can help a bit, I will."

Oliver smiled at him and nodded. "And I'll be there to protect you."

They had a good life in Croftwell. Felix did some work now and then, as he always had, mostly to keep himself from growing bored. He kept the cottage and had even managed to coax a small vegetable garden out of the reluctant soil. Oliver went out with the fishermen or helped in the village when houses needed repairs. He'd discovered that he was handy with tools. They drank at the pub with their friends and walked the moors, and at night they held each other tight in their big, warm bed. Oliver would be content with this life for as long as he lived.

And yet... sometimes they had adventures instead. Sometimes they found small ways to improve the lives of poverty-stricken Noxers. Sometimes Oliver laced up his boots and straightened his coat and became a guard again—and that was good too, especially since he knew that no matter what, he and Felix would always return to Farview.

"I'll read the letter after dinner," Oliver said.

Momentarily abandoning his cooking efforts, Felix crossed over to Oliver, wrapped arms around his neck, and kissed the top of his head. "All right. Then early to bed?"

"Of course."

"Good. And now I have a story for you. It's about two men who thought they were cursed but discovered they were the luckiest people alive. They lived happily ever after, and that is the truth."

"That's my favorite story."

"Mine too." Felix kissed him again before heading back to the stove. While tending the food, he began.

"One afternoon a man who believed himself a Noxer sat on a crowded train to Bythington. Thirty minutes into the journey, he knew he should have splurged on a first-class ticket, but by then it was too late...."

Read Julian and Kit's story!

Julian Massey has always been sickly. When the young man's parents send him to the seaside town of Urchin Cove to recuperate, he finds himself stranded in a tiny cabin with only the quirky local inhabitants for company. Then a storm blows through, and he finds an unexpected discovery washed up on the beach: an unconscious man.

After stealing a treasure, Kit Archer is taken prisoner by a ruthless pirate, Captain Booth. When a storm hits the pirate ship, Kit is able to escape, but not without serious injuries. Jules nurses him back to health, and friendship grows into desire. But Captain Booth is bound to come in search of his treasure and the man who stole it.

In a world with dragons, sprites, and wizards, it's going to take more than a little magic for Jules and Kit to find lasting happiness together.

Treasure—available now

Kim Fielding is very pleased every time someone calls her eclectic. A Lambda Award finalist and two-time Foreword INDIE finalist, she has migrated back and forth across the western two-thirds of the United States and currently lives in California, where she long ago ran out of bookshelf space. She's a university professor who dreams of being able to travel and write full time. She also dreams of having two daughters who fully appreciate her, a husband who isn't obsessed with football, and a house that cleans itself. Some dreams are more easily obtained than others.

Kim can be found on her blog: http://kfieldingwrites.com/
Facebook: https://www.facebook.com/KFieldingWrites
and Twitter: @KFieldingWrites
Her e-mail is kim@kfieldingwrites.com

Made in the USA
Coppell, TX
09 June 2021